THE DARK SIDE OF BEAUTY

Stephen McNeilly

Copyright © Stephen McNeilly 2020
This book is sold subject to the condition that it shall not, by way of trade or otherwise, be lent, resold, hired out, or otherwise circulated without the publisher's prior consent in any form of binding or cover other than that in which it is published and without a similar condition including this condition being imposed on the subsequent publisher.
The moral right of Stephen McNeilly has been asserted.
ISBN: 9798644745456

This is a work of fiction. Names, characters, businesses, organizations, places, events and incidents either are the product of the author's imagination or are used fictitiously. Any resemblance to actual persons, living or dead, events, or locales is entirely coincidental.

DEDICATION

For my beautiful daughter Eleanor, who motivates me in all things I do.

CONTENTS

CHAPTER 1 The Butcher 1
CHAPTER 2 Annabelle 18
CHAPTER 3 Room 527 28
CHAPTER 4 The Lover 46
CHAPTER 5 Home Invasion 56
CHAPTER 6 Identity 67
CHAPTER 7 Following the Trail 77
CHAPTER 8 Club 88 91
CHAPTER 9 Invitation 103
CHAPTER 10 Questions 117
CHAPTER 11 Mannequins 134
CHAPTER 12 Country Club 147
CHAPTER 13 Play Date 157
CHAPTER 14 Probable Cause 170
CHAPTER 15 Closing the Net 184
CHAPTER 16 Suicide 200
CHAPTER 17 Confrontation 212
CHAPTER 18 Epilogue 227

ACKNOWLEDGMENTS

Thanks to my friend Luke O'Connor for all your support throughout this project.

CHAPTER 1

The Butcher

This was the place. As I sat in my Sedan listening to the rain patting against the roof of my car like several tiny fingers, I watched the old abandoned country house from a safe distance. Nobody had entered or left the property since I had started watching the place and I had only a few hours of sunlight left before nightfall.

I would have to make my move now. I reached into my glovebox and retrieved my Beretta 9mm, my weapon of choice and only trusted companion, as well as a good bottle of whiskey of course.

I took a long hard look at myself in the rear-view mirror and sighed at the unfamiliar man who stared back at me. My long dark hair was unkempt as I no longer bothered to take care of it and my eyes were surrounded by dark circles which showed that I hadn't slept properly for a long time.

I wore my favorite grey trench coat which constantly gave off the unpleasant aroma of whiskey and cigarettes, a stained white shirt underneath, faded blue jeans and black boots.

I ran a hand across my rough chin and sighed again before lighting another cigarette.

The house stood isolated in the middle of a farm in Texas. I had my car parked down a dirt road that ran through the middle of a cornfield. From here I was fairly certain that nobody could see my car from the house. The car which belonged to the missing students had been located less than a few miles from here, abandoned in the middle of a field with the belongings of the two girls and the two boys still in the trunk.

I got out of my car and flicked the butt of my cigarette into the tall forest of corn and strode towards the house with a flashlight and my Beretta at my hip. The rain felt refreshing as a gentle breeze swept through my hair, but my heart was beating like a drum in my chest. As I walked, I spotted figures moving through the corn through my peripheral vision on both sides. My eyes darted side to side, but there was nothing really there.

The house was run down. White paint peeled from the wood and shutters hung from the windows. Some were missing entirely. A rusted pickup truck was parked near the house with overgrown grass on either side of it. Old rotten steps lead to a wooden porch. The mesh screen door was open, creaking eerily in the wind. Behind it lay a green door. I reached for the handle with my spare hand, gripping my Beretta tightly with my other hand and aiming it at the doorway just in case someone had seen my approach and was waiting in ambush.

*

The group of four which I had been hired to find were all college students from LA who had travelled to Mexico for a vacation. Although they never made it back, their car was found abandoned. Zach Brady was a typical college jock. The photo which I had seen of him showed him smiling smugly. He had slicked-back black hair and he was a broad-shouldered guy wearing a red soccer shirt with a blue bodywarmer over the top. His girlfriend, Melissa Lennox, was a blonde Barbie doll type of girl who wore way too much makeup on her already pretty face. In the photo, she wore a pink dress. Mike Vance was a dark-skinned young man with short black hair. He had a much smaller build than his friend Zach, but he was still part of the college in-crowd. Finally, there was Sarah Walker, whose parents had hired me to track the missing group. Sarah was a slim girl with brown hair which she wore in pigtails. She also wore glasses, which I found broken at the scene of the abandoned car.

The police had investigated the farm, yet their search had yielded no results. "The farm is long abandoned. After an extensive search of the property we have concluded that the gang of teens were never there," declared the State Sheriff whilst chewing a mouthful of tobacco. "We will continue our search, but the likelihood is that the kids broke down and hitched a ride out of the state."

The Walkers, of course, were not satisfied with the rushed and careless investigation and so they hired me. I was surprised to see that the police hadn't removed the abandoned car, but this worked to my advantage. Finding Sarah Walker's broken glasses only strengthened my conviction: the group had been taken to the house.

*

The front door creaked in protest as I slowly pushed it open and the beam of my flashlight cut through the thick darkness within. The floorboards creaked under my feet as I cautiously made my way into the front hallway. An old decrepit-looking staircase led to the upper level of the house and a doorway at the back of the hallway led into the kitchen. This is where I began my search of the house.

The smell was disgusting. Pots, pans, and plates were piled up in the sink with old decaying food still clinging persistently to them. Flies buzzed around everywhere, and I was constantly having to swat them away with my hand. The kitchen was small with a square wooden table in the center of the room surrounded by four wooden chairs. The boarded-up windows allowed for some beams of natural light to penetrate the darkness from outside to reveal the particles of dust floating through the air. Another door at the far side of the kitchen was left ajar.

I held a handkerchief to my nose and scanned the kitchen surfaces for any clues. Shadows danced menacingly across the room and as my beam passed over the doorway, I thought that I saw the silhouette of a young woman walk by in the darkness. My head started to throb, and I held my hands to my temples. "She wasn't real!" I told myself shakily, my voice barely louder than a whisper. The lack of sleep was making me hallucinate again!

I continued to scan the kitchen when I made an interesting discovery. A patch of the floorboards had been scrubbed clean whilst the rest of the floor was grimy and covered in dust. "How curious..." I muttered to myself with a smile. Bleach had been used, and lots of it. My heart sank at what this implied. I had little hope of finding the four kids alive anyway, but this discovery only affirmed what I already believed.

I swallowed a lump in my throat and continued my search,

cautiously moving towards the door at the far side of the kitchen. Upon passing the refrigerator, my nose was assaulted by an incomprehensible foul smell which made me dry heave and filled my mouth with liquid. I fought the urge to throw up and reluctantly opened the refrigerator door, half expecting to see rotting dismembered remains. To my relief the refrigerator was full of rotting food that had been left here for a very long time. I pushed onwards through the door where I had imagined that I had seen the young woman walk by.

I found myself in a dark corridor filled with clutter long since abandoned by the people who had once lived here. Boxes of musty old clothes and books and other forgotten belongings were piled as high as the ceiling. I gave them a brief look over with my torch before deciding to push on. Two doors were at the end of the corridor facing each other. No windows lined the walls and so the only light that I had was the beam of my trusty torch. One door led into a small toilet. I didn't linger as there wasn't much to see besides a dirty toilet filled with water.

The second door led me into an old living room with an open fireplace and two old sofas. Framed photographs still hung from the wall depicting the family which lived here before. An old hillbilly with a bushy beard was standing beside his wife proudly brandishing a shotgun with a toothless grin whilst his wife had a look of insincere happiness on her face. Her smile would tell any observer that she was happy, but her eyes had a haunted look to them. It was a look which I recognized very well. Other photos were of the same woman holding a baby and then of the entire family sitting around the table. Aside from the parents, there were two twin girls sitting with them with blonde hair and exaggerated grins.

I had previously been in touch with an old police contact of mine called Olivia Lockhart and she had told me the tragic history of this family. One day the two girls were playing in the corn when their own father accidentally ran them over with his tractor as he ploughed the fields. He later took his shotgun and blew his brains out in the bedroom upstairs. The wife had received an eviction notice afterwards and packed all of the family's belongings before she took herself to the old oak tree in the back garden and hung herself. It was a story writhe with tragedy.

My investigation turned up nothing of interest in the living room, disappointingly. "God damn it!" I muttered in annoyance before slumping into one of the sofas. I figured that the upstairs was the only place left to investigate when I heard it: a gentle melody that I recognized as a classical piece reverberating from a distant region of the house.

At first, I thought that it was another hallucination, as sometimes they were auditory rather than visual, but after a few seconds the music didn't fade, and I knew that the music was playing somewhere. I got down onto my stomach and pressed my ear to the ground and a smirk spread across my lips. 'Clair de lune', French for "light of the moon" a soothing piano melody by Claude Debussy, was unmistakable.

"How curious though!" I thought to myself. I didn't see any doors to the cellar at any point during my search. Similarly, the police report which Olivia faxed to me didn't even mention a cellar.

I turned on my torch again whilst still laying down and that was when I happened to see it by sheer luck: a piece of rope in the chimney breast tied to a metal handle. It was a crude invention, to be sure, but I was able to predict what would happen once I pulled that cord: the entrance to the cellar would be revealed.

I didn't hesitate. I pulled the cord and smiled when a small section of the wall popped open across from the living room door to reveal a small space behind the living room wall. I crawled through the gap and shuffled towards an opening with a crudely built ladder descending down into darkness. A quick scan with my torch revealed a dank walkway underneath the house.

I descended as quietly as I could, half-expecting someone to bash me over the head when I reached the bottom. The classical music was louder now, but still muffled. Its gentle melody coupled with the repetitive sound of dripping water from an old pipe overhead. The ground beneath my feet was muddy and wet, sucking at my boots as I slowly moved down the underground passage with my torch lighting my way and my Beretta at the ready.

To my right was a heavy-looking metal door covered in rust with a curious cloud of cold air seeping underneath. To my left was a wooden door with a hole that looked like it had been punched into it. The classical music was coming from the room with the metal door.

It was behind this door that I would definitely find whoever was hiding down here.

But this wasn't the door that I investigated first. A muffled cry of distress came from the wooden door and so I peeked through to see that a cage had been erected in a corner of the room and I recognized Mike Vance bound by the wrists and ankles as I shone my torch through the hole into the darkness.

"Mike Vance!" I whispered in relief as I fumbled with the door handle and let myself in. I briskly paced over to his cell and observed him through the bars. He peered back up at me like a deer caught in headlights, the look on his face an ambivalent mixture of both relief and abject fear. It took me a while to figure out why he didn't speak to me and why his kidnapper had not bothered to gag him: his tongue had been cut out.

"Jesus-fucking-Christ!" I muttered in disgust and horror. I grabbed the door to his cage and rattled it fiercely in a futile attempt to free him. "I need the key! Sit tight! I'm going to free you soon! You're going to make it out of here!"

He mumbled in panic. Presumably he was begging me not to leave him. Tears rolled down his cheeks and he sobbed in agony and terror.

I gave him one last lingering look of sympathy before I moved to the metal door and pushed it open. The room inside was already bathed in blue light and so I turned off my torch and held my Beretta close. I flicked the safety off and gritted my teeth. I wasn't about to ask this fucker to come down to the station quietly.

I had seen some horrific sights during my time as a LAPD homicide detective, so I had a hardened stomach for scenes of gore. Hundreds of pine tree shaped car air fresheners hung from the ceiling and a refrigeration unit hooked up to a power generator which whirred quietly in the corner, all here to preserve the severed limbs that dangled from meat hooks and mask their smell.

I moved silently towards the source of the classical music where I could see a large figure of a man standing behind a plastic curtain with his back to me. He lifted a heavy arm in the air, and I could see the light reflect off of the meat cleaver in his hand just before he brought it down with a sickening thud. The sick fuck was cutting someone up in there.

I moved closer, passing a meat hook with the top half of Zach Brady's dismembered torso hanging from it. His eyes stared at me sightlessly, frozen in their last horrible moments. His arms and legs had been removed and dangled from different meat hooks across the underground room and his guts had spilled into a pile beneath him. It was absolutely disgusting.

I brushed aside the plastic curtain and practically held my breath through fear of the huge man hearing me. He must have been at least seven feet tall. He was dressed in dirty blue dungarees with a blood-stained apron over the top.

My heart sank when I saw Sarah Walker hanging upside down. Her feet were bound with rope which had been hoist onto another meat hook. Her throat had been cut and a pool of blood gathered around a drain installed into the tiled floor. Her body was wrapped in plastic and her hair was matted with blood. Her eyes had been gauged out and her arms had been removed and presumably hung from the hooks on the other side of the curtain.

It was Melissa Lennox who was on the madman's table now. Tears stung my eyes as I realized that had I arrived moments sooner I could have saved her. She hadn't been dead for long.

"Don't fucking move, you fucking piece of shit!" I called out through gritted teeth as I raised my Beretta and aimed it at the back of his head. I was still standing near the curtain, a decent distance away so that if he spun around and swung his hatchet at me, he wouldn't reach.

He froze in mid-swing of his hatchet, turning his head slightly to glance at me through the hockey mask that he was wearing. He didn't say anything but gave an exasperated sign as though my presence was a slight inconvenience.

"That's fucking right, asshole!" I shouted, grinning a wolfish grin, full of malicious intent for this bastard predator. "On your knees! NOW! DON'T MAKE ME ASK AG-" I didn't get the chance to finish making my demands. I should've just put a bullet in the back of his skull while I had the chance. It was my own desire to let this bastard know that I'd caught him which gave him an opportunity to trip the switch.

He moved like a gazelle on steroids, diving for a switch that plunged the room into darkness as the generators whirred to a stop.

"Son-of-a…" I exclaimed, frantically diving into my pocket for the torch. I found it and shone it in his direction to see that he had discarded his mask and equipped a set of night vision goggles. He flinched as my torchlight temporarily blinded him, but he was already coming towards me like a freight train. He charged at me and tossed me into the air like a bull tossing a matador. My torch hit the floor and flickered weakly before dying completely and I was engulfed by complete darkness.

"You're going to end up on one of those meat hooks!" one of the dead girls whispered in my ear.

"NOT NOW!" I shouted at the hallucination. I rolled on the floor and clutched my chest in agony. "Motherfucker…"

Then I heard it: the sound of the Butcher starting some kind of motor with a grunt and the sound of a metallic cord sliding back. Then came the inevitable constant buzz of the chainsaw and I knew that I had to move. This motherfucker could see me, but I couldn't even see where I was going.

I forced myself to my feet and reached for my Beretta as his thunderous footsteps came running towards me at full speed. I fired my Beretta blindly and used the quick flashes of light to blind my enemy, see where he was and locate the exit at the same time.

It worked! He staggered backwards, using his tree trunk arms to shield his NVG-covered eyes. Then he swung the chainsaw wildly at me and I rolled across the ground, hearing it pass over my head.

I memorized where the door was and bolted for it, hearing him hot on my heels. I made it to the ladder and frantically climbed to the top, hearing the chainsaw fading away behind me as I crawled through the small opening in the wall and back into the living room. I slammed the door shut behind me and panted breathlessly against it. I really had to stop smoking! Then it hit me: my lighter! It was still in my coat pocket and I could use it to light my way through the dark house because my phone was ancient and useless.

I reached into my pocket and found my mobile, my hand shakily scrolling through my contacts until I reached Olivia Lockhart's number. The line rang and rang for what felt like an eternity.

"Come on Olivia, you cunt!"

"Hello, Jack," Olivia answered as I called her a cunt. "Cordial as usual…"

"Fuck off, Olivia! This is urgent!" I held the phone to my chest and pressed my ear to the small door but heard nothing. Why didn't he follow me? Had he really given up that easily? "Olivia! I found the four college kids! Three of them are definitely dead! I had to leave one of them down there! I need you!"

"Whoa, whoa there! Slow down! Jack, what's going on?" asked Olivia, sounding as cool as a cucumber down the other end of the line, as though what I had told her was a mere triviality.

"I've just fucking told you! Some maniac just tried to cut my head off with a chainsaw!" I responded anxiously. "Send help to the old farmhouse down the interstate!"

"I will contact the State Sheriff and see to it that he sends help ASAP!" she replied. "In the meantime get out of that house!"

She didn't need to tell me twice. I got to my feet and bolted for the front door. Using my lighter as a makeshift torch, I passed through the kitchen and could see the last rays of the afternoon sun shining through the front door towards me.

Then the wall underneath the stairs burst into splinters and dust and the chainsaw-wielding maniac was standing in front of me. He had removed his NVG equipment and donned his hockey mask once again. He waved his chainsaw in the air and howled like a wild animal and I could see that the entrance to the cellar under the stairs had been boarded and plastered over.

"You've got to be fucking kidding!" I stumbled backwards and grabbed a kitchen chair to use to defend myself, only for him to cut it in half with his chainsaw and stick a heavy boot in my chest, sending me flying backwards and crashing to the ground. I rolled under the table just in time as he drove his chainsaw downward into the floor where I had just been laying. Sparks flew into my face and stung my skin, but my adrenaline was through the roof.

He attacked again, growling at me like a bear and driving his chainsaw through the kitchen table in an attempt to kill me. It took him a while to cut through the old table, giving me ample time to crawl out the other side. I got to my feet and drew my Beretta 9mm. I didn't hesitate to unload the rest of my clip, sending bullets flying into the Butcher's chest. One missed and hit the wall behind him, sending flecks of porcelain from the white wall tiles flying out into the room.

The Butcher staggered backwards with each slug that hit him until he sank to his knees and fell face down onto the floor. His chainsaw flew out of his hands and skidded across the kitchen floor until it came to a stop at my feet.

I panted breathlessly and walked towards the Butcher, stepping over splintered wood so I could cautiously tap him with my foot to see if I could provoke some kind of response. The Butcher didn't move.

"Make sure you stay dead, you disgusting cunt nugget!" I exclaimed, spitting on him in disgust. This man had taken the lives of three, possibly four, young teens and fuck knows how many others that he'd dragged to this house and dismembered.

My priority now was to head back into the cellar and find the key for the cell that held the lone survivor, Mike Vance. I searched the Butcher's dungaree pockets and found a keyring with a small brass key and the keys to the rusted old pickup truck which I had seen outside.

I took the stairs which the Butcher had used to ambush me, descending into the darkness once again. I had put three clips into the Butcher and so I was fairly confident he was dead, but I felt uneasy in spite of myself. I briefly pondered over what his motives could have been, if he even had any at all.

The stairs led down to the walkway opposite the ladder which I had descended before, so this time the metal door was to my left and the wooden door was to my right. I headed straight into the wooden door, using my Zippo lighter as a faint source of light. My heart pounded in my chest as part of me expected to find Mike Vance dead in his cell. I held my lighter to the bars and whistled to get Mike's attention.

To my relief he was alive. Apparently, the Butcher hadn't thought to kill Mike before he began his hunt for me. His eyes widened and he gargled something incomprehensible in panic before I shushed him soothingly.

"Don't try to speak. You're safe now!" I assured him calmly. "I put three slugs in his chest. He was a fucking lump, but if he survived that then I'll eat his dungarees." I smiled warmly and tried the small brass key in the lock. The lock was stiff and took some gentle persuasion to unlock. I flung open the cage door and fumbled with the knots which bound his wrists and ankles. Once his wrists were free, he stretched his arms and aided me in releasing his bonds around his ankles.

"Your friends didn't make it," I told him bluntly, giving his shoulder a reassuring squeeze when his eyes welled with tears and he sobbed uncontrollably, making strange choking sounds as he heaved. Whether he was sad for his friends or happy to be free I could not know. It didn't matter.

He put his arm around my shoulder, and I helped him limp up the creaking cellar stairs.

It wasn't ideal to walk away with only one survivor out of the four, but it raised my spirits to know that I'd at least saved one and permanently put down the animal that inflicted this horror onto these students.

The shocks in this case had mounted exponentially and culminated in me putting three bullets into my assailant's chest. I thought that rescuing Mike Vance would be the end of it, but I was sorely mistaken. When we reached the hallway, I inevitably glanced into the kitchen to observe the Butcher's corpse, only to find it wasn't there! Neither was his chainsaw!

"Holy shit!" I muttered as my heart rate accelerated. Mike glanced at me with a worried expression on his face and gave a feeble whimper. My eyes followed droplets of fresh blood that lead out through the front door onto the front porch.

"How the fuck can he have gotten up and walked away from that?" I muttered as I walked into the kitchen and left Mike supporting himself by leaning against the wall in the hallway. A small pool of blood had gathered underneath where the Butcher had been lying unconscious. I deduced that my shots had put him into shock, and he had collapsed unconscious rather than dead as I had at first believed. Now I was fucked! I knew that he was out there waiting for me and Mike. Part of me hoped that he had gone off into the cornfield to bleed to death, but I knew that that wasn't likely.

I heard Mike make a break for it, his movements swift despite his limp.

"Wait! Don't go out there!" I called after him as I gave chase.

Mike ignored me and kept running. He didn't even make it to the porch steps before the Butcher started his chainsaw and brushed Mike's arm with it. Mike wailed and flew down the porch steps with a gash in his shirt that revealed the severed flesh underneath.

I grabbed a broken chair leg with a pointed edge and charged like a jousting knight until I speared the Butcher in his arm. He grunted as he could no longer hold his chainsaw. It clattered to the floor as he brought his other arm swinging into my face. I flew backwards from the impact, landing hard on the wooden decking of the porch with a thud that knocked the breath out of me. Some of my belongings flew out of my pocket, including my phone and the keys to my Sedan.

The Butcher tossed the chair leg I had used as a weapon aside and he strode towards me, grunting in pain before he stuck his heavy boot into my stomach and knocked the wind out of me completely. He then grabbed my shirt and dragged me to my feet as effortlessly as a crane lifting a pillow. I punched him in the stomach and flinched in pain when my hand crunched against pure muscle. The Butcher retaliated by wrapping his sausage fingers around my throat and hoisting me into the air. I turned my head to catch a glance of Mike Vance hobbling down the dirt path where he had spotted my Sedan parked tight to the fields of corn and picked up my keys where I had dropped them. I tried to call him a "motherfucker" for abandoning me to die, but all that left my lips was a breathless wheezing.

The Butcher tightened his grip and I coughed a mouthful of spittle down my chin and clutched his gargantuan arm in a vain attempt to remove it. My head started to throb, and my vision was becoming blurry. I scrambled at my hip and pulled my 9mm Beretta handgun from its holster and bashed the Butcher in the side of the head with it, knocking his hockey mask to the floor.

He had blood between his teeth and his right arm trembled with the strain of holding me after I assaulted him with the broken chair leg, but his left arm held steady and no matter how much I whacked him in the side of the head with my handgun he wouldn't relent in his attempt to snuff me out. He gritted his teeth and squeezed tighter,

THE DARK SIDE OF BEAUTY

staring menacingly into my eyes with intense hatred.

"Fu….ck…yoooo…." I gasped as I raised both my arms and pressed the two of my thumbs into his eyeballs. There was a sickening squelching noise as I pushed as hard as I could until he screamed and tossed me over the porch railing into the mud below.

I hit the ground with a thud and the wind was knocked out of me. I gasped desperately for air. The Butcher stomped around on the porch in agony before he donned his hockey mask and started revving his chainsaw again.

I scrambled to my feet and staggered forward towards the corn fields with the Butcher hot on my heels. I hoped to elude him in the tall forests of corn now that the last rays of sunlight had dissipated and given way to the pale rays of moonlight. I had to lose him in the corn. I knew that it was my only hope until Olivia could contact the State Sheriff.

Unfortunately, luck was not on my side. I was still dizzy from where I had come close to passing out when the Butcher choked me and so my escape was clumsy, and my coordination was terrible. I slipped and tripped and constantly had to keep picking myself up whilst the Butcher strolled leisurely behind me, chuckling to himself deeply as his long strides gained ground on me.

Then it happened.

I spurred myself forward in a last desperate attempt to escape when my foot slid from under me and I flew forward, face down into the mud. When I looked back, the Butcher was only a few paces away, brandishing his chainsaw in the air with a victorious howl.

I sighed and closed my eyes, resigned to the fact that I was about to die. I did not fear death, in fact, I welcomed it. A release from the mental torment which I suffered every day would be bliss.

Then I heard the screech of tires and I opened my eyes to see my Sedan tearing towards the Butcher. He looked startled for a moment and braced himself before the Sedan flew towards him like a bullet with a determined-looking Mike Vance behind the wheel.

I barely even had enough time to process what was happening before Mike slammed the car into the Butcher. The Butcher's head slammed into my windscreen with a sickening crack, instantly cracking my windscreen in the shape of a spider web. Then the Butcher was sent flying into the air and landed with a sound of bones breaking. Mike swerved out of control and crashed my car into the side of the porch near the house. The sound of my horn blaring constantly filled the air.

When I struggled to my feet, my first instinct was to make sure that the Butcher no longer posed a threat. His dungarees were ripped at the leg and soaked in blood with a shard of broken bone protruding through. His hockey mask had flown off and his discarded chainsaw lay buzzing near the corn. The Butcher's face was claret. He coughed up a mouthful of blood as I stepped near him and feebly swiped at my ankle with his remaining good arm. His other arm, the one which I had speared earlier, was twisted the wrong way and twitched. His eyes darted back and forth, bloodshot and delirious until they rolled upwards and he lost consciousness.

He was a threat no longer.

I ran to my Sedan and flung the door open. The front of the car was crumpled inwards and the windscreen had shattered on impact. Mike Vance hadn't been wearing a seatbelt and had smashed his head against the steering wheel upon impact. I pushed him back and winced when I saw his bent and broken nose that had exploded in a crimson waterfall down his face. Some of his teeth were strewn across the passenger side of my car.

"You crazy bastard!" I gasped. I checked his pulse and sighed with relief when I felt it still beating. I pulled him from the wreckage and made him as comfortable as possible, throwing my blood and mud stained trench coat over him to keep him warm.

Then I saw the blue and red lights flashing closer and closer. Olivia had contacted the State Sheriff and he had arrived to investigate the scene with two other police cars full of brown-uniformed officers armed with shotguns.

Most notable of the officers was the sheriff. He got out of his car and adjusted his belt before he strode arrogantly toward me, giving a curt tip of his cowboy hat.

"What the fuck happened here?!" demanded the sheriff through a mouthful of tobacco. His eyes widened when he saw the Butcher strewn across the ground. "Call sleeping beauty an ambulance!" he ordered his deputy.

"He will probably die. From what I can gather he has a broken leg and internal haemorrhaging. Not to mention three 9mm slugs that I put in his chest. Your main concern should be the young boy who's unconscious over by the crashed Sedan!"

The sheriff spat out a mouthful of black nicotine and gave me an incredulous look. "You must be Jack Cucchiano," he said. "Lieutenant Lockhart mentioned you were in distress and so we came as fast as we could." He offered me a handshake and his face turned sour when I grimaced as though his hand was covered in shit.

"This could have been avoided!" I snapped at him, unable to keep my anger in check. "Your initial investigation was a complete shambles! You neglected to search the property in the first place!"

"You watch your fucking mouth, boy! You're under my jurisdiction now, Cucchiano," he puffed his chest and prodded an accusatory finger in my chest. "I could slap you in cuffs and book you quicker than a turd can flush! And there would be nothing your contacts in the LAPD could do about it!"

"Book me for what exactly?!" I snapped back with a bitter laugh devoid of humor. "Book me for doing your job for you and actually taking the time to investigate?! Some turds flush easily, but others refuse to be flushed!"

"All turds flush," replied the sheriff levelly, his hand lingering over his truncheon attached to his belt. "Some just need to be forced down. I could book you for shooting a man three times in the chest."

I understood his threat, but I would not be intimidated by some asshole sheriff getting kicks from swinging his dick around. "Listen, you fucking idiot!" I shouted in anger. "All I'm saying is that if you'd have done your job properly all those kids might still have been alive! And as for putting three slugs in Goliath over there, he's a psychotic killer who murdered three people, god knows how many more, and tried to cut my head off with a chainsaw! You'd be doing the world a service by pressing the end of your shotgun against his skull and blowing his brains out, not sending him to a fucking hospital!"

The sheriff rolled his eyes and huffed impatiently. "He shall be taken to a hospital and treated and then stand trial like anyone else in this country. He will more than likely be found guilty and sentenced to death under state law," he replied, his tone becoming more venomous. "Now I suggest you fuck off before I decide to arrest you for being such an annoying piece of shit!"

I threw up my arms in frustration and stormed away from the sheriff before I did something that I would regret, such as ramming my fist into his face. Shortly after our confrontation, two ambulances arrived on scene and Mike Vance and the Butcher were taken to the nearest hospital to be treated for their wounds. A deputy assured me that the Butcher would be kept under constant guard and would be shot dead if he attempted an escape.

I had to call Olivia Lockhart to come pick me up as I had no money and my car was trashed. She was annoyed to be sure, but I explained that the sheriff and I had argued and that he refused to provide me with a lift into town.

"It's a long walk back to LA," he said with a mouth full of tobacco and a smug grin on his face. "Better get hiking."

"Give me your name and badge number!" I requested, my voice full of bitterness and hatred for this man.

He surprisingly obliged before he tore down the dirt road like a formula one driver, leaving me standing in a cloud of his dust. His name was Hershel Murray, Sheriff Hershel Murray. It wasn't a name that I was going to forget. I promised myself that I'd have his badge one day.

I stood in the rain for over three hours whilst the remaining deputies conducted a more thorough search of the house. The three dead students were put in body bags and driven to the coroner's office and the police closed off the country lane leading to the farm. I was asked to vacate the area as this was now a police matter. Weary and despondent, I obliged and waited for Olivia to collect me from the side of the highway.

By the time she pulled up, I was drenched. She gave me a sympathetic smile and asked about the case.

"I'd rather not talk about it," I told her as I stared out of the window. "I'm really not looking forward to telling the Walkers that their daughter is dead…"

Olivia didn't take her eyes off the road, but she rested her hand on mine and smiled. "You did everything you could, Jack," she said comfortingly "You're a good detective!"

I smiled back at her. I felt grateful that I had made such a good friend during my service in the LAPD. I glanced at her satnav and sighed at the estimated arrival time in LA: almost four hours. I settled back into the seat and fell into an uneasy, dreamless sleep.

CHAPTER 2

Annabelle

I am relentlessly haunted by the images and voices of the dead, though whether they are actually the restless spirits of those who I failed or simply visual and auditory hallucinations, I cannot say...

In particular the spirit of little Annabelle I find especially harrowing. Her unsolved murder is the defining moment that ruined my career in the LAPD and also my marriage. I could never come to accept that I had failed to bring her killer to justice and that was why she haunted me everywhere I went.

Her murder was the fourth in LA committed by the infamous 'Artist Killer', a name bestowed upon the depraved lunatic by the media. I refused to acknowledge him as such, as I believed that such a title only served to inflate his ego and confidence. His modus operandi was to kidnap his victims and mutilate and dismember them before leaving their remains in a park or one of the many patches of wasteland that littered LA. He would use their skin as his canvas and cut locks of their hair for his paint brush to paint a twisted image depicting some unspeakable scene of horror.

I was the homicide detective assigned to the Artist Killer case, alongside my partner Olivia Lockhart. Together we built a psychological profile of the suspect and established his comfort zone based on the distance between the locations of the first and second victims. However, after Annabelle's murder the killings ceased, and the killer's trail went cold.

Annabelle Green lived with her father in the Encino neighborhood situated in the San Fernando Valley region of Los Angeles. She had gone out to play in the front garden one day when her parents noticed that she was missing. A half-blind elderly neighbor claimed later that he had seen Annabelle walking down the street with a young man hand in hand. Had her killer gained her trust somehow? Her parents had informed me that she had been brought up not to trust strangers and so that left only two possibilities: either Annabelle knew her killer, or he had gained her trust over time.

Annabelle's parents received a ransom letter demanding $20,000 the day following her disappearance, which the parents tried to muster as quickly as possible. However, the so-called Artist is a fucked-up bastard and had no intention of returning Annabelle. The ransom letter specified that the parents of Annabelle Green had exactly one week to provide the money, but a man walking his dog found her naked body among some reeds near the Encino reservoir.

The evidence which I found at the scene was a partial tire tread and a hair belonging to someone who we had processed before for drunk and disorderly behavior. Chad Sullivan was his name, a young delinquent whose daddy worked as a film producer and who had too much money. Chad lived alone in a large estate which his father had purchased in Encino, only a few streets away from where the Greens lived.

I arrested Chad Sullivan and questioned him at the station. He denied ever having spoken to the little girl, let alone kidnap and murder. He also pointed out that his father was rich, and he had no need to demand ransom when he could get money from his father at any time he wanted. Chad also had a solid alibi at the time of Annabelle's death as he had travelled by train to enrol at an air force base. We had to release him and with his release our investigation came to an end as we had no further lines of investigation to follow. The ransom note had been soaked in gasoline and cleared of fingerprints, so we couldn't use that evidence either. A week later another painting inevitably arrived at the police station.

After Annabelle's death the killer disappeared. No more killings and no more macabre paintings. I became depressed and hit the bottle even harder. My drinking addiction spiralled out of control and eventually I lost my job.

*

Olivia had dropped me off at home after she took me to the Walker residence so that I could inform the parents of Sarah Walker what had happened to their daughter and her friends. They wept and thanked me profusely for my help before they offered me my fee, which I reluctantly accepted. I felt guilty for not bringing their daughter home safely to them. Thinking about it reignited the hatred that burned like a burning fire within me, hatred for the Butcher and for the neglectful sheriff who was too lazy to conduct a thorough investigation.

The first thing I did when I entered my apartment was kick off my boots and throw my trench coat in the washing machine. Then I walked into the open-plan living room and kitchen and poured a glass of neat whiskey. I drank the whiskey in one and winced as it burned my throat and chest. I poured another whiskey and made my way to my study with my bottle and glass in hand.

My study was a spare bedroom which I had converted into an office. In this room was everything that I had gathered on the Artist case. The case was my obsession. It is the only case which I could never solve as a police homicide detective and a private investigator.

During the case over two hundred people contacted the police station claiming either to be the killer or to know who the killer was. None of these calls were ever followed up on as the influx of callers only increased over the weeks and months that followed. In the end we had nothing concrete to go on.

I pulled my chair out and slumped into it. The time was almost 3 a.m., but I couldn't sleep until I had at least reviewed my notes one more time. I opened my desk drawer and pulled out a copy of the case file that Olivia had provided for me and opened it.

"The first victim…" I opened the file. "Scarlett Jones, twenty-five years of age. An aspiring actress with contacts from Bel Air. Worked in a small café in Downtown LA." I turned the page to see a beautiful young woman with short red hair and green eyes. "Disappeared April 5th and her body was found a week later on April 12th on a deserted lot at Leimert Park, South Los Angeles region of LA."

Leimert Park was developed in the 1920s as a master-planned community featuring quaint Spanish colonial revival homes and streets

THE DARK SIDE OF BEAUTY

lined with resplendent trees. "Her body was discovered by a mother walking her son to school. Scarlett had been cut in half and drained of blood. A Glasgow smile had been cut into her mouth, giving her a creepy look and flesh had been flayed from her thighs. Last seen arguing on the phone at her place of work before storming out on April 5th. The Boyfriend was the initial prime suspect. He was brought in for questioning, but later cleared as his band provided a solid alibi. A day after Scarlett's remains were discovered her belongings were found in a trashcan at Longbeach. Her purse was still in her bag, containing her apartment keys, ID and a wad of cash."

I sighed and rubbed my brow in frustration. A beautiful girl with her whole life ahead of her… she didn't deserve what happened to her and I truly hoped that her killer suffered a horrific death. I clenched my fists and then took a deep breath. "The painting arrived at the police station on the 14th. It was a painting of Scarlett. It depicted her smiling an unnaturally large grin that gave her an almost sinister demeanor. Above the image, painted in red, were the words 'A Beautiful Smile'." I paused and took a mouthful of whiskey. "But the most disturbing thing about this painting was that the canvas was made of Scarlett's own skin! The creepy red title turned out to be her blood and with the painting came a brush that was made with Scarlett's hair…"

I pushed Scarlett's file aside and looked at the second folder. The problem with the second victim was the unprecedented mystery that shrouded her. I opened the file. "Name: Unknown. Age: Estimated at 26. Nobody reported her missing and nobody was able to identify her body." I scratched my head, puzzled. "We have no idea who this woman is. Lady Mystery was found on the beach lying face up in the sand. She had been decapitated, but this was not the cause of death. The cause of death was asphyxiation, the same as Scarlett. Her eyes had been gauged out and replaced with child's marbles. Lady Mystery also had flesh professionally flayed from her thighs. A couple of days after she was discovered on June 20th, another painting arrived at the police station depicting the mysterious woman looking at herself in a mirror and clawing melting flesh from her face. Painted in blood, the title was: 'The Masks We Wear'."

I stared at the file and sighed. "Tourists and journalists arrived on the scene first, taking pictures of the poor girl. Any evidence around the body was likely trampled into the sand by the waves of spectators. No known connections within the city."

I took another mouthful of whiskey, finishing the glass with a grimace as it burned its way down my throat and left a lingering burning in my chest. "Rosita Ramirez," I said to myself as I opened her file. "32 years old. Lived in Inglewood and worked as a care nurse for the elderly in the same area. She didn't show up for work for a full week starting 11th December and was discovered murdered in her apartment just after Christmas by her landlady. Cause of death was asphyxiation. Police found her naked in the bathroom, crammed into a suitcase with flesh flayed from her thighs like the other two victims. Her eyes had been gauged out but hadn't been replaced like the previous victims. There was no sign of forced entry and the landlady was the only other person with a key to the apartment. However, I did notice tiny scratches around the lock, which suggests that the lock had been picked. Neighbors heard nothing and saw nothing, so I deduced that she was strangled in her sleep. The coroner's report supported my theory as he approximated that her time of death was roughly between 3 a.m. and 4 a.m. on the 10th of December. Another macabre painting arrived at the police station the day her death was made public depicting Rosita naked in a shark cage, her skin bubbled and flaked away like she was in acid rather than water. The title 'Dissolving the Ego' was painted in Rosita's blood and the canvass was made from the missing flayed skin. A paintbrush arrived with the painting made from cuttings of Rosita's hair, just like the previous victims."

I poured another whiskey and rubbed my temples, giving an exhausted sigh. "Annabelle Green." Her name left my lips in a high-pitched whimper. I felt the tears begin to sting my eyes as I began to imagine the horror to which these people and their families had been subjected. Annabelle was the hardest to endure for me by far. "Went missing just after new year and was found the very next day strangled at the Encino reservoir. Curiously no flesh was flayed from her body like the previous victims. A ransom note demanding $20,000, which the killer had no intention of collecting as Annabelle was already dead. And a witness who claimed to have seen young Annabelle walking down the road hand in hand with a young man. Tire treads belonging to an unknown vehicle and the DNA evidence that placed Chad Sullivan at the scene of the murder..." I tapped the file impatiently. "What am I not seeing here?! How can Chad have been placed at the scene when he had a solid alibi? Several members of the air force recruitment facility collaborated his story…" A dozen questions raced through my mind. Was the hair placed on Annabelle in an attempt to frame Chad Sullivan? And if so, to what end? Why would the killer want to see Chad take the fall for these murders? Nothing made any sense.

"A painting entitled 'Loss of Innocence' arrived at the police station after Chad was released from custody. It depicted Annabelle hanging from a tree with her own entrails. It was crudely painted, as though the killer were in a rush to complete the piece and see Chad behind bars." I drank the full glass of whiskey in one. "Then there's the ransom note! And the tire tracks, but Chad doesn't drive a car!"

That's when I heard whispering, the whispering of a little girl that seemed to come from every direction. I looked around frantically, searching for the source of the whispering. "It's all in your mind!" I told myself, somewhat unconvincingly. Then my doorbell buzzed, and I got to my feet and walked to the door, leaving my files in an unorganized pile on the table.

I pressed my eye against the peephole and gasped with shock when nobody was there. The buzzing had continued until the very moment when I pressed my eye to the door. Was someone hiding below the peephole? If so, how would they know that I was about to look through? I pulled away and spun on my heels to walk away, but as I did the doorbell buzzed again. I spun around and opened the door in one fluid motion, half-expecting someone to be standing behind it holding their finger on the buzzer.

Nobody was there.

I stepped out into the hallway and looked down both ends, scratching my head in bewilderment as nobody was to be seen. Then I heard the giggling of a little girl echoing down the hallway and the sound of little footsteps falling on the floor as if a child were running away.

The lights down the hallway began to flicker on and off, then the lights next to them started to flicker and I saw the image of a woman standing at a weird angle. Her limbs twisted and her head shook side to side at an unnatural speed. With each flicker of the lights she appeared closer and closer. The sound of her crying echoed down the hallway and filled my heart with dread. Her long black hair cascaded over her face in matted tufts with a clump missing. Her thighs had bloody patches where her flesh had been cut away.

The disgruntled spirit of Rosita Ramirez was coming for me. Her arms twisted at unnatural angles and creaked like old trees. The lights outside my neighbor's apartment flickered and she appeared at their door, the sound of her sobs filling my ears.

"I'm sorry!" I called to her before I fled into my apartment and slammed my door shut with my back to it, panting breathlessly. That's when I noticed that my bathroom door was ajar, and light seeped through the gap. I found this immediately strange because I always closed a room door when I left it and I never left the lights on. I walked over to the door and reluctantly peered inside. A suitcase was sitting in my bathtub. I stood frozen in horror as the suitcase started to unzip itself and two rotten arms sprouted from the opening. The sound of sobbing filled the bathroom and I staggered backwards and slammed the bathroom door shut.

When I turned around, I gasped and held my hands to my head at the sight of hundreds of bloody handprints covering the hallway leading to my study. The study door was closed with a child's inflatable ball constantly rolling back and forth bouncing against it.

The door creaked open when I approached it and two rotten hands picked up the ball, which turned into Lady Mystery's head when the lights in my study flickered. The study door slammed itself shut and I collapsed in a heap on the floor hyperventilating.

The hallucinations, or the spirits of the dead, were becoming stronger and more vivid. I felt like opening the window to my apartment and plunging six stories to my death.

But then who would catch the man who murdered these women and little Annabelle? I knew that it had to be me. I wiped tears from my eyes and rose to my feet. The hallway of my apartment had returned to normal. There were no more flickering lights, no more bloody handprints and no more spirits harassing me.

"I will find out who did this to you! I know that you're all upset and angry!" I shouted tearfully "I will never give up looking for answers, I promise you!" My eyes darted around the hallway and the open-plan kitchen and living room, searching for anything out of the ordinary. Then I muttered, "I promise you…" again in a quiet, but determined, whisper.

Then my doorbell buzzed again, and my head shot towards the door. My heart was pounding against my rib cage as though it wanted to escape my body. "Not again!" I called out, slumping to the floor and burying my head in my hands. I rocked back and forth and wept with fear. I couldn't bear to see another horrific image of one of the victims again, I just couldn't. "Go away!" I called out desperately as the doorbell buzzed again, more persistently this time. "Go away! Leave me alone!"

"Jack?" called a familiar but muffled voice from behind the door. "Jack Cucchiano! Open up!"

I looked up at the door with a raised eyebrow and got to my feet. I cautiously made my way towards the front door and peeked through the peephole. I thought that I had recognized that voice! My former boss, Captain Matthew Perry stood at my door in full uniform with Olivia Lockhart standing beside him.

"This is a colossal waste of time!" I heard Perry whisper to Olivia in an impatient agitated tone.

Olivia cast him a look that silenced him and he rolled his eyes before pressing the buzzer again.

I opened the door. "What is it? It's the early hours of Sunday morning!" I snapped at them, although in secret I was glad to see Olivia. She was also in full uniform. Her crystal blue eyes regarded me warmly with a vague hint of underlying concern.

"It's Monday morning, Jack," Olivia corrected me gently.

"Jack, you look like shit and you stink of whiskey!" cut in Perry. "Can we talk inside? It's important!"

It took me a few moments to adjust to the news that I'd just heard. Monday morning! How could that be possible?! How had I lost an entire day? I stammered something nonsensical and moved aside to allow Perry and Olivia to enter my apartment.

"Jack, you're wearing the same shirt you had on when I picked you up in Texas…" said Olivia with a worried tone.

I looked down to see dried blood and mud stains down my front.

I closed the door and gestured for both of them to enter and sit down. "I'll freshen up and join you in a moment," I told them before I whipped my shirt off and headed into the bathroom. Before I did, I noticed Perry and Olivia cast each other a glance of concern.

I changed into some blue jeans and a button up white shirt and rolled my sleeves up. "Would either of you like a drink?" I asked disinterested as I opened a cupboard and retrieved a fresh bottle of whiskey. I twisted the lid open and poured myself a glass.

"None for me thanks," replied Olivia curtly with a wave of her hand.

Perry just shook his head distastefully. "Let me get right to the point, Cucchiano," he interjected bluntly. "We're here because we need your help."

I lit a cigarette and nursed my whiskey as I seated myself in my armchair facing Perry and Olivia. "You need *my* help?" I exclaimed mockingly. "What could I possibly do to help you? Why on earth would I even care about the problems of the LAPD? You fired me, remember?" I glanced at Perry reproachfully and took another drink from my whiskey.

Captain Perry flinched indignantly. "I had no choice, Jack!" he explained. "Your behavior was becoming problematic for the homicide department! The mayor was practically threatening me to remove your badge."

I laughed bitterly. "I see that nothing changes! You still talk absolute fucking bullshit!"

Perry scowled at me and rose to his feet. "Fuck this!" he shouted angrily. "Come on, Olivia, let's leave this dumb fuck to drown himself in another bottle of whiskey and self-pity! What a waste!"

Olivia ushered Perry to sit. "Please, captain!" she pleaded before turning to me. "Jack, we want you to help us with another homicide."

"Not interested," I replied rudely.

"It's the Artist, Jack.... He's back," she uttered, her voice becoming more and more distant as she explained the most recent murder committed by the Artist killer after two years of inactivity.

My fingers became numb and my glass of whiskey slid through

them and landed on the carpet with a thud, spilling its brown contents and staining my cream carpet.

"Jack? Jack?!"

I raised a hand and silenced her. My temples were throbbing, and I could hear static coming from my radio.

Then silence.

"He's not well, Olivia! Look at him, he's vacant!" snapped Perry. "I'm not having him investigate this case alongside the LAPD. He's a liability!"

I glanced up at him and grinned. "Maybe so, captain Perry, but I'm still the best fucking homicide detective the LAPD has ever known! And I never fail a case!"

The Artist was back! And this time I would catch him and settle the score once and for all. For Scarlett, Lady Mystery, Rosita, and little Annabelle and finally for my own sanity!

"We'll explain on the way," said Perry with a sigh of resignation.

CHAPTER 3

Room 527

Olivia drove us to the scene of the crime in her SUV. The murder had occurred during the early hours of Monday morning in a busy four-star hotel situated in Beverly Hills. The hotel was a fairly new building and had only been open for the past year.

Rain lashed violently against Olivia's windshield as we pulled into the car park of the hotel and already crowds of journalists had swarmed at the hotel entrance to get their story.

"Have these people no respect?!" remarked Captain Perry with bitter contempt. "They're like flies drawn to shit!"

We exited the SUV and ran towards the entrance to the Budapest Hotel, where several uniformed police officers kept the baying crowd of journalists at bay. As I ran through the car park the gathering water beneath my feet flicked up and soaked the bottom of my jeans. We made it to the entrance and the police officers let the three of us pass.

The Budapest Hotel lobby was tiled with marble and had huge columns holding up balconies that overlooked the lobby of the hotel. Plants lined the walls in huge ceramic vases adorned with beautiful patterns and jewels, which were probably fake, set into the ceramic. A huge fountain stood in the center of the lobby where a statue of a woman stood holding a jug from which the water poured. The reception desk was situated underneath two sets of marble staircases that led to the next level.

A nervous looking man, who looked like he was in his late

adolescence, observed us curiously as we made our way across the lobby to the elevators. The hotel owner and manager and a security guard were standing in the lobby, both appearing anxious. The hotel manager was pacing back and forth in agitation.

I was approached by a stocky police officer with green eyes and a bushy mustache. "Name's Kenneth, first officer at the scene," he extended his hand and shook mine with gusto. "I've gathered those who might be able to offer some information in the foyer."

I patted his shoulder and nodded curtly in response, quickening my pace to keep up with Perry and Olivia.

"These three staff members will need to be questioned," said Captain Perry as we stepped into the elevator.

The steel doors slid closed and Perry pressed the number for the fifth floor. We stood in silence as the elevator ascended. A red light showed which floor we were at and I watched it restlessly until we reached the specified floor.

We walked down a corridor with rooms lining both sides. Paintings in golden frames hung from the walls and ornate vases with blue oriental patterns stood on pedestals along the corridor.

Finally, we approached the scene of the crime: room 527.

Larry King, the coroner, exited the room wearing rubber latex gloves as we approached. During my time at the LAPD we all called him 'The Grim Reaper' due to the nature of his work and his bleak outlook on everything.

"Hello, Grim!" I greeted him with a warm smile.

"Jack," he replied flatly, his voice conveying no emotion and his eyes maintaining their usual glazed expression. They said that the eyes were the windows to the soul, but the eyes of Larry King appeared soulless. It was like looking into two pools of icy water. "It's not pretty in there," he said in a monotone voice.

Larry was a tall man. At almost seven foot he towered over Perry, Olivia and myself. He was skinny, like a rake, and his remaining graying hair was combed over in an attempt to hide his rapidly receding hair line. His eyes were icy blue, and his nose was long and pointed like the beak of a bird. He was dressed in black, as usual, with a paper suit over his black shirt and trousers.

"I'll speak to you back at the morgue, detective," Larry said to me. He gave me a curt nod and then continued: "Time of death was between midnight and one in the morning."

Room 527 was shrouded in darkness. From the entrance to the room the bathroom was to the left. Two doors leading out to the balcony were opposite the entrance with large velvet curtains draped shut to block out any light from outside. The bed and wardrobes were behind the bathroom wall, next to the double glass balcony doors. A table was against the wall opposite the double bed and a fancy plasma-screen TV was mounted above it. A half-empty bottle of champagne was standing on the table with two crystal glasses beside it.

"Everything is left as it was when we got here," said Olivia from behind me. She remained standing in the hallway with Perry and The Grim Reaper as I stepped over the threshold into the room.

"Before you look around you should know that the door was locked from the inside when we arrived," said Perry. When I glanced back at him curiously, he added: "The key to the room is still in the room and only the reception has a spare."

"Interesting!" I replied. "So, either she committed suicide, or the killer works for the hotel." I was speaking in jest of course, but Perry apparently didn't see the funny side.

I walked by the bathroom and made my way to the bed where I could see the victim's feet at the end. When I walked to the end of the bathroom, where I could see the whole of the bed, I involuntarily gasped: "Son of a bitch!" The woman was a young lady with short curly brown hair. A large tuft of her hair was missing, and skin had been cut from her thighs. The fucked-up bastard had sliced open her stomach and clipped back the flesh with surgical clips so that all her organs were exposed. Her eyeballs had been removed so that two empty sockets stared back at me. She was naked as they always were.

I wasted no time. I began to investigate the crime scene. The killer had already given me a very useful hint. Initially I had built up a psychological profile of the killer and ascertained by his flaying of the skin with such precision that he was either someone who had worked as a butcher or someone with surgical knowledge. This recent murder suggested the latter. The killer had knowledge of surgery and had a steady hand for it. He was someone very calm and calculating and with a high level of intelligence.

"Thanks for the insight, motherfucker!" I muttered to myself. I inspected the body further and noticed bruising around her throat. She had been strangled, like all four of the previous victims. Larry could've probably told me that anyway.

I walked over to the small table opposite the bed and inspected the champagne bottle and the two crystal glasses. One glass still had champagne sitting in the bottom of it and the other glass was empty with lipstick marks around the rim.

"Seems our victim had some company..." I used a handkerchief from my pocket and picked up the glass with no lipstick on the rim, turning it carefully in the dull light of the room. "There you are!" I uttered, smiling as I saw a distinctive fingerprint revealed by the light. This would be used as the first piece of evidence.

I looked in the wardrobes and wolf-whistled at the spectacle within. Corsets and various other raunchy items of lingerie were inside, including sexy underwear and stockings and suspenders. Only a few articles of clothing were folded neatly on the shelves which included a skirt, knee-length boots, a beret, and a green cardigan.

A brown leather handbag was sitting on the bottom shelf and I peered inside and found a purse. I opened the purse and found the key to room 527, car keys, a driving license and an ID card belonging to the victim. "Emma Fontaine. Age twenty-one. From New Orleans, Louisiana." I glanced at the dead girl with a mournful sigh. "You're a long way from home, sweetheart," I uttered quietly. "Don't worry! I'll find whoever did this!"

I checked under the bed and found nothing. I walked towards the bathroom and opened the door to take a look inside. The bathtub was sparkling clean, as though it had never been used. Since there was no blood in the main room, I concluded that poor Emma Fontaine had met her end in this very room and then later been moved. The shower curtain was missing. The killer more than likely used it to catch any blood.

Then I walked to the balcony, stopping briefly to observe the bottom of the curtains that looked like they were still damp. A quick pinch with my finger and thumb confirmed it. I opened the doors and stepped out onto the balcony. The rain came down ferociously, bouncing on the stone handrail. I curiously noted that the room adjacent to room 527 had a balcony also, with no screen separating the two.

"Well?" demanded Captain Perry fervently. "What do you make of it, Jack?"

"Emma Fontaine travelled to LA from New Orleans, Louisiana," I replied. "She clearly had intentions of meeting with someone for a night of passion. Unfortunately, it didn't go as planned. We can't be sure that the person who arranged to meet her and the killer are the same person, but if we can find out who she shared this room with they could shed some light on the situation. Whoever was in here with her was probably the last person to see her alive."

Matthew Perry nodded in affirmation: "I agree. Now how did the killer leave the room without locking the door?"

"He jumped balconies to the room next door," I explained. "In all likelihood whoever was staying in room 526 is the killer!"

Perry and Olivia both looked unconvinced.

"I'll explain!" I continued. "The curtains over the balcony doors are damp at the bottom. Our killer most likely booked into room 526 under a fake name. And I guarantee he would've paid cash. He hopped the balcony and sneakily ambushed Emma while she showered. If we get some fluorescent lighting in that bathroom, I am confident we will see the remnants of blood covering the bathtub. She wasn't murdered in the bed; she was moved there."

"Jumped the balcony?" repeated Perry in disbelief. It was five stories to the ground. If the killer had slipped or failed to make the jump, then his spree would've come to an embarrassing and sticky end.

I asked Olivia for a torch and shone the light on the red carpet, closest to the doors leading to the balcony. "There!" I said triumphantly. We could all see it: the faintest outline of a muddy footprint. "There you have it!" I exclaimed. "Our killer came in through the balcony doors!"

"We did consider that," said Olivia, her cheeks flushing and her voice betraying her indignation. "We concluded that he never would've made the jump."

"Forensics turned up no evidence," said Perry. "Not so much as a fucking flake of skin."

"Our killer is resourceful," I explained. "He has surgical knowledge and he's well aware of how a police investigation would be carried out." I shuddered at my own sentence; I was giving this cunt way too much credit for my own liking. "Looks like he neglected to notice the footprint though," I continued. "Those balconies gather water and dirt from the guttering."

I was highly satisfied with how the investigation had gone so far. My next step was to question the hotel manager, the receptionist, and the security guard.

I left room 527, glancing up into the corner where a security camera was placed facing down the corridor. I would also need to see the security footage from this hallway camera and possibly the footage from the camera at reception.

I walked to the elevator and pressed the button to call for it. I waited for what seemed like an eternity before the elevator arrived at my floor. I entered and pressed the ground floor, anxiously watching the lights to observe which floor I was at. The elevator stopped at the fourth floor and a woman in a red jacket, red skirt, red heels, and a red summer hat tilted downwards to obscure her face entered and pressed several buttons at once, one after the other.

I pulled a face at her, something between confusion and frustration, but decided not to say anything. She stood with her back to me, humming to herself eerily as we descended towards the ground floor.

I yawned and checked my watch and sighed. It had stopped at 3:33 a.m.

There was a *bing* as the elevator stopped at an unknown floor.

"What floor is this?" I asked the woman in red, but she didn't reply. Instead she continued looking at the buttons and humming to herself. I decided, 'fuck it', and left the elevator to take the stairs the rest of the way to the ground floor. Whatever floor I was on was eerily dark. I turned back to give the strange woman a reproachful glance and she looked up to meet my gaze.

That was when I could see that she had no eyes and an unnaturally large grin that had been cut jaggedly across her face. She giggled and the elevator doors closed, engulfing me in darkness.

What the fuck was going on?! My heart started to beat as I used the walls to guide myself through the tenebrosity.

Had that woman truly existed? Was she the spirit of Scarlett Jones deliberately trying to impede my investigation and sabotage my mental health? Or was my mental health already fucked because of this case?

I frantically pressed the elevator button, but nothing happened.

When I turned around, I could see a faint light flickering weakly ahead. I made my way towards it, curiously noting that I hadn't encountered a single door to a room yet. Where the hell was I? Was this a secret area of the hotel? I reached a corner and turned into another corridor where rows of rooms stretched seemingly never ending. Each room had suitcases left outside, as though everyone were planning on leaving the hotel. I couldn't blame them after what happened, but where was everyone? Why was this all so creepy? The hairs on the back of my neck were standing on end.

I walked down the corridor and rubbed my temples as they began to throb, and my vision started to become blurry. The hallway in front of me seemed to tilt at an unnatural angle and the door of every room was numbered 527. I was halfway down the hallway when I heard a zipper. I turned around and scanned the hallway looking for the source of the noise. Then I heard another zipper, and then another one.

The air went cold and I could see my breath in front of me. Then every single suitcase in the hallway unzipped itself and my heart seemed to jump into my throat when arms emerged from all of them. Unnaturally long, rotten arms with long claws that brushed against the wall and left deep gashes in the plaster and wallpaper. A creepy woman's chuckle filled the air. It seemed to come from every direction and the tone of it denoted malicious intent.

I turned and fled down the hallway back the way I had come. The head of Rosita Ramirez emerged from every case, vibrating wildly from side to side as though she struggled to manifest herself. Her long dark hair was matted and strewn across her face. The multiple manifestations of her restless spirit croaked like they were struggling to breathe. They all scrambled out of their suitcases and crawled along the floor behind me, leaving the carpet shredded and torn in their wake.

Some of them had crawled out of their suitcases in front of me, barring my path. One swiped at my face with a scream of fury. I ducked and continued forward. Another swiped at my chest and I hopped backwards to avoid the attack, but I wasn't quick enough, and her claws ripped open my shirt and left four gashes across my chest. It was only the warm trickling of blood creeping down my chest that alerted me to the damage caused.

I swerved around another manifestation of Rosita, while the multiple manifestations behind me all crawled over one another in a tangled mass of decaying bodies.

I turned the corner and fled towards the elevator, hoping beyond hope that I could escape this nightmare. The light behind me cast the shadows of Rosita Ramirez on the carpet and walls in front of me. She had become a tangled mass of gangly arms equipped with razor-sharp claws and long-haired heads that gasped desperately for breath.

The elevator seemed to be forever put out of my reach. No matter how hard I ran the elevator appeared to move further away. Escape was seemingly impossible.

I turned to face Rosita, pulling my gun from its holster and raising it level with my line of sight. Rosita wasn't there anymore. Neither was the corridor. Instead there was just a door with the number 527 in gold. I turned back to face the elevator and the door was behind me too. In fact, it was all around me. I was now standing in a square with a door numbered 527 on all four sides.

What choice did I have? I entered the room.

Inside the layout was the same, but the room had no balcony doors and a brick wall stared back at me instead. The room was stifling, and the heavy scent of blood filled the air. Taking a single step revealed to me that the red carpet was sodden with blood. As I put the weight of my foot down it oozed out of the carpet as though I were walking through marshland. Then I heard machinery whir to life and the sound of chains coupled with the agonized screams of a woman. I ran around the corner, droplets of blood flying through the air in my wake.

It was Emma Fontaine. She was alive, albeit in profuse agony. She was upright like Jesus on the cross, her feet dangling above the bed. All around her were giant gears built into the walls, the ceiling and the floor with chains being pulled tighter and tighter as the gears turned and wound them in. The chains were fused with Emma's flesh.

"Holy fucking shit!" I exclaimed at the horror which was before me. The chains were fused with every part of her. They were fused with her face, her arms, her legs, her chest and even her buttocks. As the gears turned the chains became tauter and with every turn came an unbearable scream from Emma that filled the entire room and deafened me with its intensity.

I had no idea how I could save her from this nightmarish contraption, so I did what I thought was right. I drew my Beretta 9mm and fired two shots into her head. She became silent and her eyes rolled upwards as she died. As she expired the chains stopped tightening and the room fell silent once again.

"I'm sorry!" I exclaimed anxiously. "I couldn't see you suffer like that!"

Emma's eyelids shot open, but there were no eyeballs behind them. Instead two dark sockets stared back at me as the mechanisms came back to life and the chains again began to tighten. A grin spread across Emma's lips that sent shivers down my spine.

Her stomach exploded open, spraying me with gore. I involuntarily screamed and frantically wiped her blood from my eyes and mouth. The coppery taste of blood made me recoil with revulsion and I spat out as much as I could.

Chains sprouted from her stomach, each with a sharp hook attached to the end, and then they hooked into my flesh through my shirt. It was agonizing. She seemed to have complete control over them as she hoisted me higher as though I were a marionette. This amused her and she let out a menacing demonic laugh. She slammed me into the wall and knocked the wind out of me. Then she catapulted me across the room and the hooks tore my flesh, sending me hurtling to the floor with a thud. I scrambled for the door, but her chains were too quick. They slithered across the blood-soaked carpet and hooked into my leg. My fingers managed to brush the door handle before my leg was pulled violently back towards the bed where the malevolent spirit of Emma Fontaine was chuckling to herself with a demonic tone.

As I was dragged through the blood and carpet, I drew my Beretta 9mm and fired some shots at her face, but to no avail. The shots shattered her skull and her face erupted in an explosion of gore before it all sucked itself back together and her face reconstructed itself.

The chains holding me upside down in the air began to reel back into her stomach wherein sharp teeth had formed around the opening of her wound.

"Fuck off!" I grunted between gritted teeth as I aimed my Beretta and fired into the hole where her heart could be seen beating. Two shots hit other organs, but luckily my third shot, and final bullet, struck true and Emma Fontaine screamed in a fit of agony and rage. Her chains released me, and I wasted no time sprinting towards the door. This time I succeeded and slammed the door behind me with an exasperated pant.

"Now where the fuck am I?" I shouted in confusion. I was in a long corridor with a checked floor and large windows on the wall to my right with rain pouring down them. The windows had metal bars preventing anyone from getting in. They also stopped me from getting out. Looking outside I couldn't see anything other than darkness and my own reflection staring back at me. I looked terrible. I was absolutely soaked in blood, both my own and that of Emma Fontaine. The wall on my left-hand side was lined with golden-framed paintings depicting different horrific images of various women dismembered and covered in gore.

I scoffed in disgust and limped down the hallway. I refused even to glance at the paintings, but I knew some of them were of the victims who I knew, and some were of women who I had never seen before. That's when I realized that Scarlett Jones was not his first. She couldn't have been; his first would have been an experiment to see if he could get away with it! My fists were clenched until my knuckles turned white and my fingernails cut into the palms of my hands.

The only sound that I could hear, aside from the rain, was the sound of my shoes clicking against the tiled floor. The noise echoed down the cavernous hallway, which seemed to continue forever.

Then there was another noise. Whispers filled the air as I walked. They became louder in volume and more distinguishable.

"The Artist is a great innovator!" declared a phantom voice pompously.

"Indeed!" agreed another phantom with an extremely smug tone. "The way he encapsulates his victim's beauty in everlasting grace! What does this piece say to you? Scarlett's smile is resplendent, yet sinister. To me it denotes the duality of a person's soul. Absolute genius!"

"Quite!" agreed the first phantom.

"Will you two shut the fuck up!" I yelled angrily at thin air, unable to bare their pomposity any longer. "He is not an innovator! His work denotes that he's a sick, twisted piece of shit! And when I find him, I'm going to ram the barrel of my gun into his skull and blow his brains out of his asshole!"

"Jack?"

I spun around to see Olivia standing and staring at me with an expression of fear.

I looked around me confused. I was standing in a hallway in the Budapest Hotel. I had been shouting at a painting of a lighthouse overlooking a black and formless ocean. "I'm sorry, Olivia," I began to explain. "I suffer from bad hallucinations. I imagined that two idiots were looking at images the Artist had created..." I stopped when I could see the unconvinced expression on her face. "Look, never mind!" I said. "Let's just question the hotel manager and the other two fuckwads!"

Olivia scowled at me. "Are you sure you're up to this, Jack?" she asked me with an expression of concern. "I think that the case has taken its toll on your mental health." She placed a comforting hand on my arm. "I can get you help."

I pulled away, offended. "What the fuck, Olivia?!" I shouted angrily "Are you trying to get me to seek help from a psychiatrist?"

"Jack, I just-"

"Don't fucking bother, Olivia!" I interjected, cutting her off and storming past her, heading for the stairs. "I'm fucking fine! If you want to help, then get me a fucking drink! We've got some questioning to do, so can we please not waste any more time with this trivial bullshit!"

My clothes were intact, and I had no gashes in my chest and no wounds on my shoulders, back, arms or leg where the hooks had pierced me. There was no blood on my clothes at all. It was as though the whole thing never happened. It felt real at the time. I couldn't understand what was happening.

*

I arranged to conduct my interviews within an office in the hotel. I wasn't officially a police detective, so I couldn't ask them anything at the station. First, I decided to interview the owner of the building.

"I'm ruined!" declared the hotel owner and manager, despairing as I took him to a private office to be interviewed. "Most of the guests have already left! None will ever come to stay here again after such an atrocity!"

Already I didn't like him. A woman was dead, and all this fat little grease ball gave a damn about was his fucking profit!

"A woman has been murdered!" exclaimed Olivia, gently reprimanding him with a reproachful glower.

He looked at her as though it wasn't his problem. Beads of sweat had begun to gather on his bald head and ran down his face leaving a glistening trail in the light of the office. He had a tanned complexion and a thick bristly mustache that reminded me of a sweeping brush. His eyes were narrow and beady and immediately made me distrust him. He was wearing a pink button-up shirt with large damp patches under his armpits. The top few buttons were unfastened, revealing a thick tangled mass of bristled black hair. The bottom buttons were stretched far apart on account of his big belly.

"As the hotel manager and owner, could you tell me where you were this morning around 12 a.m?" I asked clinically. I didn't suffer fools lightly, and this man already struck me as a complete fool blinded by the innate desire to accumulate an abundance of wealth. Such empty ambitions only served to disgust me.

He tapped a chubby finger adorned with gold rings against his bottom lip thoughtfully. "I believe I was relaxing in the sauna of the hotel," he replied. "Then I headed to the bar and had a few drinks before retiring to my penthouse."

"Did you receive any complaints about noise between the hours of 12 a.m. and 1a.m?"

"Nothing. There was someone staying in room 526 next door and they didn't hear anything. There were people staying in the room above and below and neither complained of any noise at all. It was an ordinary night."

"What can you tell me about the person staying in room 526?"

He rolled his eyes and sighed like a petulant child. "How much longer is this going to take? I have things I need to do!"

I slammed my hands on the table between us. "Answer the goddamn question! I don't have time for your cantankerous bullshit!"

"No! I don't have anything to do with the guests!" he snapped back, taking me aback with his aggression. I had expected this grease ball to be a sack of shit, but it turned out that he had a pair of balls after all. "Whoever stayed in room 526 will have had to sign in with reception," he explained. "Which means they will have been caught on camera and seen by the clerk at reception. They're who you need to question!" Then he got to his feet and said with an arrogant tone: "Now if you'll excuse me, unless I'm under arrest then I trust I'm free to go!"

I sighed and rubbed my temples. "Yes," I conceded. "You're free to leave. Thank you for your time."

He left and Olivia and I both agreed that he was a complete asshole.

Next entered the spotty little Herbert from reception. He was nervous and Olivia needed to pour him a cup of coffee to calm his nerves.

"Listen, son," I said, trying my best to sound like a father figure, an old police psychology trick. My intention was to make him comfortable and make him more willing to give information. His boss seemed uncooperative and I hoped that this young receptionist would be more helpful. "You're not in any trouble," I assured him gently. "I just need to ask you a couple of questions. The more you can tell us, the easier it makes our jobs, the quicker we can catch this killer."

"O-o-okay..." he stammered anxiously.

Olivia brought me the check-in logbook and I found Emma Fontaine's name signed with the room number which she had stayed in. Then I showed the boy a photograph which Olivia had taken of her driving license. "You were working on reception last night and early hours of this morning. Do you remember this girl? She checked into room 527 on Friday."

He leaned forward and studied the picture for a long time. I tapped my finger on the desk impatiently, waiting for his response.

"I-I-I th-think so," he answered finally. "Sh-she was super flirty, and very p-p-pretty."

"Good! Now we're getting somewhere! Do you remember if a man was with her?"

He shook his head almost immediately. "No, sh-she w-w-was alone. B-b-but a man did come asking about w-w-w-what room she w-was staying in. That w-w-was Friday night, shortly after she checked in."

"Do you remember what this man looked like? Was he the same man who booked this room?" I spun the logbook around and pointed to where someone had signed into room 526 under the name 'Heinrich Wulf'.

"A m-m-man did ask about which room Emma Fontaine was in on Friday, but Mr Wulf was a different man."

"Anything strike you as odd about either of these men?" I asked as I got a cigarette out of my pocket. I offered him one and he reluctantly accepted. He choked when I lit it for him, and he inhaled deeply.

"Mr Wulf was very specific about which room he wanted to stay in. He paid in cash and said he w-would only stay in room 526."

I was starting to believe Heinrich Wulf was the killer. Obviously, a fake name. He had seen which room Emma Fontaine was staying in and requested to be in the room next door so he could hop the balcony and kill her. Still, things didn't seem to add up.

"Can you describe this Heinrich Wulf?" I asked him, getting a pen and paper at the ready. The paper was already covered in notes which I'd made so far with important details pertaining to this murder.

"He was w-well dressed. He w-was wearing a red shirt with a black jacket over the top, a fancy scarf and black pants with some fancy looking shoes. He w-w-was also wearing a trilby hat. Now that I think about it, he deliberately covered his face from me."

I decided to ask about the other man, the one who had asked which room Emma Fontaine stayed in. "Any distinguishable features? A scar? Anything?"

"Nothing. I'm sorry I can't be any more help."

"You've been very helpful," I told him, getting to my feet and offering him a handshake. He shook my hand limply before leaving.

Next I had the guy who was on security the night of the murder. He was a slim man with dark skin and a bald head. His eyes looked bloodshot and tired. He was still wearing his security uniform, a pale gray button-up shirt with brown trousers.

"Take a seat, Mr...?"

"Carl Porter," he replied, seating himself opposite me.

"You're not in any trouble, Mr Porter. I just want to ask you some questions about this weekend. Have you been working the night shift since Friday?"

He nodded in affirmation. "I work Friday, Saturday, Sunday and Monday night."

"And you work in the security room? Am I right?"

He nodded again but remained silent.

"Did you notice anything unusual over the course of the weekend?"

He yawned. "I have several monitors I'm supposed to monitor at once. I can't be expected to notice everything."

"Nothing peculiar happened at all?" I asked again incredulously.

He contemplated for a moment. "Well, there was a knock at the security office door this morning, around early hours."

I nodded. "What happened?"

He shrugged his shoulders and gave me a quizzical look. "Nothing. I went to the door and nobody was there. Later on, I fell asleep, but don't tell Mr Díaz I told you that." he replied, yawning again and holding a hand to his mouth. He set Olivia off yawning as well.

"So, you're telling me you slept on the job?" I asked, narrowing my eyes at him. Then I sighed and realized that interviewing this man was a waste of time. He didn't need to have seen anything; the camera feed would provide everything that I needed. "I trust you have a key to the security room?"

He nodded his head sleepily and searched his pockets for the keys. "I'll take you both up to the security room if you would like."

*

Olivia and I followed Carl Porter up to the second floor where the security room was situated by the staircase. Carl unlocked the door and we stepped inside the dingy room that served as a security office.

The office consisted of a few filing cabinets, a small station with a kettle and a microwave and bits for making tea and coffee. There was a leather swivel chair positioned in front of several screens that showed various parts of the hotel. In addition to the monitors there was an old PC in one corner where security footage could be viewed. Wires were all over the room crossed and tangled like spaghetti connecting all the security equipment.

"I want to review all the footage from Friday through to Monday morning," I told Carl.

He sighed and seated himself in his chair, clearly disinterested with the investigation.

We were there for several hours, during which time Larry had removed Emma Fontaine's body from her room and taken her to the LAPD morgue to conduct an autopsy. Carl begrudgingly rewound through hours of footage. I was interested in only two feeds: the reception footage and the footage from the fifth-floor corridor. Unsurprisingly, both had been tampered with.

Carl seemed aghast. "How can this be?" he gasped in disbelief. "I was here the entire time!"

"You said there was a knock at the door," interjected Olivia. "Then you said you fell asleep. Is it possible you were drugged?"

It certainly seemed plausible: a knock at the door to lure the security guard to unlock it then drug him. The only other explanation is that Carl Porter is an accessory to murder and removed the data himself.

"The killer lured him out of the security office and sedated him!" expressed Olivia, echoing my beliefs.

Carl tried to think back, but his memory of the knock at the door was hazy at best. He recalled nothing other than the knock and then waking up in his chair, by which point the killer had removed any trace of himself on camera. Very clever! This wasn't a spontaneous murder! The killer had been planning this for a long time. He probably checked in several times so he could observe the security room. All he really needed was to wait until a beautiful woman entered and then make sure he had a room adjacent to hers with a balcony. The mysterious lover who Emma had been meeting with was more than likely problematic to the killer's plans, but it still didn't ruin his plan. It merely delayed it.

As we were leaving the security office, I glanced back at the monitors to catch a glimpse of the headless spirit of Lady Mystery crawling across the ceiling of one of the corridors. I rubbed my eyes and when I looked up again, she was gone.

*

"You can't just go snooping in other rooms!" remarked the owner, Mr Díaz, snarling when Olivia requested the room key to room 526.

"We can do whatever we like!" she replied sternly but politely. "We are the police and a crime has been committed. If you don't cooperate, Mr Díaz, you will be impeding a murder investigation, which I don't need to make you aware is a serious crime!"

I grinned triumphantly. I couldn't resist sticking the metaphorical boot in. "What will it be Mr Dumbass?" I asked tauntingly. "Will you give me the key for room 526? Or will we be taking it anyway while the LAPD drag you out of this hotel the same way you came into the world: kicking and screaming?!" I chuckled at his dismayed facial expression.

Pablo Díaz sighed and slumped his shoulders. He snapped his fingers and the spotty little Herbert who I'd interviewed earlier scurried to reception to retrieve the key that we had requested for room 526.

"I should warn you though, detective," he said impatiently. "You are wasting your time. When a guest checks out maids are immediately dispatched to vigorously clean the vacated room in preparation for the next guest." Díaz shrugged his shoulders sympathetically when he saw the shared dismay of Olivia and myself. "I'm sorry," he continued. "But the room has been cleaned, vacuumed, polished and dusted."

I swept an empty mug across his office and watched as it shattered against a wall. "Goddamn it!" I yelled impulsively. "He fucking knew it! He fucking knew that he could live here and that when he committed his murder your staff would clear the room meticulously! FUCK!" I slammed my fists onto the table. Olivia assured me that room 526 would be searched by forensics, but her voice held little conviction. I could tell that she was only trying to cheer me up.

The killer played a good game, but he still made some minor mistakes. I was determined to catch him and bring him to justice, with a bullet through his head if necessary.

CHAPTER 4

The Lover

"I want you two to work closely together on this one," said Matthew Perry before he had to stand before the ever-growing masses of reporters and journalists and answer a deluge of questions. "But this stays between us, Jack! If anyone asks, you're working as a police homicide detective again!"

"Sure thing, Perry," I agreed. I didn't really care under what capacity I would investigate this case. I just wanted to find this bastard.

Me and Olivia ran across the car park to her SUV as the torrential rain thundered down relentlessly, bouncing from the asphalt and the roof of Olivia's vehicle. We slammed the car doors shut and sat there in silence for a while before Olivia started the car and drove to a nearby café so that we could both grab some coffee.

Olivia purchased the coffee and ran awkwardly back to the SUV with both plastic cups in hand. I opened the door for her, and we sat there drinking for a while and watching the roads of LA become busier and busier as commuters started making their way to work.

I checked my watch and it read 9:15 a.m. We were waiting for a phone call from Larry. He had taken the body over an hour ago from the Budapest Hotel and we had to wait for him to perform some additional tests.

Olivia's phone rang, playing a corny dance tune. "It's Larry," she said, handing me the cell phone.

"Larry, you ugly son-of-a-bitch! What have you found out?"

Larry sighed at my immaturity and proceeded to relay what his tests had turned up. "The victim was killed between 12 a.m and 1 a.m this morning. Cause of death was asphyxiation, severe ligature marks and bruising reveal that she was strangled with a piece of thick rope of some kind. I found traces of semen in her vagina."

"What else? Any DNA trace evidence? A hair? Fibres?" I interrupted eagerly.

"Will you let me finish?" responded Larry, though his voice portrayed no irritability. His voice never portrayed any emotion at all. "I sent a sample of the semen to forensics and I also found a single strand from the rope that was used to strangle the victim, it appears to be hemp. As soon as forensics examine the semen, I shall call you back and inform you as to whether or not we have their DNA on file."

He hung up before I could ask any further questions. I waited restlessly for some feedback from forensics. Olivia attempted to initiate some kind of conversation with me, but I was too distracted by the case to pay her too much attention. I nodded and grunted in affirmation in the right places to give her the impression that I was interested in her conversation, an effort that I would only ever make with Olivia. Had it been anyone else filling my ears with their mundane bullshit I'd have told them to shut their fucking mouths.

Sometimes though, I felt as though Olivia talked just to make noise. An attempt to fill the voids of silence that had grown exponentially over the years we had known each other.

Her cell phone rang again, my saving grace.

"Hello, Larry. What did the semen samples turn up?" asked Olivia. "Bingo!" she declared with a victorious grin after a moment of letting Larry speak. Then she asked: "Can I have his last known address?"

"I take it we have a match for the semen sample?" I asked rhetorically with a smile as she typed in an address into her satnav.

"Reece Pemberton. His address isn't far from the Budapest Hotel. He has been arrested twice on charges of assault and sexual assault in the past," said Olivia with a vague hint of disgust. She turned the key and fired up her SUV, the car tires screeching as she pulled away from the café sending a up a spray of water behind us.

"Well this makes things interesting!" I exclaimed. I hadn't expected Emma Fontaine's lover to have such a colorful history. I could tell that Olivia was angry; she loathed rapists and those who abused women. Personally, I didn't give a fuck what he'd done in the past, so long as he could shed some light on what had happened to Emma Fontaine.

I sat with my arms resting on my lap as we drove in silence towards the address of Reece Pemberton. I watched the road fall away through the front windscreen with a hypnotized stare.

"I need a fucking cigarette," I declared suddenly, realizing that I hadn't had one in a while. I tried to raise my hand to get my box of cigarettes from my shirt pocket, but my arms would not move. I looked down to see that they were bound to my seat with leather straps. The sound of the SUV travelling over the wet asphalt was replaced with the sound of old wheels squeaking. I looked up to see that I was no longer in Olivia's SUV, but instead I was sitting in a wheelchair, bound by the ankles and wrists with leather belt straps.

"Hush now, darl," soothed the voice of Olivia. I tried to look up at her, but a leather strap across my forehead prevented head movement. She was wheeling me down a long clinical hallway with doors on either side. The sound of maniacal laughter and screaming filled the hallway. "You know smoking is bad for your health, Mr Cucchiano!"

"Olivia?! Where the fuck am I?!" I asked in confusion and fear. I struggled against my constraints, desperate to free myself.

"Please calm down, Mr Cucchiano," scolded Olivia, trying to hide the annoyance in her tone. "We're trying to help you!" She spoke to me as though she was reprimanding a naughty child. "A quick visit to the doctor will help you feel better."

"Olivia!" I shouted.

"'Nurse Olivia!'" she corrected me.

I struggled harder. "Let me out of this fucking chair!" I yelled as I lost my temper. "Olivia, we have a case to solve! Stop fucking around!"

Olivia sighed and stopped pushing me for a moment. She walked to the front of the wheelchair, her white high heels clicking on the tiled floor, and she learned over me with a feigned smile of sympathy spread across her lips. She was wearing a white nurse's uniform that revealed her cleavage as she leaned over me to try and calm me down. She was also wearing white tights and white heels. Her lips were crimson with thick red lipstick, which seemed out of character for Olivia. She rarely wore makeup.

"You're not well, Mr Cucchiano!" she said soothingly. She placed a gentle hand on my cheek as she spoke. "We've never worked together in the LAPD! It's all a delusion you've created in your mind! We've never even met until you were admitted to this hospital!" Her solemn facial expression changed into one of exaggerated happiness and she continued: "I'm taking you to see the doctor. He's working to cure your sick mind. So be a good patient and stop causing me unnecessary aggravation!" She stood up and walked to the back of my chair, then the squeaking resumed as Olivia kept pushing me towards two metal double doors at the end of the hallway.

"The Doctor truly is an artist in his own right," said Olivia admiringly as the two doors scraped open. Standing there in the doorway was a man in a surgical gown covered in blood. The latex gloves on his hands were also covered in blood. Yet, all the blood was the least terrifying thing that I remember about the so-called doctor. The man had no face! His face was like a blank canvas, skin stretched over a featureless face. When he spoke his chin moved, but words materialized from no mouth.

"Let's get you looked at, young fellow!" exclaimed the doctor jovially, as though his friendly demeanor would make me comfortable with the fact that he had no face. "I'll take him from here, Nurse Lockhart." The faceless man took control of my wheelchair and wheeled me into the center of the circular room so that I was positioned under a fluorescent light that hung above. It was only then that I could see that the whole room was coated in plastic.

"What's going on?!" I demanded as the fear began to take hold of me. My heart rate increased to a sickening thudding in my chest.

"I'm afraid the dead girls you have been obsessing over have their worms routed deeply within your brain," explained the faceless doctor casually. "But don't worry, young sir! We have a license to perform brain surgery if we believe it's in the best interest of the patient."

"Let me go, you sick fuck!" I shouted at him wide-eyed.

He shushed me and pressed a finger covered in latex and blood against my lips. "This is for your own good!"

He began to walk away as another door opened and the silhouette of the Butcher stood in the doorway revving his chainsaw with an ear-piercing maniacal laughter that merged with my own screams.

Young Annabelle, who'd seemingly appeared from nowhere, tugged at my sleeve. I looked at her through my peripheral vision and was horrified by her rotting flesh and her menacing grin. "Wake up, Jack!"

I sat bolt upright in the passenger seat of Olivia's SUV, alarmed and covered in sweat. I wiped drool from my chin and looked around frantically for any threats.

"Jack, it's me! We're here!" Olivia's hand was still on my sleeve, with her other hand she gestured to a quaint little house with a red car parked in the driveway.

"I need a fucking cigarette," I grumbled. I snatched my arm free of Olivia's grip, much to her surprise, and fished in my pockets for my cigarettes and a lighter.

The rain continued to pour down on LA from the previous night, as though the gods above in heaven wept for Emma Fontaine. Olivia and myself had barely got halfway up the garden path before my cigarette was completely soaked and wouldn't smoke. I cursed bitterly and flicked my sodden cigarette across the garden with blatant disregard for the owner of the household.

Olivia pressed the doorbell and after a short while a man wearing a checked red and black shirt with Levi jeans answered. He looked us up and down suspiciously with a look of confusion in his puffy eyes.

"Reece Pemberton?" asked Olivia in her official tone.

He hesitated, "Yes?"

"I'm detective Lockhart and this is my colleague detective Cucchiano. We were wondering if we could ask you a couple of questions about a young woman named Emma Fontaine. She was found dead in the early hours of this morning. Can we come in?" Olivia stared at him with her piercing eyes as though she was trying to see through to his soul. Her mouth was a thin line across her face.

His face turned white as a sheet and his mouth gaped open. In that moment I could see his shock was genuine and I instinctively knew that there was no way Reece Pemberton was guilty of murder. A brief look at my colleague revealed to me that she wasn't so easily convinced.

"Emma... Emma... murdered?!" he gasped in disbelief. He held a hand to his head and staggered on the spot.

Olivia was unsympathetic. "Sir, can we come in and speak to you about it? Forensic tests revealed that you were with her the night of the murder."

"That's not true," asserted Pemberton. He fought back tears of grief and his body language indicated he was speaking in self defense.

"We're not accusing you, Mr. Pemberton," I interjected politely. I figured that if I made that point clear he would be more inclined to cooperate. However, I quickly discovered why he denied that he was with Emma Fontaine on the night of the murder.

"Who's at the door?" called a woman's voice from within the house. The voice was frail and shaky.

"It's the police, sweetie. They're making inquiries," responded Reece. "Look," he snarled quietly at me and Olivia through gritted teeth. "I was home all fucking night looking after my sick wife! If my DNA was found on Emma Fontaine, then somebody planted it there! My wife will confirm I was here all night!"

"Oh really?" I smirked at him, though my patience for this idiot was starting to thin rapidly. It was still raining, and I looked towards his car.

"Your wife's testimony means nothing against forensic evidence, Mr Pemberton. If you won't cooperate willingly then I'll simply call for a warrant for your arrest," said Olivia in a professional but irritated tone.

Both Reece and Olivia stopped and glanced at me with shocked expressions when I threw myself to the ground. I looked underneath Reece Pemberton's car and for a moment was horrified by the specter of Annabelle Green peering back at me with an unnaturally large grin on her face. Her eyes, which she still had unlike the other ghosts, were black and lacked pupils or irises. She raised a finger to her lips, warning me not to scream and then burst into flames before disappearing into a cloud of burning embers that were swept away with the wind.

"What are you doing?" asked Reece Pemberton, bewildered.

I stood up smiling. "I'm asking the questions now, dipshit! I suggest you answer them unless you want to be picking up your teeth from the driveway with a broken arm!"

Reece looked at Olivia indignantly. "Can he speak to me like that?!" he demanded, turning red in the face.

Olivia herself looked flustered and could find no words to offer him.

I stepped forward and grabbed him by the collar. I twisted him around and rammed him into the door frame as hard as I could, knocking the wind out of him. "Listen to me, you fucking prick! A young girl is dead and you not cooperating is helping the bastard who killed her get away with it! If you want to bang other women behind your sick wife's back, then that's up to you! But when said women wind up dead with your ejaculate still inside them, we have a fucking duty to that woman to knock on your fucking door! This is your last chance to cooperate before I punch your fucking pea-sized head in! Don't bother telling me you were here all night because we know that's bullshit! Your neighbor's car is dry underneath where it has been parked on the drive all night! The drive under your car is wet, indicating it hasn't been parked here all night! Now tell us the fucking truth!"

"Reece! What's going on?!" asked his wife from the bedroom upstairs.

"Nothing, sweetie!" he replied. He tried to sound calm, but his voice was shaky. He didn't take his eyes off me. "I'll tell you what I can," he said quietly.

I released my grip and stepped back out into the rain. Reece Pemberton stepped out into the rain with us. He called up to his wife and told her he was just popping out to talk to the police and then he closed the door.

"I hope you don't mind if we do this outside..." he said sheepishly.

"I don't give a fuck!" I replied impatiently. "Let's just get this over with!"

Reece Pemberton sighed as he relayed the story of the previous night's events. He spoke with tearful eyes that darted between me and Olivia, desperately seeking approval. "My wife has a debilitating illness. I care for her full time, as she won't allow a stranger to do it. But it makes me so unhappy. I met Emma Fontaine on a dating site, and we arranged to meet at the Budapest Hotel. All this weekend I upped my wife's meds so I could slip away and meet with Emma at the hotel. I figured I could be there and back without my wife knowing what was going on," he sighed and slumped his shoulders. He gave us a pleading look as he continued. "I figured I could just have a weekend of fun and then cut things off with Emma when she went back to New Orleans. I think I'm entitled to some fun, some kind of life, y'know?"

"You're a fucking scum bag!" snapped Olivia, her stony professional demeanor giving way to emotion. Her hands were balled into tight fists and her knuckles turned white.

"Olivia, please," I snapped, silencing her. I turned to Mr Pemberton. "Reece, tell us about the weekend at the hotel. I'm not interested in intimate details about your 'fun' or about any sob story about how you feel like you deserve 'a life' because I'm only interested in finding the fucker who took Emma's life away." I gazed at him seriously to make sure that he understood, and he nodded in affirmation. "Now tell me," I continued, "Do you remember anything strange during your meetings with Emma? Someone suspicious lingering around or anything like that?"

Reece stroked his stubble in contemplation. "Not really, no." Then he snapped his fingers and his eyes lit up. "There was one thing!" he exclaimed as the sudden realization struck him.

"Anything," I said, retrieving my notebook from my pocket and a pen.

"I think it was Saturday night. I was in Emma's room and there was a knock at the door. Emma answered it and a man's voice apologized and said he thought it was his room. I didn't think anything of it at the time, but now that I think about it, it was really strange. Why would he knock if he thought it was his own room?"

"Did this man have a notable accent? German for example? Did you get a look at him?" I asked.

Reece shook his head solemnly. "I couldn't see the door from where I was sitting. His accent was American, not German. What makes you ask that?"

"We're not at liberty to..." explained Olivia, but I cut her off before she had chance to finish her sentence. She pulled a face at me as though she had just licked a nettle covered in piss.

"The man staying in the room next door signed the logbook under a German name. Did you see or hear anything of the man staying in the room next door?"

Reece shook his head. "Emma mentioned that a strange man complemented her in the bar one night. He apparently told her she was beautiful, like a piece of art. She didn't mention much else about him though."

"You have a very interesting history, don't you Mr Pemberton? Sexual assault? Would it be a stretch for us to assume you assaulted Miss Fontaine before she was murdered?" challenged Olivia. Her body language had become hostile and I stepped back to allow her to pursue her line of questioning. I was convinced that this guy had nothing else to offer that would be useful.

"That's all part of my past, ma'am," he offered curtly. "I used to be a bad seed until I met my wife. She set me straight."

Olivia scoffed at that. "And you repaid her with betrayal at a time when she needs you the most?! You may have my partner fooled, but I'm not so easily convinced! We shall be looking into this further, Mr Pemberton. You are officially arrested and de-arrested. Don't leave LA and make sure you come to the station tomorrow to make an official statement, otherwise I'll have a warrant issued for your arrest! For all we know you could've lured Miss Fontaine to that hotel to her death! We'll be in touch Mr Pemberton."

Olivia spun on her heels and stormed towards her SUV. Her attitude reminded me of a petulant child.

"I didn't kill Emma Fontaine!" exclaimed Reece Pemberton with teary eyes.

I ignored what he said but thanked him for the information which he had offered with a polite nod, and then I joined Olivia in her SUV.

She turned on the heating as she drove and the hot air burst through the ventilation system and started drying our wet clothes. "I'll take you home," she said. Her voice lacked its usual warmth and her crystal blue eyes regarded me coldly. "I've got to go back to the station and do some paperwork."

We didn't speak the entire ride to my apartment block in the Downtown district. As I was leaving Olivia's SUV, she stopped me by calling my name.

"Don't ever undermine me in front of a witness or possible suspect ever again!" she warned me sternly.

I laughed nervously. "Olivia, you let your emotions and personal feelings cloud your judgment!"

She shook her head vigorously and narrowed her eyes. "I don't want to fucking hear it! You're not even LAPD anymore, but I AM! Don't let it happen again, Jack. I swear to God!"

She slammed the car door shut and took off before I had chance to respond, her tires splashing a puddle that soaked my jeans as she sped away. Despondent and utterly miserable, I entered the apartment block. I would dwell in my apartment and ponder the mounting mystery of this case while drowning my sorrows in the depths of a bottle of whiskey.

CHAPTER 5

Home Invasion

I didn't hear from Olivia for several weeks after the Budapest Hotel case. Every time I attempted to call her the phone rang continuously, or the call was cut off after a few seconds. I decided to give her some space and I went back to investigating the case alone. In the end I decided that Olivia and the police were just a hindrance to my investigation.

In the weeks that followed Emma Fontaine's murder, Reece Pemberton was questioned by the LAPD. However, they failed to convict him. Even though his DNA was found on the body it was concluded that Reece Pemberton was innocent. The rigorous questioning which he went through was a complete waste of time in my professional opinion. Reece Pemberton was many things, but a murderer he was not. Heck, what did I know? I was only the best homicide detective that the LAPD had ever had. Pemberton's innocence was so painstakingly obvious that even a blind man could see it, yet somehow the LAPD could not.

No new evidence emerged and yet again the trail went cold. I added the notes that I'd gathered from Emma Fontaine's case to the case file that I'd compiled since the beginning of the investigation.

I studied the notes repeatedly, starting from the beginning and reading right through to the most recent murder. I took a couple of days break and travelled back to Texas to present a case against the sheriff Hershel Murray. With the written testimony of Mike Vance,

THE DARK SIDE OF BEAUTY

Hershel Murray was dismissed as county sheriff for gross negligence and misconduct during a missing persons investigation.

"I'll make sure you both suffer for this!" he promised me and Mike venomously as we left the tribunal. His eyes burned with intense hatred and he slammed his truck door so hard that I thought it would fall off.

Now that turd had been flushed, I returned to LA with Mike and bought him a drink and wished him the best of luck before we parted ways.

Returning to my apartment block was when something happened that would utterly unnerve me. It wasn't a ghostly sighting or anything strange like that, but something equally unsettling which I noticed the minute I reached my front door.

I whistled to myself as I walked down the hallway. I felt jovial that I'd secured at least one victory. It might have seemed petty to most people that I had pursued the dismissal of sheriff Hershel Murray, but as far as I was concerned his negligence had caused the death of three teens. If he'd conducted a thorough investigation, then they could have still been alive.

The hallway always had a pungent odor of piss, an unfortunate by-product of the undesirable heroin addicts who I shared this building with. The muffled cries of a baby reverberated within one apartment while a young couple argued in another. I had grown used to it by now. The rent was cheap, and the location was close to an old jazz bar I usually liked to drink at when I could be bothered to brave the outside world.

I reached my front door, twirling my keyring around my index finger and as I was about to put the key in the door the door creaked open by itself.

It was already unlocked.

I drew my Beretta 9mm from its holster and held it close to my chest. Inside the curtains were drawn closed and the apartment was gloomy.

"If anyone is inside this apartment, I WILL open fire!" I called into the apartment, the tone of my voice being an ambivalent mixture of fear and anger.

I stepped into my apartment, aiming my Beretta down the hallway towards the living room and kitchen. The first door to my left was the bathroom and the second door to the left was my study. The first door to my right was the master bedroom. All three doors remained closed, as I'd left them.

As I moved cautiously. I had a quick look in the bathroom, but nobody was there. I moved to the study and creaked the door open a crack, aiming my Beretta through the gap, but the study looked untouched. Nobody had been here, or so it seemed. I moved over to the bedroom and opened the door. I turned the light on and that's when I saw it.

A painting had been framed and hung above my bed. A red ribbon had been tied around the center of the painting with a little bow. The painting was undoubtedly the work of the Artist and it depicted Emma Fontaine with her stomach opened wide. In each of her hands she held a flap of crimson flesh like she was holding open the entrance of a tent. Inside her opened stomach hundreds of eyeballs could be seen peering through the hole and Emma Fontaine was looking down at them smiling affectionately, like how a mother might smile at their infant child. The title "Look Within" was painted in blood across the top of the painting. I could tell the canvas itself was made from the stretched and tanned flesh of Emma Fontaine that had been flayed after her murder.

"Mother fucker!" I exclaimed. I stormed through the bedroom door and made my way into the living room and kitchen area, hoping beyond hope that the fucker was still here. If he had been, I'd have filled him with bullets until he looked like a colander.

Nobody was there. However, on my marble kitchen worktop was a video cassette with a sticker on the front with 'Detective' written on it in marker pen. As I didn't have a cassette player, I ignored it for the time being.

I continued searching my apartment until I was convinced that I was alone. I checked in wardrobes, under the bed and behind the shower curtain. Then I went to inspect my front door and ran my index finger over the subtle scratches around my keyhole and I realized that the lock had been picked, similar to Rosita Ramirez's front door.

This fucker had invaded my fucking castle! Now it was personal!

It wouldn't have been hard for him to find my address. All he had to do was wait for me and Olivia to leave the Budapest Hotel and then follow us around all day. We were so distracted by the case that we wouldn't have noticed a car stalking us during the busy morning rush hour. Then all he had to do was check the names on the mailboxes at the front entrance to see which apartment was mine and then make his way to my front door.

This was all speculation of course, but nevertheless the fucker had compromised my safe haven in an attempt to mock me. This was a fatal mistake on his part, though I felt nervous in spite of myself. I had to hand it to him: he was patient and resourceful.

I drove to a nearby charity shop and purchased a cheap video cassette player and then returned to my apartment. My hands trembled with trepidation as I hastily wired up the cassette player to my television.

The video started black, then a sheet was pulled from the lens of the camera and a table could be seen with a shadowy figure sitting slumped at the end directly opposite the camera.

"Let there be light!" cooed a man's voice. The voice was like velvet, though I could sense the concealed maliciousness within, and I instinctively knew that this was the voice of the killer: the fabled 'Artist'.

There was a metallic buzz and suddenly the room was bathed in bright light. Sitting at the end of the table was a man who I knew. It took me a while to recognize him, but the swollen face of Reece Pemberton stared back at the camera with silver tape over his mouth and his hands bound behind his back. He squinted and struggled side to side with muffled screams. His eyes rolled wildly, and I could see that he was heavily drugged. He was still wearing the red and black checked shirt which he had worn when I interviewed him several weeks earlier.

On the table in front of him there were four jars filled with liquid, which I assumed was formaldehyde given the contents of the jars, with two eyeballs floating in each one. Presumably they were the missing eyes of Scarlett Jones, Lady Mystery, Rosita Ramirez, and Emma Fontaine.

"I think everyone should bear witness to this momentous occasion!" announced the killer as he walked around the table towards the bound Reece Pemberton.

The killer was wearing a black overcoat with black trousers and black leather gloves. The angle of the camera was pointed forward so Reece could be identified, but the killer's head was off camera.

The killer stood behind Mr Pemberton and rested his gloved hands on his shoulders. Reece's eyes widened and he tried to squirm away in panic. Muffled screams erupted from him and I could hear the panic and desperation in his stifled tone. The killer hushed him and stroked his cheek tentatively, as gentle as a lover's touch.

"I wanted to demonstrate to you, detective Cucchiano, that nobody is out of my reach. I can get to anybody," he said, pacing back and forth behind a weeping Pemberton. "And where I've only killed women in the past, I want to make it absolutely crystal clear to you that I'm not scared of killing a man too, hence this little demonstration I've prepared for your own home entertainment!"

The killer dragged the chair back across the room and walked back to the camera. He adjusted the angle so that Pemberton could still be seen clearly and then he could be heard opening a drawer. When he walked back on camera his leather-gloved hands were balled into fists with brass knuckles on each hand. "I want you to know how powerless you are! I want you to know I have absolute control! You can't save this man! By the time you watch this he will already be dead!" The killer pressed a switch on a remote control and a song called 'Candy Castle' performed by Glass Candy started to play.

'Let's take off our masks. And be so naturelle. Let's behold ourselves. And break this evil spell. I think that I'm good just because I behave. But I've reached stalemate, I'm a self-made cage. They poked me with a stick because they wanted to see. If I was alive or just pretending to be. But my bones are in my body and not in my grave. Turns out I am free, and I pretend to be a slave..."

While this song played the Artist stretched and then launched forward, driving his fist hard into Pemberton's face with a sickening thud. The killer could throw a punch. He grunted and threw rights and lefts into Pemberton's face, jerking it violently from right to left.

He chuckled and peeled the tape from Pemberton's lips.

"Please...." pleaded Reece Pemberton pitifully with a mouthful of blood. His face was battered and swollen.

The killer responded by throwing another punch that connected sharply with Pemberton's jaw with a cracking that sent shivers down my spine. The impact of the blow sent teeth and blood spraying from Reece Pemberton's mouth and dislocated his jaw so that it hung open loosely. I wanted to look away from the brutality, but I couldn't. I was stood transfixed by the act of barbarism taking place on my television screen.

After what seemed like forever, Reece Pemberton's face was an unrecognizable bloody pulp that hung forward with strings of blood hanging like crimson spider webs from his face. His eyes were swollen to the point of being closed.

"Now I hope you can see," panted the killer breathlessly when he turned the music down. "I will destroy anyone who gets in the way of my art." The killer took off his brass knuckles and placed them on the table. He turned the music back up to full blast, then he grabbed a pillow and shoved it hard against Pemberton's face before he rammed what looked like a Glock into the pillow and pulled the trigger. There was a brief flash of light and the pillow made the gunshot a whisper. The back of Reece Pemberton's head exploded in a fountain of blood, brains and fragments of skull. The force of the gunshot sent his corpse flying backwards to the ground.

"I'll be seeing you, Jack!" said the killer, chuckling as he turned off the camera.

I fought hard to fight back the bile that was rising in my throat and eventually I could contain it no longer. I collapsed on all fours and hurled all over my cream carpet. I was trembling, through disgust, through fear and through frustration and rage. I wanted the killer dead. I wanted to do to him what he had done to Reece Pemberton and to all the women who he'd killed too.

I reached into my pocket with a trembling hand and scrolled through my short list of contacts until I found Olivia's number and I dialled. The phone rang and rang and unsurprisingly went to voicemail.

"Olivia! You have to get here! My apartment! He, the killer, was here! He left another painting on my wall! On my fucking wall! He left a video tape too! He beat Reece Pemberton and shot him, and I watched the entire thing! Please! Olivia, I need you!" I pleaded and then hung up the phone hoping that she would call me back soon.

"Don't cry, Jack!" begged a child's voice.

I looked up to see Annabelle Green staring at me with a warm smile on her face. She rested a comforting hand on my shoulder. It felt warm, as though she were really there. "You'll catch him eventually!" she said. "You have to keep trying!" She looked normal, how she might have done when she was alive. She was wearing her red pinafore dress that she had worn when she disappeared.

"Thank you, Annabelle," I replied, looking up at her blurred form through teary eyes and placing my hand over hers. "I will find the bastard who killed you, I promise!"

Her smile faded almost immediately. "Killed me? You mean, I'm..."

We both looked down to see the puddle that had formed around her feet, making my carpet sodden wet through. Annabelle looked at her hands and watched horrified as her flesh began to rot before her eyes.

She began to smell like death and decay and that's when I knew that I had to run. I broke free of her grasp and frantically crawled across the carpet towards the hallway leading to my front door. When I was out of her reach, I scrambled to my feet while Annabelle vomited a black tar-like substance that stained her pinafore and chin.

I reached the front door of my apartment and froze in horror when I saw that thick chains ran through metal loops attached to either side of the door frame and the door, sealing it shut.

"Where are you going, Jack?" asked Annabelle. Her voice was a mixture of an innocent little girl's voice overlapped with a demon's voice.

When I turned around, she was standing right behind me with her hands by her side. Her hair was sodden wet through and dripping stagnant water all over my carpet. Her pinafore dress had gone really dark from damp and hung from her skeletal frame. Her eyes were black, and her mouth looked like a cartoon grin stretched across her small face from ear to ear.

"Come play with me!" she giggled playfully and then burst into flames before erupting into flaming embers, disappearing completely.

I heard squelching noises and looked down to see wet children's footprints appearing down the hallway towards the living room and kitchen. "You find me, Jack, and I'll come find you afterwards!" Her childish laughter filled the air and made the hairs on my arms and the nape of my neck stand on end.

"I don't want to play, Annabelle!" I stammered nervously. "I need to find your killer so I can avenge you!" I still wasn't sure whether Annabelle was a specter or a figment of my fucked up imagination, but one thing I knew for sure was that an encounter with Annabelle was one where any damage that I sustained was carried over into reality after the encounter or hallucination. I was wary of upsetting her.

Annabelle rematerialized and ran around the corner back down the hallway as though she were getting fast-forwarded. Each step she took squelched and left a damp footprint on my carpet. She stopped inches in front of me. Her eyes were twisted with rage and her mouth was turned downwards in an angry grimace.

"You WILL play!" she demanded angrily. The demon part of her voice was most dominant. She jabbed a sharp fingernail in my knee. The pain was excruciating, as though someone had stabbed me in the knee with a drill.

"Okay, okay, okay!" I conceded in agony. "I'll play with you."

Annabelle's fingernail shrunk away from my knee and her smile returned. "Thank you, Jack!" she said sweetly, her voice resembling that of a little girl again.

I searched for Annabelle in the bathroom first, inspecting behind the curtain and checking in my washing basket. Then I searched my bedroom, glancing at the painting of Emma Fontaine with absolute hatred for the monster who had painted it. Annabelle wasn't here either. I made my way to the kitchen and happened to glance at a gap between two cupboards, one that was way too small for any person to squeeze into, even someone as small as Annabelle, but this was where she was hiding. Her black eye stared through the small gap at me.

"You found me!" she declared playfully. "Now you have to stab me to death."

Annabelle placed a large kitchen knife in my shaking hand, and I stared back at her in disbelief. "I can't do that..." I told her.

"Then die!" replied Annabelle with a shrug of her shoulders. My hand involuntarily moved the blade to my throat until I felt the cold steel against my flesh.

"Okay!" I said with a lump in my throat. Then I had control of my body again and I plunged the knife into her chest repeatedly, screaming while I did so. "I'm so sorry!" I stammered before dropping the knife and sobbing uncontrollably.

Annabelle's lifeless body was covered in blood and her lifeless eyes stared at me as though she were questioning why I had done something so horrific. Then she burst into flames and vanished. The blood that soaked my sleeve and carpet vanished too and Annabelle was standing beside me just as suddenly as she had vanished.

"It's your turn to hide now, Jack!" giggled Annabelle as the knife appeared in her hands. "If I find you, I stab you to death. That's the rules!"

I stared at her in disbelief and was spurred into action when Annabelle started counting down from ten.

"Ten. Nine. Eight..."

I ran to the bedroom and hid myself in the cupboard, sliding the door closed with a small gap to peek through.

"Ready or not, here I come!" I heard Annabelle's ghost call from the next room.

It didn't take long before the bedroom door creaked open and the silhouette of Annabelle's shadow was cast across the back wall by the light of the hallway. I watched through the gap in the door as Annabelle moved silently through the bedroom. Her movement reminded me of a Claymation character. She peeked under the bed and looked under the covers. She lingered in the bedroom for a very long time before she walked through the bedroom door and into the hallway again.

I listened to her wet footsteps falling down the hall and I sighed with relief and then suddenly her eye was there peeking through the gap.

"Found you!" she said in an unnaturally deep voice.

I was propelled forward out of the cupboard and sent hurtling across the bedroom. Annabelle lunged at me, swinging the knife wildly. I lifted my arm to defend myself and she sliced through my shirt and cut my arm with several swings.

I sprinted for the door and flung myself into the bathroom and braced the door behind me.

Annabelle threw her body at the door repeatedly and it took all my strength to keep her out.

"Let me in!" she demanded furiously. "I FOUND YOU, I FOUND YOU, I FOUND YOU!" Her voice was back to the deep and demonic voice that sounded more like a man than a little girl. "I'LL FUCKING KILL YOU! YOU CHEATING FUCKING BASTARD!" With every frustrated scream, the ghost of Annabelle's attempts at getting in the bathroom became less energetic until they ceased completely.

I sighed with relief and rested my head against the door. My heart was hammering furiously in my chest. I checked my arm and grimaced in pain when I prodded the slashes in the flesh. My shirt sleeve had been shredded completely and so had the flesh underneath. The white of my sleeve had turned red. I used my foot to drag a towel across the bathroom floor and when it was close enough, I used my other arm to wrap the towel around my wounded arm in an attempt to make a tourniquet to stem the bleeding. I didn't dare to move away from the bathroom door.

Suddenly there was a knock at the bathroom door.

"Jack? Are you in there?" It was Olivia's voice.

"Olivia?! Is that you? How did you get in here?!"

"The front door was open. I let myself in because I listened to your voicemail and I thought you needed my help," replied Olivia. "Open the door, Jack!"

"I need a minute, Olivia!" I gasped breathlessly. I pulled my cigarettes from my pocket and lit one, breathing in a deep lungful of nicotine. I decided that I couldn't let Olivia see the state of my arm since it would only freak her out and make her distrust me more so than she did already.

"Just open the door!" yelled Olivia again.

I was about to get up and open the door when my cell phone rang. I looked at the name displayed on the screen and my mouth gaped open. The name read 'Olivia Lockhart'. I answered the call numbly.

"Hello, Jack," she greeted me warmly, as she used to before the incident at Reece Pemberton's place. "I got your voicemail message and me and Perry are on our way over right now!"

"Sit tight, buddy!" I heard Perry call out.

"Jack, I'm sorry," said Olivia. "Maybe I did overreact a few weeks ago! You know how stressful these cases can be. I'll give you a big hug when I see you!"

"No!" I replied, still in shock. "Don't worry about it! Just get here quick!" I hung up the phone and braced the bathroom door. The thing outside was *not* Olivia!

"Jack, let me in!" said Annabelle in Olivia's voice. She kept up this facade for hours until she eventually gave up and burned into another fit of rage. After a few hours I passed out because of exhaustion and when I woke up, I was holding a kitchen knife in my left hand which was stained with my own blood.

I cleaned myself up as quickly as possible and when Perry and Olivia arrived, I explained to them everything that had happened since I arrived home, excluding the ordeal with Annabelle. I used superglue to close the wounds on my arm and then used bandaging to hide them.

Perry called for forensics to come to my apartment and search for any fingerprints or clues that might help us to identify the killer. In the meantime, I would gather my case files and move in with Olivia temporarily. The painting and the video tape were seized as evidence by the police.

CHAPTER 6

Identity

I didn't stay at Olivia's place for long. As soon as forensics had dusted my place for prints and searched for any other forensic evidence, I had my lock changed and I moved back into my apartment. I considered laying traps and installing surveillance in preparation for the unlikely event that the killer would infiltrate my apartment a second time. In the end, I concluded that his psychological attack had already served its purpose and that he had no need to invade my home a second time. Still, paranoia is a cruel mistress...

Olivia had a tendency to walk about her apartment in her underwear. I'm not sure whether this was an attempt at being provocative. Perhaps she intended for me to initiate some kind of romantic entanglement with her. However, her attempts to entice me, if that is indeed what they were, were met with an awkward embarrassing silence. I averted my eyes every time she would walk by the sofa that I slept on wearing nothing but a red lacy bra and panties. I even confronted her at one point, asking her if she could protect her modesty a little better when in my presence. I told her that she was like a sister to me and seeing her walk around in the nude made me feel uncomfortable.

"This is my house," replied Olivia with an impassive shrug. "If you don't like it you know where the door is!"

I took her response as my welcome wearing itself out and I took my leave as soon as I could face going back home. Olivia was my greatest friend, my only friend, but there was only so much of each other we could tolerate.

*

I decided to drink myself into oblivion the weeks following my harrowing home invasion. Instead of drinking at home I spent several weeks getting blitzed at the Blue Bell Tavern, which was a dingy little jazz club a short walk from my apartment block. The outside of the bar had a bell that turned into a saxophone illuminated in blue neon light. The name 'Blue Bell Tavern' lit up above the saxophone bell. A couple of lights had busted and hadn't lit up for months.

The inside of the bar was gloomy and felt cramped with its low ceiling and poor lighting. At one end of the bar was a mahogany stage where a jazz band played every Saturday night. These nights were usually the busiest. The bar itself had tacky-looking neon lights across it and dirty-looking stools lined across the front of it. A pool table was at the other end of the tavern in a smaller separate room with no door.

It was a Saturday night when I went there, and tonight was a special night. I wouldn't be drinking much tonight and the reason for that is a specific band was playing. The Brass Bulls was the name of the band and the lead singer was Dean Costello, a Frank Sinatra tribute singer and Scarlett Jones' former boyfriend. He was the prime suspect during the initial investigation.

He was already at the bar when I walked in, laughing and joking with his band members. He was a short fella with slicked-back black hair that had more shine than his black shoes. He was wearing a cream suit with a brown waistcoat and a black tie. His jovial party spirit disappeared when he saw me approaching the bar.

"What'll it be, Jack?" asked the barmaid. She was a round young thing with dark eyes and curly black hair who looked like she swallowed her twin.

"The usual, Shelly. Whiskey on the rocks," I replied. I then nodded at Dean and his cronies with an insincerely earnest smile. "How's it hanging, Deano?" I asked.

Dean Costello nodded back. "Not bad," he replied bluntly. I could tell with his body language and the tone of his voice that he saw me as an irritant who he would rather not converse with. His experience with me during the investigation of his dead girlfriend wasn't pleasant. I didn't get on well with people who didn't like to cooperate.

"You're performing tonight?" I asked, pretending that I didn't already know that he was.

"You bet, Detective," he responded, stony-faced.

I held out my hands and offered a friendly smile. "Relax, Dean! I'm just here to have a few drinks and enjoy some good music," I told him dishonestly. In truth, my being here was part of my investigation. Scarlett Jones had the voice of an angel and while she worked through the day at a café called 'The Toast Office' she would sometimes come here and sing a duet with Dean or sing alone. I'd watched her a few times and the girl definitely had talent. Plus, she was beautiful.

Dean didn't respond. Instead he drank the rest of his whiskey and stormed off towards the bathroom. I gave it a moment and followed him.

The male toilets assaulted my nostrils with the overpowering pungent odor of urine. There were two cubicles inside the toilets and one of them was out of order and the other was occupied. Dean Costello was hunched over one of the cisterns of the out of order toilet snorting lines of cocaine.

I took out my phone and recorded him. "Powdering your nose before you go on stage, sweetheart?" I asked mockingly.

He turned around, shocked, with cocaine still clinging to his nostril. He stammered, flustered and embarrassed.

"Relax, Dean!" I said smirking slyly. "I just wanted to talk about Scarlett!"

Dean sniffed and threw his hands in the air angrily. "This again?! How many times do you want to have this conversation, detective?! I was cleared of all charges! I was with the boys in Vegas!" he replied, speaking with his hands and gesticulating every sentence.

"Calm down, Costello!" I snapped, eyeballing him. "I know the nature of the argument which her colleagues at the café heard her having with you on the phone right before she died. She wasn't happy with you going to Vegas. I wanted to talk to you about a well-dressed and well-spoken gentleman who might have approached her at some point, either at The Toast Office or here at the Blue Bell. Did she mention anything, before she disappeared?"

Costello's attitude changed. Now he seemed intrigued. "Have you got a new suspect?" he asked wide-eyed.

"Witnesses have described such a man at his latest victim's murder scene. And I've seen him myself on... Err..." I paused, searching for the right words. "I've seen him on security footage."

Costello's eyes brightened. "Yes! She called me and told me she'd been offered a job by a Hollywood film producer. She had always been an aspiring actress and when she told me about this job offer, I'd never heard her so excited. That was why she was angry, because I was going to Vegas instead of sticking around to celebrate with her." His eyes began to well up. "Of course, she never made it to that interview."

My eyes narrowed. "Whoever posed as this film producer was definitely the person who killed her," I squeezed his shoulder reassuringly. "Don't worry, I'm getting closer to the truth! I'll catch the man who killed Scarlett!"

He nodded, but I think that he was unconvinced. He wiped tears away and walked towards the restroom door. "Delete that video of me snorting coke!" he snapped, his hostile demeanor returning.

"My phone camera doesn't work anyway!" I assured him. I waited until he left the restroom and then I deleted the video. I splashed cold water on my face and sighed. I'd gotten absolutely nothing from that conversation. What was I hoping for? Did I truly expect him to offer some new information because I threatened him with a video of him inhaling cocaine?!

"You're losing your touch, old man!" I told my haggard reflection. I stared transfixed at the beads of water that snaked their way down my beard and then I heard someone snivelling in the occupied toilet.

It was the sound of a woman. The snivelling quickly turned into uncontrollable sobbing.

I made my way to the cubicle door and knocked gently. "Hello? Are you okay in there? You know this is the guy's toilets, right?"

She ignored me but continued to sob.

I thought about knocking again but resisted. Either this was a specter or a woman who wanted to be left alone or another hallucination that wanted to torment my mind. Either way, I wanted out of this restroom. I paced to the exit and then the cubicle door creaked open before I reached the door.

Every fiber of my being told me to flee the bathroom, but some innate part of me felt compelled to go look inside the cubicle and see what was in there, whether it be a woman in distress with mascara streaked down her cheeks or a harrowing ghost.

It turned out that it was neither. When I reached the cubicle there was nobody in there. I knew that it had been a specter or an auditory hallucination. I reasoned that there was never anybody in there and that Dean Costello had decided to ingest his cocaine in the cubicle that was out of order to prevent anyone who might have needed the toilet from disturbing him. He probably didn't expect me to follow him since I'd ordered a whiskey and he assumed that I would be off duty. I was never off duty.

When I turned, I gasped at the sight of Scarlett Jones sitting on the toilet with tears of blood pouring down her face. They fell from eyeless sockets and left red streams on her cheeks. She looked up and if she had eyes, they would have locked onto mine.

I couldn't take my eyes from the mirror. Even when Scarlett's crying stopped and she pointed an accusatory finger at me with her grin stretching wider and wider, I remained transfixed. Then my hair started to fall out in thick clumps and my flesh began to melt from my face. I screamed and clawed at my face desperately, watching in horror as my hands pulled away thick clots of melting flesh as though it were melting candle wax.

The restroom door opened, and a burly man stared at me for a few moments before shaking his head and walking to the urinal. I looked back at the mirror. My face was back to normal and the toilet cubicle where Scarlett had been was empty.

*

Dean Costello was a good singer. If I hadn't known any better, I'd have thought that he was Frank Sinatra himself. A large group of spectators had now gathered in front of the stage where Dean stood and his band played. It was around this time that the bar started to get busy.

I sat alone, as I always did. To the youths who frequented the bar I must've appeared as a sad old fucker who didn't know what went wrong. I downed another whiskey. My head was already buzzing pleasantly, and the pain of everyday existence had been subdued to a significant degree.

I had thought that this night would have been the same as always, but as it turns out tonight would yield some interesting information pertaining to the case.

At first, when the young man approached me, I suffered a hallucination. As he seated himself in front of me, I envisioned his face to be a writhing mass of tentacles that squirmed and squelched underneath his hood. Then I rubbed my eyes and massaged my throbbing temples and the man was normal.

"Are you detective Jack Cucchiano?" asked the man. He looked nervous. He looked around the busy jazz bar to make sure that we weren't being watched.

"Who the fuck is asking?" I barked. My voice had a drunken slur and I could smell the whiskey on my breath.

"I'm a private detective, Mr Cucchiano." he replied sternly, digging around in his Parker coat and producing a driving license.

I snatched it out of his hand and examined it sceptically with one squinty eye. "Nicolas Brown, eh?" I studied him carefully. He was a young man in his thirties with dark brown eyes, clean shaven face, quite stocky in stature. "What can I do for you, detective Brown?"

Nicolas took his driving license from my hand and put it back in his pocket. He smiled at me from the corner of his mouth and I felt like he was sizing me up, trying to figure me out. "You seem like a straight-talking guy, Cucchiano, so I'll get right to the point," he said, leaning forward. "I'm investigating a case that I think you should be familiar with: the case of the Artist serial killer."

I couldn't hide my shock. Who was this man? Who hired him and why was he questioning me? Was I a suspect in his investigation?

I regained my composure and narrowed my eyes at him suspiciously. He was momentarily distracted by Dean Costello finishing his version of 'My Way' by Frank Sinatra. The band, a black guy with sunglasses and dreadlocks with a brown suit playing saxophone and another guy in a black suit with sunglasses playing drums started a new funky tune while Dean clicked his fingers and stomped his foot.

"Who hired you?" I asked when Nicolas Brown turned back to face me.

"I'm not at liberty to divulge such information, but I think I could make an exception in your case. I was hired by the parents of Annabelle Green to find her killer. They offered a handsome reward. And besides, I've taken a personal interest in this particular case." Nicolas Brown smiled enigmatically, lacing his fingers together in front of him. "You were the homicide detective investigating the murder for the LAPD at the time," said Nicolas, pointing a finger at me. "I recognized you the minute I walked in."

"I take it you finding me here was no accident," I replied dryly. "How did you know where to find me?"

Nicolas leaned back in his chair, his body language indicating that he was ready for a confrontation. He looked down at me. "I know everything about you, Cucchiano. I know you're one of the best homicide detectives the LAPD has ever had. Your success rate at solving cases is an impressive feat. Your intellect is matched only by your tenacity." He sat forward again, leaning closer. "It all went wrong though, didn't it? Disgraced detective dismissed for gross misconduct for drinking on the job!"

"Fuck you!" I exclaimed, snarling back at him. I gritted my teeth and clenched my fists before anger gave way to curiosity. "How do you know about me?" I asked him.

He rolled his eyes as though what I'd asked him was incomprehensibly stupid. "I'm a detective!" he reiterated. He smiled at me before his facial expression became one of grave seriousness. "Listen, Jack, I know you did your best to catch the Artist Killer. From what I can gather, you're the only homicide detective in the LAPD who is capable of catching such a resourceful killer."

"You almost sound like you admire him," I retorted bitterly. I took another mouthful of whiskey and washed the bitterness away.

Nicolas shook his head vigorously. "I'm simply a realist. The Artist *is* resourceful, and he *is* intelligent. Me saying that isn't a statement that denotes admiration, but rather simply a statement that is the unfortunate truth."

I huffed and buried my head in my hands. My frustration and curiosity were mounting in equal measure. "You sure do like to talk, detective Brown! Please! Get to the fucking point already!"

Nicolas Brown stared at me blankly for a moment before he cleared his throat and spoke. "As I said before, I've been hired by the parents of Annabelle Green. I want the reward they're offering for the capture of the Artist killer. I would like to propose that we share certain information pertaining to the case. In other words, I propose an alliance of sorts. Two great detectives collaborating as one! What do you say?"

I sniggered bitterly. "I say fuck off! I'm not in this for monetary gain, unlike yourself, a pseudo-detective with no fucking repute whatsoever. Nicolas Brown? I've never even fucking heard of you. The truth of the matter is that you've got fuck all information and you learned that I had police connections! Do me a favor and get the hell out of here!" I waved a dismissive hand at him, as though I were swatting away a fly. Then I finished my drink and began to rise to my feet to leave. The chilled ambiance of the jazz club contrasted strongly to the tension at our small table in the corner.

Nicolas Brown was no pushover. He wasn't prepared to give up that easily. He slammed his hands on the table and jumped to his feet to block my exit. "Anyone would think you don't want this case to be solved!" he snapped in annoyance. His patience for my bad attitude had dissipated completely. "I'm proposing that we work together and share information so that we can both move closer to solving this case!"

"You have five minutes to convince me," I told him bluntly, sitting back down. "And I want another whiskey," I added.

Nicolas complied. "Thanks for hearing me out," he said, placing the whiskey on a coaster in front of me. "Here's what will convince you." The enigmatic detective Brown continued a sly smile: "The second victim, the one whose identity remains a mystery to yourself and the police, I know who she is!"

My jaw dropped. I couldn't contain my shock. "Why didn't you go to the police?!" I asked in disbelief. "That kind of information could have helped forward the case!"

"Simple," replied Nicolas. "I don't trust the police. And neither should you!"

His words confounded me. I asked him why, but my questions were swept away by the audio tsunami of a saxophone solo. "Why?!" I called out louder.

"Not so fast!" warned Nicolas, holding up his index finger. "First I want some information from you! Since you were unwilling to cooperate at first, I want you to go first. Tell me what I want to know, and I'll tell you the name of the second victim and where you can find a contact of hers. And then I'll tell you why you shouldn't trust the police."

"What do you want to know? Seems you know more than me!"

"The police are withholding information pertaining to the most recent murder. I feel this information could help me with my own investigation. Are you ready to play ball?" asked Nicolas, with a raised eyebrow.

"The victim was a woman from New Orleans. Her name was Emma Fontaine," I began to explain. "She was strangled with hemp rope, just like the other victims. The killer has surgical experience." Nicolas's eyes were transfixed on mine. "It might be an idea for one or both of us to visit various universities in the area to see if we can find anything out," I continued.

"What else did you find out?" asked Nicolas eagerly.

"The killer had booked a room next door to the victim under the name 'Heinrich Wulf'. He somehow drugged the security guard and deleted the footage from any camera that had recorded him."

Nicolas widened his eyes at that last piece of information. "Drugged? Did the police test him for drugs?"

I shook my head. What was he trying to get at?

"Detective Cucchiano, I'd like to offer a personal theory and an explanation as to why I never shared the information that I had gathered about the second victim with the LAPD. I think the killer is exponentially wealthy. I also think that certain high-ranking members of the LAPD are on the killer's payroll," alleged Nicolas.

His words hit me like a freight train. Could it be true? Could Perry and Olivia be on his payroll if that was the case? My mind was flooded with a deluge of questions. The worst thing about what Nicolas had said was that it would make a *lot* of sense! My thoughts went to Carl Parker and his claim that he had been drugged. What if he had simply been paid a considerable amount of money to take a walk?!

"Thank you for sharing that information," I replied coldly. I felt like I'd been betrayed, even though there was no evidence to support his claims.

"And thank you for the information you have shared with me," replied Nicolas, offering me a handshake and getting to his feet. As he turned to walk away, he turned to me and said: "Mary O'Reilly." He stuck his hand in his Parker coat and produced a small envelope. "Inside are two addresses, one is Mary's father's address and one is the address of a friend of hers, a girl called Rebecca. My card is also in there. Call me if you want to work together sometime." Nicolas Brown gave me a two-fingered salute and pulled up his hood before he paced towards the door and left. After he left, I raced home as quickly as I could with the file clutched tightly under my arm. I first looked up the house phone number of the parents of Annabelle Green and inquired as to whether they did actually hire a detective by the name of Nicolas Brown.

They confirmed his story: he was a private detective who had offered his services in order to obtain the cash reward on offer. This wasn't something that they would have told just anybody, but the Green family trusted me after I investigated the death of their daughter. They sounded in high spirits, confident in the abilities of Nicolas Brown. He seemed resourceful, but his warning about the police had unnerved me. Now I felt like I couldn't trust anyone, not even Olivia Lockhart...

CHAPTER 7

Following the Trail

The folder which Nicolas Brown had given me contained everything that he had promised it would: a written address for Rebecca Valentine, a written address for Mary O'Reilly and a simplistic laminated contact card for Nicolas Brown.

I travelled by bus to Compton where both addresses were located. It was a beautiful day. The sun shone brightly, and rays of brilliant light cut through the dark clouds and dispersed them, giving way to a blue sky. It was a welcome change to the relentless downpour that LA had seen in recent weeks. To me, the sun and brightness were synonymous to my investigation regarding Mary O'Reilly. At first her identity was shrouded in darkness with dismal prospects of discovering the truth, but now that shroud of darkness had disappeared and given way to bright rays of hope as her identity was illuminated.

I felt very happy today. It seemed like the weather not only reflected the case, but also my mood. Everything seemed more colorful and vibrant despite the fact that I was travelling by bus through a particularly rough area of LA. I wore a clean white button-up shirt and jeans with brown shoes.

Compton was home to several of LA's more notorious street gangs. I stared through the dirty bus window and could see groups of African Americans congregating in large groups. Their specific gang alignment was unknown to me, nor was it of any interest.

First, I would go speak with Rebecca Valentine. I got off at the bus stop a few blocks from where Nicolas Brown had claimed her address was in his notes. From here I would walk a few blocks to the home address of Mary O'Reilly.

A group of tall African American youths were the only people I could see in the neighborhood. They were dressed in shorts and vests, kicking a football to each other up and down the street. They laughed and swore at each other in jest as they chased the ball, panting breathlessly. Their jovial playfulness made me smile.

A Rottweiler barked angrily from behind a chain link fence, startling me. I jumped back away from the fence swearing involuntarily, evoking chuckles from the African American teens.

As I kept walking the aroma of Caribbean jerk chicken curry made my mouth salivate and I briefly imagined myself as a Disney cartoon character floating through the air as the scent of delicious food drew me towards its source. As my stomach grumbled in complaint like an angry bear, I had to stop and try to think back to the last time I had eaten properly. To my surprise I realized that I'd been so busy with this case that I hadn't eaten a proper meal in weeks.

Rebecca Valentine lived in a small house with a black fence around her property. The windows and front door had white bars in front of them to prevent anyone breaking into her property or causing any damage. The lawn was neglected and overgrown, with long blades of grass reaching up into the sky. Ivy had crawled up the walls and surrounded the front window, forming a partial shield to prevent nosy passers-by from peering inside.

I entered the garden through a small waist-high black gate that groaned in protest. I approached the front door, opened the white gate and rapped the brown door. It didn't take long before a pretty girl opened it and looked at me with a wooden expression.

"Rebecca Valentine?" I asked her with a cordial smile. "A friend gave me your address and said I should come speak to you. Apparently, you may be able to help me with something." As she continued to look me up and down with a blank stare I added: "Can I come inside?"

Rebecca smiled. It wasn't a welcoming smile, rather one void of any joy. She flirtatiously leaned against the door before walking into her house and leaving the door open behind her. "Come in," she sighed.

She was a bonny girl. She had long black hair, which bounced behind her. Her eyes were emerald green and had regarded me warily with a degree of lust. Her body was slim and voluptuous. She was wearing tight gray yoga pants that accentuated her ass. Her green vest revealed her cleavage and complimented her slim figure. I found myself attracted to this young lady, even though I was most likely ten years her senior.

The house was decorated with potted peace lily and pink crystals. Symbols of peace had been painted on different canvases and hung on the walls. Incense sticks burned in every room and the entire house smelled like lavender. Rebecca led me into her living room, a small room with two green sofas a few bookshelves containing self-help books and books about spirituality. A yoga mat was on the floor in the center of the room and Rebecca made her way straight to it.

"Put your money on the table by the door," she said as she entered the down-facing dog pose. Her yoga pants stretched, and I could see the faint outline of her red French underwear underneath.

I stammered awkwardly before responding: "I don't know why you think I'm here, but I'm a private detective and I'm only here to ask you a few questions about Mary O'Reilly."

"Terrible what happened to her," said Rebecca, forlornly. She stood back upright and gestured for me to sit. She sat on one of the green sofas and I sat beside her. "Who are you?" she asked.

I sighed heavily. "My name is Jack Cucchiano. I'm a private detective investigating the case of the Artist serial killer. Have you heard of him?"

Rebecca shook her head fervently. "I don't watch the news or read the papers, there's too much negativity. I know what happened to Mary though. Another private detective turned up not long ago asking all sorts of questions."

Rebecca buried her head in her hands and wept. The thoughts of her murdered friend all came flooding back. Her back rose and fell as she sobbed for her lost friend. I sat staring at her awkwardly before I placed a hand on her back. I was useless at consolations.

"I'm so sorry," I said while squeezing her shoulder in an attempt to comfort her. "That's why I'm here. I want to catch the killer and avenge those he's taken away. I want to make him pay for all the suffering he's caused! With a bullet in his gut if necessary!"

"How can I help?" asked Rebecca, looking up at me with puffy eyes and streaks of mascara running down her cheeks.

It was show time. I took out my notepad and pen and prepared to make some notes. "When was the last time you saw Mary?" I asked, the tone of my voice changing from caring and passionate to clinical and professional.

"I don't remember exactly," said Rebecca with a sympathetic shrug. "She had come over and we blazed a few together. She was really upset. I remember that."

I raised an eyebrow. "What was she upset about?"

"Her father!" spat Rebecca bitterly. "He's a preacher at the local church. He hates me. He said I lead his daughter down Satan's path and made her a whore!" Her lip curled at the mention of Mary's father. "I went to his house once with Mary because he was out. We put salt in his drinks, put bleach on his razor blades and rubbed his toothbrush around mold gathering around the windowsill. I'm spiritual, detective. I believe in peace and love. But I despised Mary's father for what he put her through."

I kept silent and allowed her to continue.

"He believed in self-flagellation and he forced Mary to do it while he watched," she explained shuddering with revulsion. "She told me that he used to touch her as a child! I wouldn't be surprised if he got some kind of sick sexual gratification from watching her beat herself just so he could 'save her soul'." She leaned towards me, her piercing eyes meeting mine with fierce intensity. "If she needed protecting from anyone it was that horrible fat cunt!"

I was taken aback by her hostility. Still, this was getting interesting. "Should I consider him a suspect? Does he share this address?" I showed her Mary O'Reilly's address written by Nicolas Brown.

Rebecca wrinkled her nose as she squinted to read the hastily scrawled note. "No," she said with a determined shake of her head. "That's her current apartment. *Was* her apartment. I don't know who lives there now. As for her father, I can tell you where to find him. He'll probably be at the local parish."

"Thank you, Rebecca," I said with an appreciative smile. "Is there anything else you can think of that could help me?"

"Well..." Rebecca tapped her lips with her index finger thoughtfully before she snapped her fingers and her eyes brightened up with a sudden realization. "Mary kept a logbook of all her clients hidden under the floorboards at her apartment. Maybe you could go there and take a look through it?"

"Just so there are no misunderstandings allow me to ask one more question. This profession you and Mary were into, was it prostitution?" I had half-expected Rebecca to become indignant at my question. I didn't want to make assumptions. Assumptions were the mother of all fuck ups!

To my surprise Rebecca just smiled. "Yes, detective. Why would we serve some corporate elite when we have all the natural resources we needed to get by in this society?" Her tone became somber. "We both knew the risks. When Mary disappeared, I hoped beyond hope that she'd met the right guy and he'd whisked her away to the Caribbean. When that other detective came asking questions it only confirmed the niggling suspicions I had that poor Mary had picked up the wrong guy!"

Rebecca gave me the address of the parish and I thanked her for her help. She saw me to the door and lingered in the doorway as I walked across the garden path.

"Take my cellphone number, detective!" added Rebecca hastily. She ran back inside and grabbed her cellphone. I waited near her front door. "I want to help any way I can. I gave the last detective my number too, but he never called."

I saved her number into my phone and smiled at her before turning and walking away.

"One more thing, detective!" called Rebecca with a sultry smile. "I like my men rough and rugged like yourself. If you feel the need to release some stress just give me a call and I'll give you a discount!" She waved playfully and blew me a kiss with a wink before closing her door.

I couldn't help but feel flattered that she would even consider a guy like me, but then I remembered that she was providing a paid service. I shook the feelings of lust from my mind and decided to focus entirely on the investigation.

"Watch out, old timer!" called out a voice suddenly, following a thud. I looked up in horror to see the severed head of Mary O'Reilly flying towards me. Her empty sockets stared sightlessly as the head flew through the air. Her teeth were like the jaws of a shark, sharp and gnashing violently. I raised up my hands to protect myself. The head rammed into me and the African American teens laughed hysterically when I let out a yelp as their football bounced off of my forearm.

I didn't give a shit! I let them laugh it up and I left the block in search of my next destination.

I walked a few blocks to a large apartment block where Mary O'Reilly had lived before she was brutally murdered. Outside was a large courtyard surrounded by chain link fencing where several youths were loitering near their cars and smoking weed. They all regarded me with mild distaste when I nodded at them in greeting.

I found Mary's old apartment and knocked on the door and wasn't surprised when a large-framed African American woman answered with a suckling babe at her breast.

I introduced myself and informed her who I was and why I was there. At first, she wasn't interested in aiding me whatsoever, and I wasn't surprised; I wanted to snoop around her home to look for something that *might* have been left behind by someone that had lived there two years ago, maybe longer. In the end I was forced to speak a language that everyone understands: the language of money! I gave the housewife over a hundred dollars which I had in my wallet just to walk into her bedroom and search for a loose floorboard.

The woman tailed me closely like a shadow as I conducted my search strictly in the bedroom. I walked around, navigating my way around children's toys, piles of clothes, and miscellaneous items to find the hidden compartment which Rebecca had mentioned. Several questions flooded my mind.

Did Nicolas come here? Did he find Mary's notes already? Had the killer attacked Mary here?

"Five minutes! Then you go or I call the police!" barked the housewife at me. Her tone was harsher than the barking of the Rottweiler which I had encountered earlier. I looked at her and could find no words. On the one hand I was angry at her for impeding my investigation, on the other hand I couldn't be surprised that the homeowner wanted a stranger to leave.

"Five minutes and I'll leave," I reluctantly agreed. Luckily, I wouldn't need five minutes. As I probed the flooring with my foot a certain section of the floorboards creaked, where the others did not. This provoked a triumphant smile. I crouched down and slid my fingernails into the gap between the floorboards, grunting with the effort of pulling up the loose section. Underneath was a small compartment with a leather-bound diary covered in dust and a small envelope. I took all of them, thanked the woman and left her house as quickly as possible.

Next, I made my way to the parish. I sat in a café across the road drinking coffee as I looked through Mary O'Reilly's diary. She had logged the names of all her clientele and the services they'd required plus the money charged. A name that appeared frequently towards the end of the diary was a man who Mary had nicknamed "Bright Eyes". She had written that his name was "Ralph Lawrence". I skipped all other entries as I read through and only concentrated on this "Ralph Lawrence" aka "Bright Eyes" character.

"May 1st Ralph Lawrence. Required me to lie on my bed naked with my eyes closed while he stood over me for the full 20 minutes. He was breathing heavily, but I don't think he was masturbating. He wasn't doing anything besides looking at me. I've had some weird requests, but this one was slightly uncomfortable. Afterwards he paid me 20 dollars and left."

"May 14th Bright Eyes was back again. He requested that I lie naked on my bed with my eyes closed. This time I felt him climb in bed next to me, but he didn't touch me, and I didn't hear him unzip his trousers. He just lay next to me breathing heavily and I felt really uncomfortable. The timer seemed to take forever to go off! Afterwards he made small talk with me and I immediately felt at ease. Turns out Ralph is really well-spoken, polite and even charming!"

"May 18th Bright Eyes requested that I lie naked on my bed with my eyes closed while he sketched images of me in his notebook. We talked the whole time and even when the timer went off, signalling the end of his time, I ignored it and allowed him to finish his sketches. He was polite and charming, and I found him very flattering and alluring. He said I was 'aesthetically pleasing' and he even compared me to a beautiful piece of art."

"May 24th Ralph said that he wants me to become his next art project. He told me that I'll never have to work again. I can just imagine his paintings of me

hanging in some kind of gallery or getting auctioned away for a handsome sum of cash. We had a lengthy conversation about how things work in nature. He told me I had beautiful eyes and I returned the sentiment. Then he went on to explain how the human eye is similar to a camera in how it functions. He made his request again and this time I said I wouldn't charge him. He warned me not to open my eyes and I obeyed him. I lie there in the dark like usual, I was so used to it now I was fighting sleep after several minutes, then I yelped when something cold touched my flesh. It was steel. He was pressing the flat of a knife against my stomach! It wasn't just the cold of the blade that made all my hairs stand on end! It was just very creepy. This man who I was beginning to trust had made me very uncomfortable! Afterwards I confronted him, and he stormed out of my apartment angrily. What the fuck is it with men?!"

"May 25th Ralph came back with a bunch of tulips and profusely apologized for upsetting me. He said I'm something special and compared me to a diamond in a cesspit. I accepted his apology and told him that I wouldn't be providing a service to him again if it involved a knife. He agreed and asked me to take off my clothes so he could sketch me again. I agreed. My trepidation began to leave me and once again I began to feel comfortable. Then, before he left, he asked if I would lie down naked on the bed. I reluctantly agreed and set the timer for 10 minutes instead of 20! I laid there in the darkness, listening intently to his heavy breathing, trying to determine whether he was going to step closer. I couldn't hear his shoes clicking on my wooden floor, but I could hear his leather gloves making noise like he was tightening his fists and then releasing them."

"May 26th Ralph came to my apartment while I was busy with another client. I had forgotten to chain the door locked and Bright Eyes just walked right in. He had a confrontation with my client and ordered him to leave. Then he stared at me angrily for a few moments before his grimace turned into a deranged smile. He kept balling his leather gloved hands into fists. I could feel the anger and hatred emanating from him. At first, I was angry he'd shooed my client, but seeing this side of him really frightened me and my anger turned to fear. He ordered me to lie on the bed naked again and I refused. He stepped into very close proximity of me and told me to lie on the bed again. This time I complied, and he mounted me. He told me to close my eyes and warned me not to open them. He stated that 'something bad would happen' if I opened them. I felt his cold leather gloves slide around my throat and I thought he would choke me to death. I struggled and he hushed me and tenderly stroked my cheek. He leaned in close so I could feel his hot breath on my neck, and he whispered a quote from scripture into my ear. That's when I went mad! I tossed and turned and clawed at his eyes in a futile effort to get him off of me. He allowed me to throw him off in the end and he left *my apartment willingly, bursting into fits of hysterical maniacal laughter. Ralph Lawrence is a deranged lunatic!*

"May 27th His Octavia is still parked outside. I know he's peering back at me through the darkness inside his car. I was awake all night watching his car through the window, I'm too paranoid to sleep! I'm starting to believe that Ralph Lawrence is a crazy goon hired by my father! I should go see Rebecca and tell her about my fucking father trying to ruin my life again! Does he really think I'll continue to be afraid of this fucking whack-job? I can easily get a gun! I'll do what I must to protect myself! I went to see Rebecca and told her about my father. She was stoned, and I don't know how much of what I said she actually took in. As I walked home, I noticed Ralph's Octavia crawling behind me the whole three blocks to my apartment. He's trying to spook me out! I called the police, but they didn't even show up. I don't think they take me seriously!"

"May 28th I woke up in shock to see Ralph Lawrence standing over me with a psychotic grin plastered across his smug face! How fucking long had he been in my apartment?! Was I not safe anywhere! I screamed and Ralph sprinted for the door and drove away in his red Octavia. I wept for hours afterwards. Later that day he posted his sketchbook and I flicked through it to see that it was empty. He'd never made any drawings with the exception of one. A picture of three coffins with the words 'pick one' scrawled across the bottom. Was this a threat? And if so, was it directed at me?! I called my father and we argued for hours about Ralph Lawrence."

"May 29th Bright Eyes is parked outside again! This is it! The police are doing nothing and I'm sick of my father's goons trying to intimidate me! I'm going out there to confront him!"

This was the last entry... I can only surmise that the killer, Ralph Lawrence, must have drugged her and shoved her in the back of his red Octavia during this final confrontation.

Mary O'Reilly's journal had provided some insight into the killer's state of mind. He is intelligent, charming, and well-spoken, but also obsessive, narcissistic and aggressive. He sounded to me a tad unhinged. Despite the insight which the journal provided me with it also created more questions. Was Ralph Lawrence a killer for hire? Was Ralph Lawrence even his real name? And did the killer have any idea that Mary kept a journal of her clients?

I closed the journal and looked in the envelope where Mary had kept notes about her father that she had planned to hand over to the police. According to Mary's files, her father was a pedophile who abused her as a child. She claims in her notes that several others were involved in her father's circle. She had overheard them all confess the same sins over and over and when they did her father would take them into the church cellar.

I think that it's time for me to meet this priestly predator.

I finished the rest of my coffee and screwed up the paper cup before tossing it into a trashcan by the café door. I left the waitress a tip and wasted no time at all. I stormed across the road with fierce determination driving me forward.

The church was a warm and welcoming-looking place. It was fairly modern-looking with its white walls that looked like they had been renovated fairly recently. Stained-glass windows depicted several important scenes from the Bible and were a blend of several different colors that seemed to radiate bright light from the glaring sun reflecting from them.

A small cobbled path led up to a heavy wooden door that looked freshly painted in black. Either side of the path were several headstones that looked neglected and crumbling. Newer headstones of black granite were compacted together towards the back end of the church with the remnants of a dead oak that had been struck by lightning hanging over them all charred and dried out.

The church was indeed a warm and welcoming-looking place in contrast to some of the gang-controlled streets that I had walked merely a few blocks away. I guessed that many people found solace coming to this place. To them it must have been a sanctuary away from the relentless influx of gang warfare that took place in these streets of LA.

They never would have guessed that one of the biggest threats to their safety was the man who represented the God who they worshipped. This man, this priestly predator of children, was a monster! He wasn't the same kind of monster as the Artist. But he was a monster, nonetheless.

"And what do I do to monsters?" I asked myself with a malicious grin on my face. "I teach them a fucking lesson!"

I opened the wooden door and stepped into the interior of the church. The smell of incense immediately struck my nostrils. It was a sweet smell that always reminded me of Sunday mass as a child. I could hear a few people coughing and a softly spoken conversation over by the altar. The lighting in the church was dim. The stained-glass windows didn't allow much light to enter and so candles had been lit and distributed around the church. Their flickering lights made the church seem more welcoming and gave a cozy feeling.

I spotted the priest almost immediately. He was standing by the altar talking with a small elderly woman. It seemed as though she clung to his every word. I walked by rows of empty benches where only a few people sat scattered, muttering prayers in silence.

The priest spotted me approaching and gave me an exaggerated smile in greeting: "Welcome! Yours is a face I have not seen before in this church! I am Father Michael O'Reilly!" He spoke with a slight Irish twang in his accent and shook my hand heartily with gusto. "All are welcome in the house of God!"

"I wish to confess," I said bluntly. I wanted this over with as soon as possible. I had to know whether what Mary had written about her father was true and whether he was linked to my investigation.

His face changed from one of exaggerated joviality into a sly smirk with a raised eyebrow. He immediately dismissed the elderly woman and he headed towards the confession booths.

"Please," he gestured towards the booth with a chubby hand. "Confess, my son!"

Michael O'Reilly, a fat bald priest with beady little eyes, a bulbous nose and fat lips. His ears were large and looked to me like a pair of wings attached to the side of his shiny bald head.

I stepped behind a red curtain where myself and Michael O'Reilly were separated by a flimsy mesh. I sat down on a stool and placed my hands on my lap.

"Forgive me father, for I have sinned," I said, trying my best to sound convincing.

"Speak, my son!" encouraged the priest. "Allow your sins to be absolved through confessing to God! Through my ears he hears your confession! And through my lips he speaks his forgiveness!"

I narrowed my eyes and curled my lip in a snarl at the round form of Michael O'Reilly's head through the mesh. It was time to see whether Mary's notes had any truth to them. She had spent several years living with her father and during all those years she overheard several conversations between her father and his circles. The secret code, from one client to Michael, would be the form of a confession.

"I have tasted the forbidden fruit of God, and I wish to try more."

Michael was silent for a while before he answered. "You are forgiven, my son!" he said. "Wait until the church empties and I shall give you holy communion!"

With that he got to his feet and left the confession booth, leaving me sitting in shock. Mary was right! This fat fuck was a pedophile! What had I stumbled across here?! I waited until the church emptied, seating myself strategically at a pew near the rear of the church so I could remain unnoticed by the parishioners. Whenever someone happened to glance curiously in my direction, I simply pretended to be busy with prayer.

"Follow me," beckoned Father Michael. He walked with his hands clasped together, his chubby fingers interlaced as he rapidly made his way to a wooden door at the back of the church. I followed him through the doorway and down some cracked stone steps, which led to a corridor with several doors on either side.

"This is where I host Sunday school," explained Michael with a touch of pride. "That's how we separate the children from their parents."

I froze in terror as Michael walked by Annabelle Green. She regarded him with abject hatred until she screamed and burst into ashes.

"What kind of pictures are you looking for? We have little girls and little boys, aged between six and ten. I'm assuming you are aware of my fee?"

He turned to face me and was met with my fist slamming hard into his nose. The impact of my punch sent him reeling backwards with blood gushing over his white robes. He squealed like a pig and tried to crawl across the stone floor towards the staircase behind me. I grabbed his ankles and dragged him back across the floor. He squealed again and his fingernails scratched across the floor.

"Who sent you?!" demanded Michael in panic. His beady eyes were wide with alarm and sweat glistened on his bald head in the pale light of the basement.

I laughed at him maliciously. "Your daughter had all the information I needed! You baldy-headed fucking cunt!" I stuck a heavy foot into his stomach and Michael cramped up, gasping for air.

"My daughter?! I have no daughter!" gasped Michael in exasperated anger. "My daughter can rot in hell for all I care!"

I grabbed his robes and dragged him to his feet. He offered no resistance. I tossed him across the corridor into a wooden door, which opened when Michael's weight slammed into it. I followed him into a small room where several small chairs were grouped in a circle and a camera and tripod stood in the corner. "You know your daughter is dead, right?!" I shouted as I rammed my knee into his oversized belly. "She was fucking murdered by a lunatic! He cut off your daughter's head and left her naked and mutilated body in the sand at Longbeach!"

"She did Satan's work!" wheezed Michael. "And so she attracted one of Satan's minions! I am not surprised she is dead!" His face became contorted with rage as he continued. "She was a whore! She lived a whore and she died a whore! She lived and died by the sword! All puns intended!"

I punched him again, and for a moment I seemed to have lost contact with reality. Even when Michael was on the floor and his face was swollen and covered in blood, I kept punching. Eventually, I managed to get back control. I looked down and the fucking bastard was actually smiling at me!

"Kill me! I want to be with my Lord up in heaven!" he said with blood between his teeth.

"Not until you talk first! Who the fuck is Ralph Lawrence?!"

"I've never heard of that name..." said Michael. His eyes began to roll, and consciousness began to leave him.

I slapped him gently to keep him awake. "Did you hire Ralph Lawrence, or a man by any other name to kill your daughter?"

"No!" came his stern reply. "I am a man of the cloth! I do not kill! Nor will I kill using the hand of another! I disowned my daughter and that was the end of it! She will be festering in hell now for her fornication!"

"And you're going to fester in prison! You and all your buddies! I have a list which I found in Mary's notes naming all of your circle! The ones who you used to make her dress up for while you overlooked the operation!" My hatred flared up inside me like a roaring fire, and the desire to kill this man grew stronger and stronger with each passing moment.

Michael stared at me with a condescending grin across his face. "You don't know all of them! Mary only knew a handful! Our group extends beyond the county borders of LA! I won't give up a single name! You'd have to kill me first! Go ahead, I'm not afraid to die! What I did broke no commandments, broke no laws of God!" As he spoke, spittle and blood flew from his mouth. I punched him again and knocked him clean out.

It didn't take me long to find the pictures of the children stashed in a hole behind a picture of the Virgin Mary holding the baby Jesus. I immediately called Matthew Perry and unleashed the full fury of the LAPD on Michael O'Reilly and his circle of pedophiles. Arrests were made all over LA in the following days and I slept easily knowing that I played a vital part in bringing some justice back to the streets of LA. The Artist was still at large, but I was confident that I would put him in jail soon enough.

CHAPTER 8

Club 88

I worked closely with Matthew Perry and Olivia and assisted them in uncovering the identity of pedophiles that comprised of Michael's circle. The operation was relatively successful, despite Michael O'Reilly's unwillingness to cooperate. Once the LAPD had discovered some of Michael's closest associates, they initiated a plan to arrest them all before word travelled and gave them a heads up. I only remained involved until several names were exposed and then I left the LAPD to continue this revenue of investigation.

I kept in touch with both Rebecca Valentine and Nicolas Brown, both of whom had congratulated me on my most recent discovery of Michael O'Reilly's antics. Shock waves rippled through the community as the shock of Michael's true nature astonished and appalled people that had once respected him and had seen him as a pillar of the community.

I met with Nicolas Brown at the Blue Bell the following Saturday where we discussed what we had learned so far. It was a bonus that I had uncovered the truth about Michael and his circle, but he wasn't my target. Even knowing that the Artist was still out there made my victory seem minor.

I explained to Nicolas what I had found. I informed him of my discovery of Mary O'Reilly's diary and Nicolas listened earnestly as I read to him the entries of Mary's diary that concerned Ralph Lawrence. I also informed him about Rebecca Valentine and how

Mary had compiled evidence against her own father and his peers.

All around me the tables were beginning to fill up with groups of patrons arriving to see the night's performance. Their voices all merged together to make a cacophony of noise that made my head hurt. Dean Costello wasn't performing this Saturday, but I noticed him at the bar, eyeballing me and Nicolas from time to time. He had noticed we had both brought folders containing information pertaining to the case and for some reason this seemed to hold his interest. Even when one of Dean's friends initiated a conversation with him, he would ignore them, nodding with disinterest as his eyes remained firmly fixed on me and Nicolas. Nicolas seemed not to notice that we were being watched, or at the very least he pretended not to.

Was I being paranoid? A feeling in my gut told me that something was amiss.

"I remember Rebecca Valentine," Nicolas mused with a vague grin. "Pretty girl."

I nodded in agreement. "Still perplexes me why you never followed Rebecca's lead. If she even gave you one." My smile vanished and I looked at Nicolas with a hint of distrust.

"She did," Nicolas promptly replied. "I found her information to be unreliable and I abandoned that avenue of investigation. Besides, somebody else occupied Mary's old apartment and I couldn't gain access," he frowned at me before continuing. "Do you still not trust me?"

I sighed, it was a combination of the noise and the feeling I got from Nicolas that evoked my sigh. "I believe in being direct. I don't trust you. How did you even know about Mary O'Reilly in the first place? Or Rebecca Valentine for that matter? You also said not to trust the police, could you elaborate on that for me?"

"I was approached by one of Mary O'Reilly's old clients. A dirty old pervert whose name eludes me. He knew Mary O'Reilly and he had a run in with the aforementioned Ralph Lawrence you mentioned from her diary. Of course, the dirty old bastard didn't know Ralph Lawrence's name. He just told me of a confrontation that had ensued. He was quite bad on the drugs, he claimed he tried going to the police to inform them he could identify Mary O'Reilly and he was dismissed so he came to me instead. I investigated the lead as much as I could, yet I yielded no results. I don't trust the police because of how disinterested they are in helping people when it comes to this particular case. The case of The Artist seems to be kept in deliberate obscurity. I've attempted to initiate contact with this ex client of Mary's since speaking to Rebecca Valentine got me nowhere. Imagine my shock when I learned he was dead. So, man goes to the police to identify a murder victim and is dismissed and then found dead of an alleged drug overdose less than a week later. Coincidence? Or something more sinister?" Nicolas took a drink of his beer and let out a sigh of frustration. "I believe some of the high-ranking police officials must be in the killer's pocket, either that or they're covering for someone among them. That's my theory, take it or leave it."

I nodded with no expression on my face. I didn't want Nicolas to know what I was thinking. The truth of the matter was that I didn't know what to think. I decided to continue working with him for now and secretly investigate him whilst also being cautious around police officials such as Olivia and Perry. In the end, the only person I could truly trust was myself. Then I briefly considered what Nicolas himself could be thinking. He suspected that there was a possibility that the killer was connected to the police and that they were covering for him, either that or the killer was exponentially rich and paying police officials bribes. I did have a connection to the police, which led me to consider the possibility that Nicolas could be keeping me close because I was a suspect in his own investigation.

"I think we should consider the possibility that our killer is a killer for hire. I think there's a remote chance that the Artist could have been hired by Michael O'Reilly to silence his own daughter before she reported him to the police. Then again, this is only speculation. I've based my deductions on what I've read in Mary's diary," I said, changing the subject back to the case.

"May I study the diary for myself?" Nicolas asked with a raised eyebrow. Something about the way he asked led me to believe that he didn't take my word for it.

"Next time we meet I shall let you read through it," I declined politely. "I still need to study it for myself, perhaps I can look into the client you mentioned. I should be able to cross reference what you've told me with the name of Mary's client using her diary entries."

"But he's dead," Nicolas objected with a snigger. "What could you possibly hope to achieve from such a pointless investigation?" Nicolas shook his head but said nothing else on the matter. He retrieved his own folder from his Parker coat. "Whilst you were gallivanting around Mary's old apartment and exposing pedophile rings, I was actually investigating the case!" he grinned flippantly before opening his folder and scanning through the contents. Inside were handwritten notes, photographs and newspaper clippings. "I went to the Budapest Hotel to see if I could find some leads. I questioned the security officer and the owner of the hotel to find out what they knew. In particular, I was interested in trying to ascertain whether or not Carl Porter was actually drugged as he claimed. His story was consistent with what you told me. He claimed someone had waited outside and had drugged him once luring him out of the office!" he lounged back in his chair and grunted with satisfaction when his back cracked.

The crowd had begun to get rowdy. Drunken cheers echoed throughout the bar as the night's performance had begun to take their position on stage. I glanced to the side and caught Dean Costello still watching me and Nicolas from the bar.

"There is one thing I didn't share with you before," said Nicolas as he leant forward and slammed a polaroid photograph down on the table. "I suspect you will recognize the individual in this photograph," grunted Nicolas with narrowed eyes. "You've already investigated this individual once because there was DNA evidence found on the body of Annabelle Green."

I used my index finger to pull the photograph across the table. I knew it was going to be a picture of Chad Sullivan, but I wasn't expecting to see the sign for the Budapest Hotel in the same picture. "What is this?" I demanded in confusion.

Nicolas snatched the photograph out of my grasp. "Ever since the initial investigation conducted by yourself and officer Olivia Lockhart, I remained fervently convinced that Chad Sullivan is the Artist Killer. What I didn't tell you during our first encounter was that I was following Chad Sullivan for several weeks prior to the murder of Emma Fontaine. Chad was present at the Budapest Hotel the night of the murder."

"Chad Sullivan was acquitted of all charges!" I pointed out, raising my voice slightly as to be heard over the rising noise of blues music and drunken cheering. "He had a solid alibi."

"I think his father's money could buy any amount of witnesses, Jack. If you don't believe that then you're naive! We have to consider the facts! Chad Sullivan fits the description of the Artist Killer! He has bright blue eyes, like Mary described in her diary. He has access to exponential wealth through his father, which is congruent with my personal theories! And not only that, his DNA was found on the body of Annabelle Green!" Nicolas ran a hand though his brown hair and licked his lips before he persisted. "I'm telling you, Jack, this is our guy! I think you were right to suspect him. I've been continuing to tail him and every week he attends the same nightclub in Central LA." Nicolas reached into his folder and tossed a handful of Polaroids on the table between us in one fluid motion. The pictures fanned out and I scooped them towards me like a poker player collecting his winnings.

I considered for a moment what Nicolas was suggesting as I idly glanced over the photographic evidence he had compiled. The pictures had been taken from a car window and captured Chad entering Club 88 with a small entourage of suited men with sunglasses on.

"Eye color and Chad's presence at the Budapest Hotel isn't enough to convict him for the murders of all those women," I said nonchalantly. I slid the photographs back across the table to Nicolas, then with a wry smile I said: "Today is Saturday. Be rude not to pay my old pal Chad a visit now, wouldn't it?"

Nicolas Brown's eyes beamed like a child's that had just been told he could have ice cream. "Excellent!" he exclaimed with a grin. "So, what time should we leave to question him?"

I laughed and shook my finger from side to side. "I work alone. If I need you, I'll call."

Nicolas shrugged his shoulders and got to his feet. "Suit yourself, old timer!" grinned the younger man. "I have some errands to run anyhow. Call if you need anything."

Nicolas gave me a two-finger salute and left the Blue Bell, leaving me to sit and ponder my next move. My car was still impounded and seriously damaged, so I needed to take a train to get to Central LA from Downtown. Before I left the Blue Bell, I glanced back over at

Dean Costello and took note of the fact that he was no longer standing among his peers at the bar.

*

Club 88 was a fairly new club on the rave scene in LA. It must've taken me almost ten minutes of standing in line before I gained access to the club. Inside strobe lighting flashed white in tandem with the beat of the rave music. The dance floor was a sea of bodies all tightly crammed together raving with their arms thrown in the air. The smell of sweat permeated the air, coupled with stale alcohol.

A DJ with bright illuminous green headphones nodded his head back and forth and reached out a hand to the mass of ravers situated on the dance floor beneath him. He looked like a creep, wearing a woolly beanie hat despite the stifling heat of the nightclub. He was also wearing expensive sunglasses, which to me was puzzling considering how dark and dingy this place was.

Cages hung from the ceiling; each cage contained a young woman dancing seductively wearing nothing but a bikini. Their skin glistened in the strobe lighting. When I took a second glance the cages were full of severed body parts with blood dripping through the mesh onto the dancers below. When I rubbed my eyes and looked again everything was back to normal.

I remembered why I didn't like raves or nightclubs. The noise was too much, the lighting was disorientating and traversing the crowd was infuriating. The atmosphere made me feel uncomfortable, glancing into the crowd on the dance floor I could see the forms of all the Artist victims floating above the crowd with their eyeless sockets watching me.

I surveyed the scene, trying not to allow myself to be distracted by the young women and their skimpy outfits. Somehow, I managed to spot Chad Sullivan dancing his way to the bar, escorted by a 6ft tall, bald headed black guy with massive shoulders. Chad was wearing a dark red button up shirt with a black blazer over the top of it, a black pair of trousers and black shoes. His accomplice, who I assumed was his bodyguard, was dressed all in black.

My eyes locked onto them and I followed them through the crowd until they reached the overcrowded bar. Chad had linked arms with a tall blonde in a tight pink dress and pink heels. She looked like a typical bimbo that liked to wear too much makeup and dress provocatively to attract attention. With Chad being a primary suspect as the Artist Killer I thought to myself that the blonde girl had attracted the wrong sort on this occasion.

I pushed my way through the crowd. Progress was infuriatingly slow. People congregated in large groups, dancing and shouting in each other's ears to be heard over the unnecessarily loud music.

I finally made my way to the bar, standing concealed from Chad's view by the crowd of people waiting to be served drinks. Back here the floor was sticky, and the smell of beer and spirits made me crave an alcoholic beverage and a cigarette.

I lingered in the crowd, ushering others behind me to go in front and get served first. From where I was standing, I could see Chad Sullivan laughing and talking with the blonde girl in pink. He rested a hand on her bare shoulder and let it linger there. Then she turned away for a split second to greet someone she recognized and that's when I saw Chad make his move.

His smile vanished and in the blink of an eye he dropped something into her cocktail glass and bubbles fizzed to the surface.

"Son of a bitch!" I cursed loudly. My curse was stifled by the loud music and drunken cheers. I don't think a single soul heard me.

Blonde finished her drink and then Chad draped his arm over her shoulder and escorted her to a red curtain where two more goons stood in suits with sunglasses on.

I knew I had to stop him. Whether or not the kid was the killer wasn't relevant. He was a menace that needed putting down. Not being able to recall when I last had a drink or a cigarette only added the metaphorical fuel to the fire.

"Excuse me," I addressed the two bouncers near the red curtain once I made my way through the crowd to them. "I'm a friend of Chad Sullivan, and I need to speak to him urgently."

One of the bouncers sniggered and shook his head. "Nobody goes through. This is the VIP lounge, sir."

"But I..."

I was cut off by a hard shove that made me stagger backwards.

"Are you deaf, cunt?" snapped the bouncer. His stance denoted hostility and his friend stepped forward. "I told you nobody gets through! Now fuck off you tramp!"

I kissed my teeth and nodded. My shoulders slumped as I walked away from the red curtain in defeat.

I made my way to the bar and ordered a bottle of beer. It only took a moment to drink it. It was cool and refreshing and it made me feel a little better. Only a little.

I decided to try plan B! I walked back to the red curtain with another beer. Slightly dancing with each step. The two bouncers could see me approaching, but their expressions were hard to read with their sunglasses on. One of them regarded me with very little interest while he was chewing gum like a cow chewing cud.

I gestured for the aggressor from before to lean in so I could speak to him yet again.

"What do you want now?!" he stepped forward and leaned in close, then he spoke to me in a level tone and spoke as softly as a lover. "Take a hint, guy. If you don't get out of here in ten seconds, I'm going to ram that beer bottle into your forehead so you look like a goddamn unicorn!" he flared his nostrils and his grip tightened on my arm.

I smiled at him and tried my best to look intimidated, which seemed to amuse him. Then, I threw my arm around the back of his neck and sharply pulled his head down with all my strength until his face met with my rising knee.

The second bouncer looked astonished but was too slow to react. I rushed towards him and smashed my bottle of beer across his head in an explosion of green glass and spraying beer. He collapsed to the ground unconscious with blood trickling down the side of his head, matting his hair.

The first bouncer was scrambling to his feet. His nose was bent and gushing blood. I dashed towards him and threw my fist into his gut twice before bringing my elbow down on the back of his head. He went down and stayed down.

Several ravers had noticed the commotion and stood staring in shock with hands raised to their mouths. Some of them were calling the police. I didn't have much time.

I paced through the red curtain into the "VIP" area. The other side was a poorly lit corridor with two doors and a fire escape. One door was open and peering inside revealed a carpeted room with a large sofa bed. Blondie was asleep on the bed with her empty cocktail glass on a small coffee table beside of her. A camera had been set up in the corner of the room and was aimed at Blondie with a red light blinking. Lamps were positioned behind the bed to provide optimum lighting.

No sign of Chad Sullivan.

I picked her up and carried her into the main dance area and handed her to a group of young men crowded around the unconscious bouncers. "Get her to a hospital! Don't worry about these bastards! They drugged her so I knocked them the fuck out!"

The youths stared at me in disbelief as I handed the incapacitated Blondie over to them. Then I rushed back behind the red curtain in search of Chad Sullivan.

Further down the corridor were two sets of toilets for male and female. I lingered outside the restroom and listened intently. Inside two voices were chatting and laughing.

I kicked the bathroom door as hard as I could, and it flung open. I was half expecting someone to be standing behind it, but I was wrong. Chad's bodyguard was washing his hands, staring at me in the mirror fastened above the sink. I could hear a stream of urine hitting the water within the bowl in one of the cubicles.

The bodyguard rushed at me, swinging his fist at my face. I ducked and brought my own fist into his stomach. He grunted but kept his footing. He threw another punch and this one connected sharply with my face, sending me staggering into a metal trash can that clattered loudly to the ground, spilling its contents.

"Rocco?!" A panicked Chad called out from the cubicle.

Me and Rocco ignored him and continued to struggle fighting. He had his hands on my shoulders and flung me towards the sinks. I used my hands to grab the sink and steady myself, turning in time to dodge another swing of Rocco's fist. I punched him in the stomach and then in one fluid motion spun and grabbed the back of his neck in the palm of my hand, then I forced his head forward until it crashed into the mirror with a crash. Rocco collapsed to the floor unconscious.

"Rocco? What's happening you great silver back?" the sound of his urine began to break, and Chad grunted to try and squeeze it all out as quickly as he could.

I kicked the toilet cubicle door open and he yelped like a dog. I grabbed his jacket collar as he hastily tucked his pecker away. I couldn't resist the more vengeful nature of my soul. I forced him to his knees and grabbed the back of his head and forced it down the toilet.

"How's that Chad? Gonna get daddy to pay your dry-cleaning bill when you have to get all that piss washed out of your fancy suit?!" I forced him to look me in the eye to confirm his eye color matched that of the mysterious 'Bright Eyes', his eyes were bright blue, like two pools of icy water.

"Do you know who my father is..."

I dunked him, using my bodyweight to pin down his thrashing body. "We're going to play a game!" I told him once I'd allowed him to emerge from the golden depths of the toilet bowl. "I'm going to ask you some questions and if I'm satisfied with your answers then I won't shove your fucking head down the toilet! Understood?"

"You're going to be sorry..."

I dunked him. "Let's try this again," I said with an exaggerated sigh. "Why were you at the Budapest Hotel the night Emma Fontaine was murdered?"

Chad's eyes widened. "I don't know what you mean!" he claimed in panic. When I went to dunk his head under the water again, he begged me not to. "I'll talk!" he pleaded, "Please, I'll talk. I was there visiting a friend!"

"Who was this friend!" I demanded.

"It was your fucking mother, you son of a bitch!" he grinned petulantly. "You are so fucking dead! You don't think I don't recognize that haunted look? Former detective Jack Cucchiano! Wait until my father hears about this! You're so fucking dead!"

I ran my fingers through his black hair and then gripped it tightly so he had to try and stand a little to alleviate the pain. Then I punched him in the side of the face. "You deserved that you little prick!" I told him with a reprimanding finger prodded in his face. "Now stop..."

WHACK!

I collapsed to the ground. My head was spinning out of control and I could see Rocco standing over me holding the metal trash can with two hands. The bastard had woken up and got the drop on me. He was sweating and panting. His sunglasses had broken and his dark eyes regarded me coolly.

Chad smiled a sharkish grin full of malice. He got to his feet and straightened out his lapels. "Thank you, Rocco!" he exclaimed. "Get him outside! Let's teach him a lesson!"

Two more bouncers appeared along with a guy in a blue shirt and long hair. Chad referred to this guy, presumably the owner of Club 88, as Deacon Swaine. I wouldn't be forgetting any of these names or faces anytime soon. For the meantime though, I had little choice other than to be beaten senseless in a back alleyway hidden behind the nightclub.

Deacon Swaine watched the beating nervously, while Chad Sullivan watched with glee and amusement. Rocco showed no emotion at all.

Blood filled my mouth as I was punched by one bouncer and went staggering into another bouncer who held me while his friends worked my ribs.

"Alright! That's enough!" an angry voice shouted once I had been punched and collapsed into some dustbins. I looked up with one swollen eye and saw the alarm and horror on Deacon's face and the faces of his goons.

Nicolas Brown was standing in the alleyway pointing a small handgun at my assailants. "Get on your feet, old timer! Let's get out of here."

Rocco stepped forward. "Come on, buddy! You're not going to shoot anyone." He spoke softly and reached his arm out gesturing for Nicolas Brown to calm down. "Why don't you just put the gun down?"

Nicolas cocked the hammer on his handgun and stepped forward towards Rocco, violently shoving the gun in his direction. "Are you fucking kidding me, big man? Try me! I want to see all your hands in the air right fucking now!"

Rocco raised his hands and backed away, licking his lips nervously. The rest of the group raised their hands too, including Chad and his associate Swaine.

"Thank fuck, Nicolas!" I tried to say as I staggered to my feet. Instead all that I managed to produce was a nonsensical incoherent babble. My world was spinning. I'd taken one hell of a beating! I staggered over to Nicolas, regaining my balance as I went. My world began to steady itself.

"You won't get away with this!" Chad's voice echoed down the alleyway behind us. "My father is going to hear about this! The police will too! You guys are so fucked!" with his warning he burst into hysterical laughter, which we heard all the way through the alley until we reached Nicolas's car at the other side of the street.

Nicolas started the car and sped away as the faint sound of police sirens began to sound in the distance.

CHAPTER 9

Invitation

"What the fuck were you thinking, Jack?!" Matthew Perry demanded angrily. He paced back and forth in front of the desk I was seated at within an interview room at the LAPD. "You crazy son of a bitch!" he added, shaking his head in disbelief. "Several counts of assault, trespassing and making threats with a firearm! What the fuck am I supposed to do with you, Jack?!"

Olivia stood leaning against the wall by the door with her arms folded. Her facial expression was one of profound disappointment.

"Walter Sullivan is pressing charges! You could do time for this, Jack! I hope it was all worth it, you fucking idiot!" added Perry.

I forced myself to smile at him in sarcastic defiance.

"An arsehole to the bitter end!" retorted Perry with a weary sigh. "Suit yourself, Jack! You can play the silent type all you want, but it won't do you any good when this goes to court!"

"I told you what happened already," I snapped at him. "Chad slipped something in that girl's drink and I tried to save her! I don't regret what I did. I used reasonable force!"

Perry laughed bitterly. "Reasonable force? You smashed a bottle over a guy's head, giving him a severe concussion and you smashed another guy's head through a bathroom mirror!"

"Come on," I chuckled, recalling the event with some amusement. I was confident that I would be out of police custody within the next

24 hours. "They drugged a girl and I saved her! I was there following a lead and when I saw a girl in danger, I acted on it! The girl should be at the hospital, she should be able to support my story."

Perry rubbed his eyes, but it was Olivia that spoke; "We already spoke to her. She claims she wasn't drugged, and she witnessed you go ape shit and start attacking people for no reason."

I recoiled in shock. That statement had taken me unawares. I was certain that Blondie would jump at the chance to incriminate those who drugged her and were prepared to do God knows what before I intervened. "What?! Then Chad's old man had her threatened or paid off!" I retorted indignantly. I was furious that Blondie would betray me like that after I saved her. "Fuck her!" I said angrily, "and fuck Chad and his old man!"

Perry leaned on the chair positioned opposite me. "Looks like you're the one that's going to get fucked, Jack! You and your new buddy have to face the music on this!" Perry's eyes narrowed. "What's your friend's name and where can we find him?"

"I don't know his name and I don't know where to find him," I answered with an impassive shrug.

Perry slammed his hand on the table, causing me to jump. "Fuck sake, Jack! Give him up! He pointed a lethal weapon at six people! That cunt could be looking at some serious time for that! Is he so good a friend that you'd be willing to do time in his place?"

"We can help you, Jack," added Olivia. Looking at her painted nails with vague disinterest. "If you tell us who the guy with the gun was then we can get you a reduced sentence or get you away with it completely. But that's only possible if you cooperate with us."

"The gun wasn't even loaded! I was getting pummelled in the alleyway and the other guy used an unloaded gun with the intention of scaring my assailants! How are they not being questioned for beating the shit out of me?!" I said, fighting back the fury I felt burning within. The part about the gun being unloaded was actually true. I had chided Nicolas for his decision to come in all guns blazing and in response he showed me the empty chamber to prove he never intended to kill anyone.

"Regardless of whether the gun was loaded or not it is still an offence to make threats of menace with a lethal weapon. Come on,

Jack! You know the law!"

I told them nothing they could use during the taped interview. I wasn't prepared to drop Nicolas in the shit, when he'd saved my arse from a worse beating. After a while they were forced to release me as they didn't have enough evidence for a prosecution.

I was at home when Perry and Olivia had arrested me at the early hours of Sunday morning. It was something I was expecting anyway after the events that had transpired at Club 88. What I hadn't anticipated was Blondie's false statement wherein she declared I was the aggressor, oppose to her rescuer. The stupidity of people never fails to astound me.

*

I returned home late Monday afternoon, picked up my mail and cautiously and ritualistically inspected my front door for signs of lock picking. Since the Artist had already infiltrated my apartment, I took the liberty of replacing the locks and had a hidden security camera installed above the door. No scratches were visible around the keyhole, something that I checked for every time I arrived at my apartment and I would check the footage afterwards to see whether someone approached my door.

I sighed with relief and opened my apartment door thinking everything was going to be normal.

I walked into the kitchen and tossed the mail on the kitchen table before I poured myself a glass of whiskey full to the brim. Then I slumped down into a chair and began to look through my mail. They consisted of nothing interesting besides pizza menus and bills, or some other corporate vultures demanding money from me.

There was one envelope that immediately caught my attention. A brown envelope with my name handwritten across the front. I savagely ripped it open as eagerly as a child opening their Christmas presents. Inside there was a letter and a card.

I inspected the card. It was an invitation to a fashion show taking place within an art gallery in LA.

I unfolded the letter and mumbled the words as I read through.

"Detective Jack Cucchiano,

I hope this letter finds you well. I know you do not understand the vital expression which drives me to create such resplendent and enduring images of the women I choose. I've enjoyed our little game so far and I wanted to even the playing field a little bit with this next game. Enclosed is an invitation to a fashion gala at an art museum Wednesday evening. I shall also attend this event and choose a new project. You have until Wednesday to figure it out and save her. Bring your A game detective."

I read the letter twice in disbelief. The killer was directly challenging me. This was the second time he had been to my apartment, to my knowledge anyway. Underneath was a handwritten cipher.

"I n o k t y l e   l v s
   a t t   a e i   r s a   l a ! Y u w l   e e   a e h   r
   w   m   C t c   r o   i n r v   e"

I stared at the letter for a long time, carefully pondering my next move.

The cipher was a simplistic one, although it took me a few hours to solve. It used an encoding technique known as 'Rail Fence' where the message is spread across the three lines of seemingly random letters. The message was intended to be read as: 'I want to make it Crystal clear! You will never save her".

I sighed and rubbed my forehead in frustration. The answer to the killer's cipher was a slap in the face. Taking another drink from my glass of whiskey made my head buzz pleasantly. I studied the decoded message a little longer and stroked the stubble on my chin in contemplation.

"Why has the word 'Crystal' been capitalized?" I asked myself with a curious groan. Could it have been a mistake? No! That's inconceivable! This guy didn't make mistakes like that. This was deliberate! "But what is the purpose of it? A name perhaps?" with a smug smile I folded up the letter and added it to the case notes in my study and immediately proceeded to contact Perry and Olivia.

*

The day of the event arrived. I was dressed in a black short sleeved shirt with jeans. I figured I would make some effort for the occasion. Perry agreed to do things my way, which was a huge relief considering I wasn't on best terms with my former colleagues. The plan was for me to wear a wire and enter the event as a guest, from there I would search the gallery for clues related to the cipher and determine who the intended victim was. The police would be surrounding the building, including the main gate, which was the only entrance to the gallery. Anyone leaving the event would be subjected to a mandatory stop and search.

My plan would hopefully trap the killer or catch him unawares leaving the premises with incriminating evidence such as a Glock used to kill Reece Pemberton or a length of rope.

I checked the time on my phone. The event would be starting soon, and I had to meet Olivia at the entrance to my apartment building. I stepped forward and froze when a crippling pain throbbed in my head. I perceived waves rippling through my apartment like the walls were the surface of a lake disturbed by someone throwing rocks. It felt like forever, but the experience only lasted a moment.

That's when I heard the noises. Mechanical noises that sounded like heavy machinery coming to life. Stranger still was the appearance of a door that never existed in my apartment before. It was situated next to my study.

Confused and nervous, I made my way to the door with a sense of dread. The doorknob felt ice cold to the touch and sent shivers running throughout my body that made the hairs on the nape of my neck stand on edge.

The door creaked open to reveal a featureless stone staircase descending into darkness. The sound was much louder now that the door was open. This staircase should have gone into the apartment below, but it didn't. The door and the staircase defied all logic and reality.

As I continued in my descent the doorway behind me was a rectangle of light in an abyss of darkness. I continued for what felt like a very long time. I looked behind me and the doorway to my apartment looked like a pin prick in a black sheet. I used the light on my phone to light the way. I could hear something banging, like a loud heartbeat. It's rhythmic beating somehow made me feel more at ease. My own heart was racing and was not in sync with the mysterious beating I could now hear.

The walls on either side of the stairs became chain-link fencing with several television screens packed closely together on either side behind the chain-link. They all showed static, then they showed images of Annabelle's smiling face before each screen repeatedly shown the Artist Killer shooting Reece Pemberton through the head. Every time the killer pulled the trigger I flinched involuntarily.

It felt like forever until I reached the bottom of the staircase, a seemingly endless loop of stairs and gunshots. I felt drained by the end of it.

The stairs ended at a pink door covered in stickers and plastic flowers. I opened the door and found myself standing in a little girl's room. The walls were covered in floral pink wallpaper and a fluffy pink carpet covered the floor. A four posted bed with pink bedding was inundated with teddies of all shapes and sizes. Bears, unicorns, and other creatures, both mythical and real, littered the bed in a neatly organized pile. They stared at me with sightless button eyes and innocent smiles on their stuffed faces.

I walked around the room to where a huge wooden doll house stood on a small white table in the corner. I lazily inspected the different rooms and gave an impressed murmur at the intricacy of the tiny pieces of wooden furniture inside. Then I remembered where I was and felt uncomfortable.

I jumped and let out a yelp of alarm when the light went out and a small lantern on a bedside cabinet began to play creepy music whilst projecting small animal shaped lights all across the room. Whispers filled the room and a sudden chill came over me. My eyes darted to the bed where a lump had materialized under the duvet and was growing until it was the size of a small child. There was a chilling giggle and Annabelle called my name as she floated above the bed with the duvet still over her.

I sprinted for the door and slammed it shut behind me. I was now back in my apartment. I screamed and fell to the floor when I looked towards the kitchen and see a group of people sitting at my dining table. There was Scarlett Jones, Rosita Ramirez, Emma Fontaine, and Mary O'Reilly. They made no move to attack me or interact with me in any way, instead they just stared across the table at each other.

I shook like a shitting dog as I gingerly got to my feet and cautiously made my way over to the table. The four ladies continued staring straight in front of them with wide tooth baring grins on their faces.

I reached forward and tapped Fontaine's cheek with my knuckle. It made a hollow sound, like she was made from porcelain. I scratched my head in confusion.

"What the fuck is..." I trailed off when I looked out of my apartment window and observed that in place of skyscrapers and bustling streets was the same pink floral wallpaper and pink carpet from Annabelle's room. From the perspective of the room I deduced that I was inside the dollhouse somehow.

"Give me a fucking break!" I muttered to myself, wiping perspiration from my brow.

A giant eye appeared at the window; it was all black with no iris. Annabelle pulled back her head with a malicious grin on her face. "Forever my plaything," she said with a cackle.

Annabelle reached over the roof of the building and the whole apartment shook like there was a giant earthquake and the roof was ripped from the building to reveal Annabelle grinning down at me. I tried to run but her index finger and thumb found my ankle, knocking the table and chairs aside with the porcelain women the Artist had killed. I was dragged into the air with my arms and free leg flailing wildly in desperation. Annabelle opened her mouth and dangled me above the opening where I stared at her giant tongue and teeth. I screamed and the next thing I knew I was falling into the abyss, the darkness of Annabelle's stomach. Acid splashed my face and I tried to scream as my skin bubbled and peeled away in the darkness.

*

I woke up on my sofa. I looked around and saw that my table and chairs were empty, and my roof was still intact. Outside the usual view of skyscrapers and traffic replaced that pink wallpaper and carpet of Annabelle's room.

I took a deep breath and rubbed the cold sweat from my brow with the sleeve of my shirt. I called Olivia and within the hour she was waiting outside my apartment in her SUV.

"Perry is setting up surveillance vans around the gallery," Olivia informed me as we drove to the art gallery, her tone was still frosty towards me after what happened at Club 88.

She parked her SUV a couple of blocks away and we walked to the front of the art gallery where a crowd of people in fancy attire stood waiting to be allowed entry into the event. Plain clothes police officers loitered around the streets, I recognized them from my days on the force.

One of them was a guy called Barry Monroe, a fat prick with a bad coke addiction and a relentless body odor issue. He had beady eyes, a pointed nose, and a thick red beard. He stared at me with disapproval as we passed.

I made my way to a plain white van where Perry and a small group of officers sat cramped together amidst several monitors, listening equipment and wires that crossed and tangled like spaghetti.

"Remember to try and stand as close to any suspects as you can," Perry informed me as Olivia taped the wire to my chest. "We'll apprehend and search anybody that leaves the event. Don't worry, Jack. We'll get the fucker! He won't be expecting us!" Perry indicated to the gallery on one of the monitors. "He's in there somewhere, the sick fuck! Time to bring him in folks! It's show time!"

*

I walked to the main gate and queued with the rest of the guests. I felt severely underdressed in my shirt and jeans. The other guests had arrived, wearing tuxedos or expensive dresses adorned with jewellery. The bouncers at the gate looked bewildered when it was my turn to approach.

"Sorry, sir," said one bouncer, holding out a gargantuan hand to bar my path. He grinned at me and chewed a piece of gum, his mouth clicking loudly. "This is an invitation only event!"

"Not a problem," I countered and pulled out my invitation.

The bouncer with the gum checked the list and with a grunt he pulled aside the red rope across the gateway, granting me entry.

I stepped into the gallery courtyard with a forced smile and a curt nod.

Many of the guests were heading straight for the main entrance, but some lingered in the courtyard, marvelling over some of the abstract sculptures and designs that littered the grounds.

"*Jack!*" Captain Perry's voice came through my earpiece. "*Can you hear me?*"

"I read you loud and clear," I muttered in response, angling my head slightly so the wire would pick up my voice.

"*Your orders are as follows: You are to simply ascertain who the intended victim is and escort them to safety. Jack! That's all you have to do! No heroics and no fucking bullshit! Do I make myself clear?*"

"Crystal," I responded with a roll of my eyes.

I walked around the side of the building into a car park where several vans were parked in disarray. A young Asian man with black hair with the topknot style. He was wearing pink glasses and a purple jacket over a black shirt. His trousers looked like they had had an argument with his shoes and exposed his bare ankles. He frantically dashed from van to van, desperately trying to organize his crew. I could tell that he was the overtly flamboyantly gay types. I didn't take offence to gay people, but the ones that flaunted it and pranced about like little fairies pissed me off!

"Oooo hurry, hurry, hurry!" He fanned his face with both of his hands as different crew members scurried hectically like ants to unload their vans.

"Can we have a quick word?" I asked as I gently tugged the man's sleeve. The name displayed on a sticker across his velvet jacket read 'Sato'.

He pulled his arm free and looked at me as though I was something nasty he had just stepped in. "Unhand me, sir!" He barked. "I'm a very busy man!"

"Listen here you little fruitcake!" I began stepping towards him but stopped myself once I remembered that Matthew Perry and his team were listening in. My voice became more amicable and I tried again. "Listen, I'm a homicide detective investigating a case undercover!"

Sato's eyes widened, but he said nothing.

"I'm investigating the case of the Artist Killer. We have a strong lead that the killer will strike again tonight at this very event. I want you to save me some time and effort by providing me with the names of all the models that will be participating tonight as my personal belief is that one of them will be the intended victim."

Sato mulled over my words and stared at me for a few moments before he replied with some bullshit about seeing my identification.

"Just fucking do it!" I snapped impatiently. "Do you really want one of your models to die because I didn't show you a fucking badge? Give me their fucking names right now!"

"*Jack!*" sharply came Perry's voice through my earpiece.

Sato snapped his fingers and a young assistant came trotting across the car park towards him. "Alyssa, fetch me a notepad and a pen or pencil please."

"I'd appreciate as much discretion as possible," I added calmly. "I don't want the killer to know we have him boxed in."

Sato hastily scribbled down the names of 13 female models and shakily handed it to me. "Good luck," he said before he clapped his hands and continued to oversee the preparation of the event.

I left Sato to his business and walked around to the front entrance and made my way inside, pushing my way past crowds of men and women in expensive suits and dresses as politely as I could.

Golden-framed paintings hung from the walls, surrounded by spectators who sipped at their wine and marvelled over their interpretation of the art's meaning.

I stood and examined a peculiar painting which consisted of different colored squares, silently attempting to see some kind of hidden artistic depth which I could not find. To me, the painting looked as though it was something a child had conjured up. It lacked imagination as far as I was concerned. How could a few different colored squares constitute as art and be hung in a gallery? I didn't get it.

"Composition with Red, Blue, and Yellow," a stranger's voice declared behind me. "Piet Mondrian, 1930. A fine piece of art, though not everyone's eye is proficient in seeing the beauty of art in even its most simplistic forms."

I detected a hint of mockery in the man's voice, like he could tell just from looking at me that I didn't know shit about art. I spun around to face the man with a raised eyebrow. He was a tall man, about 6ft with blonde hair that was neatly combed to the side. A huge pair of golden horn-rimmed glasses sat on his nose. He regarded me with vague amusement. He was wearing a tuxedo with one hand behind his back and the other cradling a glass of red wine.

I turned back to the painting. "It just looks like different colored squares to me," I replied, trying to hide my annoyance. "It looks like something a child painted!"

The man chuckled to himself, bemused, and took a step forward so he was standing beside me. "Piet Mondrian is no child! He is considered one of the greatest artists of the 20th century! Some might say that he's a pioneer of 20th century abstract art!"

I grunted and nodded with very little enthusiasm.

"Forgive my impertinence," said the man with exaggerated shock. "I completely neglected to introduce myself! My name is Larry Gyllenhaal," he offered me a limp handshake and a forced smile.

"Jack Cucchiano," I mumbled back to him.

Larry smiled smugly and swirled his glass of wine under his nose before taking a drink. "As I was saying, Mr Cucchiano, Piet Mondrian adapted his painting style over time, transforming his work from a figurative painting style to a more abstract style of painting. Eventually, his artistic vocabulary was reduced to simple geometric elements. You see, Piet believed that art should be set apart from reality. In 1914 he said: *'Art is higher than reality and has no direct relation to reality. To approach the spiritual in art, one will make as little use as possible of reality, because reality is opposed to the spiritual. We find ourselves in the presence of an abstract art. Art should be above reality, otherwise it would have no value for man'.*" The corners of Larry's mouth curled up into a shark-like grin. Then he continued, "So when we look at this painting, we can see that Piet Mondrian believed that, aesthetically, minimalist art offers a highly purified form of beauty. Just look at this magnificent piece! It doesn't pretend to be anything other than what it is: Order, simplicity, and harmony. There is beauty in simplicity. That is why, dear Cucchiano, Piet Mondrian reduced his art to the three primary colors; red, blue, and yellow. The three primary values; black, white, and grey and the two primary directions; horizontal and vertical. Do you understand?"

I narrowed my eyes and stared at Larry Gyllenhaal with questions spinning in my head. None of them pertaining to abstract art or Piet Mondrian. Who was Larry Gyllenhaal really? What was his angle? Was he really approaching me to give me a tedious lecture on art or was his true purpose to play some kind of game with me?

"I understand," I said.

"Good!" Larry lifted a hand to his ear as a classical melody began to play in the next room. "The gala is about to begin. Can you hear the beautiful melody calling to all the guests? I believe the tune is called 'Serenade for Strings'. This is certainly a song with culture! True artistic expression in the medium of music." Larry grinned and lazily glanced at me. "Fashion itself is a form of art. Don't you agree, detective? The women are like a blank canvas and Sato dresses them in his designer outfits and dresses, expressing his artistic creativity through these women. Isn't that beautiful?"

I turned so we were face to face. Through gritted teeth I asked him: "I never told you I was a detective, Mr Gyllenhaal! Care to explain how you know who I am?!"

Larry closed his eyes and took a sip of his wine. Then he let out an involuntary chuckle. "I know who you are, detective! Did you really think I wouldn't recognize the man who was investigating one of the most infamous crimes of the 21st century?! The case was highly publicized so it shouldn't come as too much of a surprise that I know who you are." He smiled enigmatically and stared intently at me.

Was that sweat on his brow? What was making him nervous?

"What you said," I began, eyeballing him suspiciously. "about women being canvasses. I've heard something similar said before by the Artist Killer himself! He compared women to pieces of art or canvasses or some bullshit like that!"

"What are you insinuating?!" Recoiled Larry with a look of disgust, the look was momentary and his smug demeanor returned almost immediately. "The Artist Killer is obviously someone who has a deep appreciation for art. Unfortunately, his method of expression is deluded and utterly insane!" He rested a hand on my shoulder as he began to walk away. "Good luck solving this case, detective," whispered Larry with a suspiciously wide grin and bulging eyes. "I think you've already lost to be honest with you, but it will be interesting to see how things go." Larry Gyllenhaal heartily patted me on the back before finishing the remainder of his wine and walking with the flow of guests that moved towards a set of previously closed double doors.

"Did you get all that?" I muttered into my wire as I watched Gyllenhaal disappear into the main hall.

"*Every word*," came Perry's stern reply.

"I want him apprehended after the event," I informed Perry. "There's something suspicious about him."

"*Agreed! For now, continue to search for the intended victim*," said Perry. A short burst of static erupted in my ear and then there was silence.

I took the piece of paper Sato had given me and examined it. I figured that the killer could never know who would be attending unless his predetermined victim was a model who the killer knew would be here tonight to model the new clothing line designed by SOAR. One name immediately leapt out at me and I knew who the intended victim was.

I walked through the double doors that had recently been opened and followed the crowd into a huge hall where a stage had been erected with red curtains at the back to hide the models.

Sato walked to the end of the catwalk with a microphone in his hand. He tapped it with sweat glistening on his forehead and he liked his lips nervously. "Hello, ladies and gentlemen. Welcome to this momentous occasion here in one of the most amazing art galleries in L.A!"

The crowd cheered and applauded lightly.

"SOAR's new clothing line will be presented to you all tonight! So, the only thing I can encourage you to do is eat and drink from the bar prepared in the room next door, be merry and enjoy the visual feast we have prepared for you esteemed guests this evening," Sato said.

The lights dimmed as Sato left the catwalk and disappeared behind the curtain. Smaller lights were turned on, illuminating the catwalk and leaving the rest of the room much dimmer. Music was turned on and I was partially deafened by the speakers which had been spread around the room.

The first of the models appeared, she had blonde hair that was full of wax or gel because it stood up straight like a yellow flame. Her long shiny legs crossed one in front of the other as she confidently strode to the end of the catwalk to be bathed in the flashing light of cameras.

My eyes momentarily glanced over at the opposite side of the catwalk where they met Larry Gyllenhaal's. He was grinning with a menacing look of excitement in his eyes. He raised another glass of wine in acknowledgement and winked at me before turning and disappearing into the sea of people.

I swallowed a lump in my throat as the sense of foreboding overwhelmed me. Was Larry Gyllenhaal the Artist Killer?

CHAPTER 10

Questions

I frantically scanned the crowd in search of Larry Gyllenhaal, but the tide of people swept him away out of view. I thought I saw him walking into the bar room.

Another model took to the catwalk. She was wearing a black feathered top which had a large feathered shoulder piece. Her skin was the color of ebony and I found my eyes involuntarily staring at her shiny slender legs. Her dark brown eyes scanned the room and she had a sultry smile on her face. She didn't flinch when a wave of photographers flooded her with flashing lights.

"Crystal is by far one of the hottest models SOAR has in its menagerie!" said a meat head to his friend with a chuckle.

I want to make it Crystal clear! You will never save her!

This was the intended victim judging by the clues I deciphered from the killer's letter. Beads of sweat rolled down my face and into my eyes and stinging them. Pools of sweat stained my white shirt and I gave off an odor which must have been a mixture of sweat, booze and cigarettes.

Now I had a choice; I could wait for the main event to finish and find Crystal, or I could keep track of Larry Gyllenhaal's movements. A brief scan of the stage area and the surrounding security indicated that sneaking backstage would be impossible without causing a commotion. Crystal was safe for now and surrounded by witnesses.

I pushed my way through the crowd and into the bar area where I found Larry Gyllenhaal stood chatting with a young couple. All of them were laughing with what seemed like exaggerated pomposity. It was as though they were competing for status of the most pompous.

Larry spotted me leaning on the wall with my arms folded watching him. He grinned and continued his conversations as normal. I raised an eyebrow. I tapped my foot impatiently.

Why the fuck wasn't he making a move?! He was just standing around talking bollocks!

A sudden realization hit me! Larry Gyllenhaal could have been a red herring! A mere distraction intended to divert my attention from the victim! Could there be two of them working together?

Larry Gyllenhaal glanced back at me and noticed the momentary uncertainty on my face. His grin widened and he broke eye contact to give another guest a half-hearted handshake.

By now over an hour has passed and Sato was making another speech. He thanked the guests for coming before a round of applause followed his departure from the stage. The models had already begun to mingle with the crowd and I desperately weaved in and out of the crowd in search of Crystal, but she was nowhere to be found. I spotted a feathered shoulder piece that must have been Crystal's and I rushed towards the woman who was standing with her back to me as she conversed with two female guests. I put my hand on her arm and she sharply turned around.

"Sorry," I said when I was met with a stranger's face. "I thought you were somebody else."

I searched and I searched, but Crystal was nowhere to be seen among the guests. I rushed back into the bar room, my heart racing, and I could see Larry Gyllenhaal was still chatting with other guests and drinking red wine.

"Perry! I've lost Crystal! I believe she is the killer's next victim!" I uttered urgently into my wire.

"*No female models have left the venue yet, Jack,*" reassured Perry. "*We have the building surrounded! Nobody gets out without us intercepting them! Lookouts are posted in the building opposite overlooking the gardens and car park around the front entrance. No models have left via the front door.*"

I shuffled my way across the back wall towards the edge of the bar where a door was positioned with a notice pinned to it informing guests that the area was out of bounds. When I was convinced that the bartender, lingering security guards, and Larry Gyllenhaal weren't looking I slipped through the door and closed it behind me.

I was standing in a corridor with pieces of art hung intermittently all way down the hallway. They depicted images of still life, portraits, and landscapes. However, I didn't have time to squander on viewing paintings! I thought I knew who the victim was, and she was missing!

I walked down the corridor, beginning my search. I passed a room where the door was left ajar. Behind the door was Sato and Alyssa. A quick peek revealed the other side of the red curtain.

Crystal must have come through this door for some reason! But why?

"It was a disaster; I just know it!" said Sato. He followed his sentence up with a bout of exaggerated hyperventilation. His assistant Alyssa tried to reassure him and calm him down.

For a moment I considered asking them for help in my search for the missing model, but then decided against it.

*

I searched the entire fucking building! The entire fucking gallery and the model was nowhere to be found! I narrowly avoided getting caught by roaming security guards. I was flummoxed! How does a person just disappear into thin air like that!

I re-joined the main party and already the number of guests had started to thin out considerably. So much so that Larry Gyllenhaal was the first face I saw. His eyes were slightly glassy from drinking too much wine. He immediately approached me.

"I see your investigation has yielded no results, detective!" he said with an enigmatic smile. "I'm afraid the event is coming to an end and still you have no suspect and no victim." With a sly grin and a malicious tone, he said: "Looks like it's game over, detective!"

I felt the fire burning within me. My urge to break his glasses and smash his head through his precious paintings was overwhelming! I took a deep breath and forced myself to smile back. "It's not game over yet, Mr Gyllenhaal. I still have a few tricks up my sleeve. Mind if

I ask you what shoe size you are?"

Larry raised an eyebrow and looked confused for a moment. Then he smiled again. "Am I obliged to tell you that, detective?"

"No," I answered honestly. Then I placed a hand on his shoulder and squeezed until he squirmed uncomfortably like the little worm that he was. "But I've got a feeling we're going to be seeing each other soon. And when that day comes, you'll tell me everything I want to know!"

"Well..." grunted Larry uncomfortably, pulling himself free of my grip. "If I never see such a boorish brute such as yourself again it will be a day too soon!"

*

The event was over. Matthew Perry and his team apprehended Larry Gyllenhaal and a few others were detained under suspicious circumstances and held in custody.

"Tomorrow we can question some of the more suspicious characters in a taped interview," Perry informed me as we both stood in the pouring rain. Perry with his umbrella and me sodden wet like a drowned rat. "Hopefully we will be able to yield some results. Either explaining where Crystal is or what the true identity of the killer is."

"Yeah," I sighed, feeling somewhat defeated already. "What was Larry like when you arrested him?" I wanted to know what kind of reaction the smug art connoisseur had once he was unexpectedly apprehended.

"He's a strong suspect!" Said Perry. "You'll get chance to question him tomorrow. As of tomorrow, you're an acting homicide detective. It's a position you'll need to have to conduct the recorded interviews alongside Barry. So, no drinking tonight! Am I making myself clear?"

"Yes, Perry," I would play along for now, but I would still conduct the investigation on my own terms.

"Oh, and Jack!" Perry called after me as I began to walk away. "We arrested someone else at the venue that you might find interesting."

I turned to face him with a raised eyebrow, my curiosity piqued.

"Chad Sullivan was caught leaving the venue and apprehended and detained as a suspect. I wasn't sure what to make of the whole confrontation between him and yourself, but him being here is most certainly suspicious," Perry narrowed his eyes. "I'm not much of a believer in coincidences..."

Chad Sullivan and Larry Gyllenhaal! Both present at the event. The strangest thing was that I had not seen Chad Sullivan at all during the event. Could it be that the two of these suspects were working together?

"We'll find out tomorrow when we question them," I said, more to myself than to Matthew Perry. I turned and walked home, leaving Perry's team to conduct a search for the missing model.

*

The next day I was awake at the crack of dawn. I made myself a quick cappuccino and slung on some pants and a stained shirt that was strewn among a disorderly pile of both clean and dirty washing on the floor.

Once I was ready, I took a bus to the LAPD building where Perry was eagerly waiting for me in full uniform. He offered me a sturdy handshake and smiled.

"You look fresh this morning," observed Perry with a sigh of relief.

"I want to be on top form," I told him with a wan smile.

Perry nodded and gestured for me to follow him. "Chad Sullivan is in interview room one and Larry Gyllenhaal is in interview room two."

"I'll interview Gyllenhaal first," I decided. Where Chad had actual evidence attaching him to the site where Annabelle Green was found, something in my gut told me that Larry Gyllenhaal was either the Artist Killer himself or a close ally of the killer. His behavior was extremely suspicious to both me and Perry. "I want to speak to him."

We entered the observation room attached to interview room two and on the other side of the one-sided mirror I could see Larry Gyllenhaal sitting at a table. His demeanor was relaxed. He had a smug grin on his face, and he was slouched in his chair. He was wearing the same clothes he had worn to the fashion gala the previous night.

"God damn it!" I growled in annoyance. I had expected to see him squirming. "Why the fuck is he so God damn smug?!"

"Beats me," replied Perry. "He must be pretty comfortable. We found no incriminating evidence on him when he was detained, and we have nothing connecting him to any of the murders."

I narrowed my eyes. This bastard was connected somehow and I had to find a way to catch him out.

I entered the interview room with Barry Monroe and we seated ourselves opposite Larry Gyllenhaal. My eyes met his and he regarded me with vague amusement.

"Mr Cucchiano! It is so good to see you again!" he declared with enthusiasm.

"Hate to interrupt this touching reunion," Barry cut in drily. "But we've got to ask you some questions about last night."

"I'm not obliged to answer any questions at all, but you can answer some of mine; why am I being detained? What law have I broken?" replied Larry with a sly grin.

"You said some suspicious things at an event where we believed the killer had attended. A woman has gone missing! Disappeared! Vanished into thin air! Now do us all a favor and cut the fucking bullshit! If you have nothing to hide, then fucking cooperate with us and help us to clear you as a suspect!" I snapped impatiently. Larry's uncooperative, cocky attitude was pissing me off already. One glance at Barry Munroe indicated that he felt the same.

Larry looked astonished, though whether his shock was genuine or feigned was something I could not tell. "Are you accusing me of murdering all those girls?! I never said anything to you, detective Cucchiano, other than enlighten you on the work of Piet Mondrian." He leant forward and regarded me carefully. "You should be thanking me," he uttered with a forced smile.

I kept my anger in check. "I was wearing a wire at the event, Mr Gyllenhaal. We have audio recordings of you using particular words and phrases that are suspiciously synonymous to things said by the Artist Killer in his letters to me."

Larry Gyllenhaal was silent for a moment. It was as though he was letting that information sink in. Could it have been a complete oversight on his part? Perhaps he thought it would be inconceivable for me to have been working with the police. He sighed and finally said: "Look, I had a little too much wine last night."

I ignored him and produced a photograph of a portion of the letter the killer wrote to me that said, 'bring your A-Game, detective.' And I slid it across the table so Larry could take a look at it. "You said to me: 'You have no suspect and no victim, looks like it's game over detective'. I am of course paraphrasing, but I'm sure the audio recording will clear up any discrepancies." I cast Gyllenhaal a vicious grin.

He looked at the photograph with an expressionless face before he slid it back across the table towards me. He shrugged impassively and said, "It's a coincidence. Like I said, I was drunk and acting in a deliberately provocative manner," he looked at me sincerely. "I'm so sorry, detective! It is just a coincidence."

Barry sniggered aloud, clearly conveying his doubt. "That's fair enough, but what gets me is how you even knew there would be a suspect or a victim. Detective Cucchiano didn't tell you he was there investigating any kind of crime. So how did you know there would be a victim or a suspect to begin with?" Barry rested his chin on his hand and raised his eyebrows.

"Well?" I prompted, eager to hear his explanation.

Larry looked at the two of us with his mouth agape for a second.

"What's the matter?" Barry chuckled. "Cat got your tongue?"

"I'm just astonished at what you're implicating!" Larry countered indignantly. He placed his hand on his chest. "I hold truth very close to my heart. It is a value of mine! Allow me to be crudely blunt with you both. I went to the gallery because I have a deep appreciation for art, I said as much to detective Cucchiano. I also acknowledged that the killer has his own view on artistic perfection, which I stated was wholly perverse and sickening! You should have that on your audio tape as well! Unless of course you intend on removing that part to strengthen your conviction that I am indeed the Artist Killer! I find these accusations absolutely repugnant! I approached detective Cucchiano because I immediately recognized him. I had kept track of the killings menacing our metropolis and I was disappointed that Detective Cucchiano had just given up and resorted to drinking himself into oblivion!" he sniggered bitterly. "You're a joke, detective Cucchiano! You turned your back on those girls and thought you could wash away your shame." He folded his arms and looked away. "You disgust me!" he uttered the sentence with such bitter contempt I could feel the hatred emanating from him.

I fought back bitter tears and clenched my fists.

"And how did you know there would be a suspect or a victim?" asked Barry. He cast me a sideways glance, though there was no concern for my wellbeing within that look because Barry Monroe hated me.

"Come on! Jack Cucchiano having an appreciation for art?! It's obvious he was there investigating. Why else would he be there? Unfortunately, he's all washed up and drowning himself in alcohol. There's no way he was ever going to find anything."

"Fuck you!" I snapped angrily through gritted teeth.

"That's all the questions for now, Mr Gyllenhaal," said Barry as he gathered his things. The two of us got out of our seats and left the interview room.

We entered the observation room attached to interview room one and saw Chad Sullivan seated next to a smaller man with large round glasses and a tuft of curly black hair.

"His name is Moe Goldberg," Matthew Perry informed us. "Walter Sullivan made sure his boy has a top-notch lawyer to represent him. Moe Goldberg has gotten so many people away with so much. He's fucking scum, like those he represents."

Barry grunted and noisily slurped a cup of coffee in his hands.

"Don't worry. I've got quite a lot of evidence against him," I said, not taking my eyes from Chad. If only looks could kill...

"Moe Goldberg won't make things easy," responded Perry with a drawn-out sigh.

Barry and I entered the interview room and seated ourselves opposite Chad and his lawyer.

Chad had his arms folded and slouched into his chair with a defiant look on his face. He was wearing what he was wearing to the fashion gala, a black suit with a bright red shirt.

Moe scrutinized Barry and myself as we seated ourselves and twiddle his fingers impatiently. "Let's get this over with, shall we?" he snapped impertinently. "My client is well aware of his rights, as I'm sure the two of you are well aware also! So, let's dispense with pleasantries and get straight to it."

I grinned and produced a small envelope that I laid out on the table before me. A surprise for young Sullivan.

"Let's begin with asking where you were during the time Annabelle was missing," Barry said.

"We've been over this already!" Chad snapped, he screwed up his face and looked at his lawyer with an exaggerated shrug.

"In light of new evidence, we're obliged to revisit this avenue of questioning," sighed Barry.

Moe whispered something in Chad's ear and Chad replied; 'No comment.'

"What were you doing at the fashion gala?" I asked. "I was present and I didn't see you the entire evening! So, where were you?"

Chad kissed his teeth and leant back in his chair. "I was avoiding you!"

"Are you sure you weren't there to kidnap one of the models?" my voice was calm and composed. Though inside I was welling over with hatred for these people.

"What kind of question is that?!" snapped Chad angrily. "No fucking comment!"

I held up my hands and pretended I hadn't intended to piss him off. "Okay... Ever been to the Budapest hotel, Chad?"

He looked uncomfortable but denied it.

"Then how come I have this?" I opened the envelope I had placed in front of me earlier and produced a photograph of Chad Sullivan outside of the Budapest Hotel. It was the photo Nicolas Brown had taken during his investigation into Chad Sullivan. A quick phone call the previous night and Nicolas agreed to give me the photograph for my interview.

Chad's eyes widened as though I had just pulled a gun out on him. He licked his lips nervously and cleared his throat.

"With respect, detective," Moe Goldberg hastily intervened, "but that photograph could have been taken at any point since the hotel first opened."

"But I took this photograph myself!" I lied. "I had received an anonymous tip from somebody working for Mr Sullivan. Informing me that Chad would be at the Budapest Hotel. That was the same night that Emma Fontaine died. So, you see, Mr Sullivan I can connect you to at least four of the murders!"

Chad's mouth gaped open and he recoiled in shock. "This is fucking bullshit!" he exclaimed like an indignant child that had been caught out.

"There was DNA evidence connecting you to the murder of the young girl, Annabelle Green! I have photographic evidence, irrevocably proving you were there at the Budapest Hotel the night Emma Fontaine was murdered! You were present yesterday at the art gallery when Crystal Hayes disappeared without a trace! How do you explain that?!" Every time he tried to speak, I cut him down. "I investigated Mary O'Reilly's apartment and discovered her hidden diary!" I showed them photocopies of pages from Mary's diary. "She described a man whom visited her frequently, a man of your description! In particular with regard to your eyes."

It was Moe Goldberg who responded. He pushed up his glasses with his eyes blinking rapidly. "Again; with respect, detective, but that evidence is all circumstantial. With regard to Annabelle Green, my client was already acquitted of all charges due to witness testimonies that cleared Chad Sullivan of suspicion. He couldn't have been in two places at once. So that's one victim disassociated with my client. The diary could have been written by anyone and I'm sure my client isn't the only young man in LA with bright blue eyes."

Olivia Lockhart entered the interview room and whispered in Barry's ear. His eyebrow raised in response and a grin appeared on his face. "Please excuse us one moment," he said. He gestured for me to follow him and I gathered my things and entered the observation room where Perry, Olivia, and Barry had gathered.

"Okay, so I have dug up something interesting about our friend in interview room two," said Olivia with a large beaming smile. "Turns out he teaches university students surgery. He's been a surgeon himself for several years!"

"Olivia, I could kiss you!" I declared excitedly. This was an encouraging development in the case. More and more coincidences were beginning to pile up. As the evidence began to mount, I became more and more convinced that these two were our guys.

Me and Barry entered interview room two again. Larry offered us a wan smile as we seated ourselves opposite him.

"Any developments, detectives? Has the missing girl been found?" inquired Larry Gyllenhaal.

"You could say that!" chuckled Barry. "We just found out that you were a surgeon, which is extremely interesting to us."

"A few of the victims, as you will know, were mutilated or dismembered when we found them," I continued. "The precision in these lacerations denotes someone of a steady hand and experience with a blade. We have recently discovered you're a surgeon! These coincidences just keep piling up, don't they Mr Gyllenhaal?!"

"But I'm innocent..." Larry murmured in disbelief. "I can't believe you're accusing me of these monstrosities!"

Barry recoiled with feigned shock, "Whoa there! Who accused you of anything?! We're just asking some questions!"

"Does the name Heinrich Wulf mean anything to you?" I asked in a slightly aggressive tone.

Larry shook his head in response.

"Let the record show that Mr Gyllenhaal responded with a shake of his head," said Barry into the tape recorder.

"What about the name Ralph Lawrence?" I pressed, not believing a word that came out of his mouth.

"No."

"Okay..." I paused and smiled. It was time to try a new approach. I had the two people I suspected the most of being the killers and neither of them had any idea what the other would say. This was something I intended to use to my advantage. "What about the name Chad Sullivan? Does that mean anything to you?"

Larry considered the name and shook his head thoughtfully. "Doesn't ring any bells."

"Bullshit!" I slammed my hand on the table, making him jump. I wanted to make him feel these walls closing in on him. I wanted him to suffocate under the weight of all his lies. I wanted him to feel fear like those poor girls felt in their last horrible moments. "You know Chad Sullivan! He's your little apprentice, isn't he?! He helped kidnap Crystal Hayes whilst you distracted me with your bullshit talk about paintings!"

Larry shook his head fervently. He shuffled awkwardly in his chair and cleared his throat. "The name does sound familiar, actually. Wasn't he implicated in the fourth murder? Yes! That's it! He was under investigation and proven innocent."

"We have him in the room next door!" I told him with a menacing grin. "He's spilled the beans, Larry, it's over! He told us how you taught him surgery and how he helped you with the kidnappings and murders!"

Larry shrugged his shoulders. "What can I tell you, detective, he's lying! I've heard of his father, a very rich and powerful man. He could have had anybody teach him surgery. I think Mr Sullivan would rather pay for a top surgeon flown from abroad opposed to myself."

"How many people in LA have you taught?" inquired Barry. "If you wish to cooperate then you could provide us with a comprehensive list of all those you've ever taught."

Larry buried his head in his hands and exhaled a long drawn out sigh of frustration. "I've taught countless students, detectives. I can't be expected to remember all of them." He paused for a while and then offered an alternate explanation. "The killer might not even have been exclusive to my class; he could have been part of another class. He may not even have been taught in this country. All I'm trying to say is that there's no point in speculating!"

I persisted with my lie. If he was guilty then this tactic would put huge pressure on him, which would hopefully cause him to make some kind of slip up. I scowled at him intensely, as though I was trying to cut through his facade with looks alone. "What you don't understand, Mr Gyllenhaal, is that Chad Sullivan has already implicated you on tape. You could make a deal with us now and make a confession for a lighter sentence."

Larry scoffed at that. "And what actual evidence is there to undeniably prove that I am the killer? I'm not an idiot, detective Cucchiano! I know that I can't be arrested for several counts of murder based solely on the testimony of some trumped up little daddy's boy!" he became enraged, though whether it was genuine or an act, I couldn't be sure. "Am I under arrest for the murder and kidnapping of those women and that child?!" he demanded angrily.

Barry was the one who answered. He answered with a blunt "no" that made Larry smile with smug gratification.

"Then I am free to leave. Unless you plan on detaining me here unlawfully," said Larry more calmly.

He was right! We had no real evidence that implicated Larry Gyllenhaal aside from the fact that he has surgical knowledge and he made some suspicious remarks at the art gallery. It wasn't enough to implicate him. We had to cut him loose. Perry apologized for any inconvenience caused and Larry politely dismissed the whole 'misunderstanding', as he put it, and he walked out of the police station a free man.

As he was leaving, he turned to me and made a flippant remark about how he isn't responsible for doing my job for me. I flipped him off and he left with a huge smile on his face.

I was fucking pissed off! I stormed back into the interview room where Chad and his lawyer were sat patiently waiting, kicking the door open with my foot as I entered. Barry followed behind me, slurping noisily at his coffee.

"I fucking know it was you!" I told him through gritted teeth. His cocky attitude evaporated, and he gulped nervously at my hostility. I completely blocked out Barry and that cunt nugget, Moe Goldberg. Only Chad and I were present in the room. I could see cracks appearing in the fortress walls.

"Scarlett Jones was an aspiring actress, that was well known! Then it would be safe to assume that she contacted your father at some point, since Walter Sullivan has been a huge producer in Hollywood for the past few years!

Mary O'Reilly, victim number two, described a young man who named himself 'Ralph Lawrence' who I believe is the killer because of how her diary became centered around him and her description of him is a doppelganger for you, Chad! Or should I say: Bright Eyes!

Victim number three, Rosita Ramirez, was a carer for the elderly. Before that she was a cleaner for rich arseholes like your dad! Is that how you chose her? Or did she attend your cess pool nightclub?

Annabelle Green lived in your very neighborhood! You couldn't resist the opportunity to take her, could you?! What was it you entitled your painting?! The loss of fucking innocence?! You sick fucker!" I was practically screaming in his face by this point. He meekly tried to interject and protest his innocence during my outburst, but I ignored him! I don't listen to flies buzzing in my ear! No, I fucking squash them!

"Your DNA was found on the body of Annabelle Green!" I continued. "I fucking know you killed her!"

"Would you tone it down, detective?!" Moe Green barked defiantly.

I ignored him. "You were present when Emma Fontaine was murdered at the Budapest Hotel and you were also present tonight when another woman disappeared! Explain how all this is coincidence!"

"No comment," replied Chad.

In the end we also had to let Chad go due to lack of evidence. Despite what I felt in my gut, we didn't have enough to make a strong enough case against either Larry Gyllenhaal or Chad Sullivan. I left the police station late that night, feeling totally dejected. I refused a lift home from Olivia, preferring instead to catch the bus.

I walked to the bus stop with my overcoat drawn tightly around me to block the crisp wind that blew through the streets carrying the scent of rain. A woman stood at the bus stop shivering slightly in the drizzle.

"Excuse me," she said softly. "Do you think I'm pretty?" she blinked rapidly and smiled at me nervously. She had sad looking eyes that frequently darted away and broke eye contact.

I cleared my throat and answered with a stammer, not because what I said was a lie, but because her sudden question caught me completely off guard! "Ummm... I...I guess so."

She smiled and offered me a nod of gratitude. "Thank you." She reached into her handbag and produced what I thought was lipstick, rubbing it side to side rapidly in my peripheral vision.

"What about now?" she asked again.

When I turned to look at her, I noticed the item in her hand wasn't lipstick, as I first thought, but was in fact a shard of glass dripping with blood. The lady had sliced her mouth wide open from ear to ear, giving herself a Glasgow smile. Her eyes were wide open, staring sightlessly forward with psychotic glee.

I watched in horror as a gigantic beast with two glowing eyes as bright as two suns gripped the road with gigantic claws that ripped the tarmac open like huge gaping wounds. The claws were attached to large leathery hands that were as black as obsidian and the creature's arms were long and gangly and stretched disproportionately to the beast's body. It crawled the corner slowly and sped up before slowing down as it approached me and the psychotic lady.

I was too frozen with horror to even scream! Let alone flee! The beast stopped beside us and hissed monstrously. The silhouette of the woman was still standing frozen until her head began vibrating from side to side so fast it had become a blur. She burst into flames and disintegrated into burning embers that were carried away with the wind.

I slowly turned my head to face the beast that still growled at the side of me and see a heavy-set man with a patchy beard chewing gum like a cow chewing cud. He raised a questioning eyebrow, but he said nothing.

I got on the bus and paid the driver to take me to my street. A young couple were sitting at the back of the bus, a young man in a woolly hat and a green parker coat draped his arm around a slender girl's shoulders. She was wearing a blue raincoat with a hat that had big fluffy pompoms hanging from it. The young man coughed and eyed me warily.

An elderly man with a beige jacket and unkempt grey hair and beard sat coughing in a window seat in the middle of the bus. His chest sounded like he'd swallowed a rattle.

I sat by the window, shaking uncontrollably from fear. I sighed and looked out of the window, watching the lights fly by as blurred colors.

The bus stopped again, and the doors hissed open. This time a young girl entered the bus and made her way to the very back of the bus behind the young couple. She walked silently with her hands in front of her and a look of melancholy on her face. She looked like she had been crying. Her black hair cascaded down her back and across her face, obscuring most of her face. I thought nothing of her.

We travelled by another stop and then I heard a voice whispering behind me "Excuse me!" Immediately my nostrils were filled with the faint scent of whiskey and sweat. "You got a light?"

"We can't smoke on the bus," I muttered back impatiently. I huffed aloud and closed my eyes, wanting nothing more than to be left alone.

"You fucking give that back!" yelled the old man as he struck me sharply across the back of the head.

I leapt to my feet. My face burning red with fury. "What the fuck is wrong with you!" I howled furiously.

The old man got to his feet and screamed back in my face with equal fury. "You stole my fucking wallet, you little cunt!" he shouted back at me. He gritted his teeth and swung for me, but the motion of the bus threw him off balance.

I grabbed the collar of his jacket as the bus screeched to a stop and the huge bus driver was striding towards us with a look of utter fury.

"Get the fuck off of my bus right now, you fucking hooligans! I mean it! Fucking get!" The bus driver hollered. He raised his fist and held it above us as we both scarpered for the doors.

The couple were watching with shocked expressions on their faces and the young girl kept looking down at the floor of the bus, her black hair concealing most of her face. Only the thin line of her lips was visible along with her narrow chin.

The bus doors closed, and the bus pulled away, leaving me and the old man standing in the pouring rain. It also meant I was stranded in Compton, with no more buses coming through at this hour and no money to pay for a cab.

I spun around to face the old man, "What the fuck was all that about, you crazy old bastard?!" I shouted at him angrily. My anger was only matched by my confusion.

The old man now looked calm. He straightened out his coat and looked at me seriously. "You should be thanking me! I just saved your life!"

I shook my head in utter disbelief. "What the fuck are you talking about?" I demanded. "Because of your outburst I have to fucking walk home in the rain! Thanks!"

The old man waved his hands frantically in front of me. "You don't understand! I see things! That girl who got on the bus was a fucking ghost and if I didn't get us off of that bus, we'd be fucking ghosts tomorrow! Everyone on that bus is fucking dead!"

I can tell he was serious. But could I believe him? He certainly believed what he was saying was real, I could tell that from the passion in his voice. Did he really see ghosts, just like I did? Or is he just some delusional crackhead?

"I see things too," I told him. "Ghosts of the dead haunt me."

He vigorously nodded his head. "If I didn't cause a ruckus like that then the ghost would've known I could see through her disguise and she would've killed us all!"

"She looked alive to me," I remarked flippantly. I had considerable doubt that the girl who entered the bus was in fact a ghost.

"Then you're not very observant!" he snapped back. "It's fucking pouring down and she got on the bus bone dry! Not a drop of rain in her hair or on her clothes. She wasn't even shivering in the rain. And I'm pretty sure she hovered across the floor to her seat. Nobody even noticed..."

My encounter with him left me with several more questions than ever before. He raised his hand and gave me a half-arsed wave as he turned and left.

"You're welcome..." he uttered as he walked away with his hands in his pockets, silently muttering to himself about what an ungrateful arsehole I was.

Did ghosts really exist? Was the old man a delusional lunatic whose delusions just happened to be similar to my own hallucinations? Perhaps the old man really did see ghosts. Perhaps he just saved my life...

CHAPTER 11

Mannequins

I stood in the rain and considered my options: I could either walk home from Compton, utterly exhausted and soaking wet through or I could call in a favor from a newfound friend. It didn't take me long to decide on the latter of my two options.

I had spent the night at Rebecca Valentine's. She answered her cellphone almost instantaneously and eagerly offered me a place to stay for the night. When I arrived, she answered the door and ushered me inside where she had run me a hot bath which I sank into with a satisfied sigh.

We made love that night, long into the early hours of the morning. I awoke sometime in the late morning with Rebecca already awake next to me, tenderly tracing her fingernail up and down my chest.

"Morning handsome!" she cooed soothingly with a gentle smile. "I usually charge for that kind of service," she joked with a chuckle. "I charge extra for overnight stays."

I smiled and lit a cigarette, watching the spirals of blue smoke rise and hang heavily in the air. I knew full well that she knew that I had no money to pay for said services.

"I guess that means I'll be in your debt?" I asked, genuinely uncertain of whether she was joking or not.

"With daily interest," she replied giving me a sultry smile and biting her bottom lip seductively. "I'll let you pay me back in kind, Jack!"

"With daily interest it sounds like we're going to be very busy," I said. We both chuckled at that. She jumped out of bed and took delicate steps towards the bathroom wearing nothing but a lacy pair of red French underwear. She squealed with delight when I slapped her bottom as she passed.

I felt invigorated and full of life! Rebecca encouraged a part of me to resurrect that which I thought had died a long time ago. I felt a great happiness in her company, but at the same time I knew that I could never truly have a meaningful relationship with her on account of her profession. Despite knowing that my feelings for Rebecca could never amount to anything meaningful, I decided to savor the moment and enjoy it while it lasted.

I finished my cigarette and got dressed into my clothes which Rebecca had dried for me the previous night. She made me a breakfast worthy of a king, a fry up with all the trimmings! Sizzling bacon, sausages, fried eggs with perfect golden yokes, beans, fried tomatoes, and mushrooms with a side dish of pancakes and syrup. She also made me a coffee with an assortment of biscuits for dipping. The array of aromas sent my senses into overdrive and I began to salivate like a wild animal with a ravenous appetite.

I devoured the majority of my breakfast, stopping only when my stomach had stretched to capacity. We talked the whole morning, discussing various topics from the case to conspiracy theories and even paranormal phenomena.

"Ghosts are just energetic parasites which feed from emotions," explained Rebecca. "I believe in reincarnation, and believing ghosts are souls of the dead who have nothing better to do than tease the living conflicts with the reincarnation belief. It makes much more sense that ghosts are energetic parasites which evoke emotions and feed from them." Rebecca pointed at me. "You told me that the victims of the Artist Killer haunt you from time to time. They can evoke powerful energy from you, Jack," she continued. "Your sorrow, your fear and your anger. These entities are feasting on your soul, Jack!"

"Interesting theory," I grunted. "But how can you be so sure that's what they actually are? They could be the souls of the dead that are too angry to let go. I feel like they are punishing me for my failure to bring their killer to justice!" I sighed and slumped my shoulders, my mood suddenly becoming somber. "There is the possibility that I'm just a fucking madman! That these apparitions are just figments of my imagination!"

Rebecca vigorously shook her head. She reached across the table and took my hands in hers, squeezing them gently to comfort me.

"Listen to me," she spoke in a commanding tone staring at me intensely. "I believe you, Jack Cucchiano! You are not crazy! I could never fall for a crazy man!"

A smile forced its way onto my face. "So now you're falling for me?" I ventured, trying to stifle my smile which persistently forced the corner of my mouth upwards.

Rebecca squeezed my hands again and gave me a perplexing smile which denoted sorrow or sympathy. Then she got up and started clearing the table. "I want to help," she finally responded while she was standing at the sink with her back to me. Her voice was expressionless. "I want to help you catch the person who killed Mary."

I nodded thoughtfully, carefully considering whether I should expose her to the gory details of the case and the potential danger that came along with it.

"Listen," she pleaded as she spun around to face me. "I know it might be dangerous, but I know capoeira! I can defend myself! Plus, I'm a smart girl! I can help you with your investigation!"

I considered her offer for help and I decided to accept her into my little investigation clique, which so far consisted of Nicolas Brown and myself. I would invite Rebecca Valentine into our group to form a trio. It would be dangerous, but Rebecca was a grown woman who has a personal stake in this case.

"The next time me and Nicolas meet I'll invite you along," I informed her. "We compare the progress of our investigation and share what we've discovered."

Rebecca sat back down across from me. She nodded her head earnestly as she listened to my words. "I can try and contact some of Mary's old clients, see what I can dig up about this Ralph Lawrence you mentioned."

I agreed and after another quick coffee I called for a cab and Rebecca gave me the money to pay for it. She passionately kissed my lips as I was leaving.

*

When I arrived home, I noticed that an envelope had been slid under my front door. I checked the locks for scratches and signs of lock picking, but it appeared as though my door hadn't been tampered with in any way.

I carefully picked up the envelope with a cloth and placed it on my table in the kitchen. I produced a flick knife and sliced across the top of the envelope. I tipped the envelope upside down and shook it gently to encourage its contents to fall out.

A small piece of paper with nothing more than an address fell onto my table. I looked up the address online and could see that this was an address to an old closed down factory which had produced different brands of clothing.

It was obvious to me that this envelope had been sent by the killer. Everything was connected! Fashion event, model of clothing brand, abandoned clothing factory. My only concern was the safety of Crystal Hayes. The nature of this address had dire implications in my mind.

Now I faced a dilemma. Should I call Olivia and Perry and gain the support of the LAPD? Or should I investigate the old factory alone. There was the possibility that this was a trap, an ambush orchestrated by my enemies; Chad and Walter Sullivan.

I hastily left my apartment, taking some money and my Beretta 9mm for self-defence. My footsteps thundered down the hallway of my apartment block and I panted breathlessly, silently reflecting on the negative impact which smoking and drinking had on my health. By the time I reached the street my chest was already burning.

I hesitated for a second, indecisive of which way I should go and what method of transport I should use. A bus? A cab?

I grabbed my cellphone and called for a cab to drop me a couple of blocks away from where the factory was situated. In total it took me half an hour to get there and even that felt like it took forever. I would have to buy a new car as soon as I could so that getting around would be much easier.

I paid the cab driver and didn't hang around for my change. I sprinted off in the direction of the factory as fast as my legs could carry me, ignoring the lactic acid that burned my legs and stomach as I continually propelled myself onwards. A life was at stake!

The factory stood isolated down an old industrial estate with patches of wasteland on either side of the road. It was bigger than it looked in the pictures online. It was only two floors, but there was a lot of ground to cover. A chain-link fence surrounded the abandoned factory about eight feet tall with tangles of barbed wire around the top. A large gate was secured shut with a beefy metal chain as thick as an athlete's thigh and a sturdy iron padlock. A sign on the gate stated that the building was condemned and due to be demolished.

How would I get in? There was no way I could climb over and digging underneath the fence wouldn't be possible because the ground was concrete with posts holding the metal panels cemented into the sidewalk.

The fence was only the first hurdle. Once on the other side of the fence I would have to find a way into the building. From the sidewalk I could see that the entrance doors and windows had been covered by metal sheets to prevent trespassers from breaking in or squatters taking residence.

I followed the fencing around the building, scoping out the area for potential access routes. I made a mental note of a tree that stood next to the building which I could use as access to the roof.

Around the back of the factory I made a series of interesting discoveries. Firstly, one side of one of the chain-link panels had been cut with something halfway across the bottom of the panel and halfway up one of the sides, so that it was possible to peel the fence away and create a small opening.

The second discovery which I made was tiny droplets of something that I assumed was dried blood. There was no way I could be certain that these droplets on the asphalt were indeed droplets of blood, but I'd have put money on it. There wasn't enough to suggest heavy bleeding, but someone had definitely been cut. The trail of them started at a random point of the asphalt and led towards the chain-link fence.

The third discovery was a small piece of fabric which had snagged and ripped on the chain-link fence, a piece of black fabric which had been torn from a garment. The same black garment which Crystal

Hayes had worn the night she disappeared perhaps?

I scanned my immediate surroundings and in my mind I pieced together what had happened here. A thick wall of foliage concealed the back end of the factory from neighboring houses, which meant that there would be no witnesses. With this information in mind I surmised that the killer had driven here with Crystal Hayes in the trunk of his car. He cut the fence with bolt cutters or something and then he forced Crystal Hayes through the gap in the chain-link fence.

There was no time to lose! Police forensics could examine the blood and collect samples when I contacted them later. For now, I would investigate the factory alone. There was no car parked close by, so if my deductions were correct then it must have meant that the killer had left. Had he taken Crystal with him? Or was she inside this factory somewhere?

I ducked through the gap in the fence, careful not to disturb the piece of fabric which was hanging from the jagged edge of the fencing. Once inside I was standing in a parking lot which was intended for the factory workers. I walked across to the main building and searched for a similar opening in the metal sheets that covered the windows and doors.

I attempted to climb the tree and gain access to the building through the roof. I jumped and grabbed hold of a branch with both hands, my eyes widened as I heard a *crack* and suddenly I was falling to the floor with the branch still in my hands. I hit the floor with a thud that knocked the wind out of me. I rolled around and groaned in pain until I snapped myself out of it and got back to my feet. The tree was rotten and climbing it would be dangerous, especially when it came to crossing a branch to the roof of the factory. That avenue was a last resort.

I continued walking around the building until I came to the loading bays where garments would be loaded into vans and shipped out to retailers. There was a door with a red arrow spray-painted on the wall pointing inside.

"Looks fresh..." I mumbled to myself. I narrowed my eyes and nervously bit my lip before I entered the factory.

The door creaked open and a beam of light penetrated the thick darkness within. Dust particles could be seen once they passed into the light. I entered and walked across the dispatch area with my Beretta 9mm in both hands.

A sudden creaking noise behind me caused me to spin on my heels and aim my handgun at the door which I had come in through. The beam of light narrowed, and the door slammed shut, engulfing me in complete darkness. I ran to the door and tried to open it, but it was jammed.

What had happened? Had someone locked me in? Or did the door just slam shut on its own?

I used the torch feature on my phone and decided to continue my investigation of the derelict building. I felt uneasy and my mind had already started playing tricks on me with shadows and things moving in the peripheral of my vision. I suddenly realized that I was very cold and a sudden sense of anxiety gripped hold of me.

From across the dispatch room I could see a wooden door with light seeping through underneath where there was a small gap between the door and the floor. I could hear music playing faintly from another area of the factory. It was indistinguishable, but I was sure that there was the sound of violins. Some classical music most likely. Was it real or just another hallucination?

I approached the door cautiously, aiming my phone torch and handgun at the door. With a strong feeling of trepidation, I slowly reached for the brass door handle and burst into the room, quickly scanning it for any threats.

The room was empty, save for a few cardboard boxes stacked in one corner of the room. A small lamp illuminated the room, but the light was dimming. The most unsettling thing about this room was the lone mannequin that stood in the center of it. The mannequin was dressed in grey yoga pants and a green vest. A black wig had been draped over its head and someone had smeared lipstick all over the mannequin's lips so that it looked vaguely like a clown.

There was something strangely familiar about this mannequin. It took me a few moments to realize, but this was exactly how Rebecca Valentine looked when I first met her. Did the killer set this up for me to see? Was he telling me who his next intended victim was? Was Rebecca Valentine in danger?!

I had to warn her! I checked my phone and cursed aloud when I could see that I had no signal. Panic began to take hold of me, coupled with an overwhelming sense of guilt! I had failed Crystal Hayes and I had failed Rebecca Valentine! I should have known that my attraction to her would've put her in danger! I cursed myself for my stupidity, for allowing myself to let my emotions cloud my better judgement. And I cursed myself for underestimating this killer!

There was a second door across from me and I decided to investigate what was on the other side of it. I pulled it open and peeked down a long and featureless corridor.

Then I saw someone move in the darkness.

I was almost considering calling out to them, but if it was the killer then I didn't want to alert him to my presence, although I was fairly certain that the killer would know that I was already here...

I moved down the corridor and slowly closed the door to the previous room behind me. I got halfway down the corridor when I heard an ear-piercing scream that made me go cold and made the hairs at the nape of my neck stand on end. It was a woman's scream, a scream so shrill that it sounded like someone was either in immense pain or sudden danger. It was really close. It came from the room where I had just come from, the one with the Rebecca Valentine mannequin.

I darted back up the hallway and threw open the door, desperate to save whoever was in danger.

I froze.

The Rebecca Valentine mannequin was lying on its back with stab wounds covering its torso and face. A red liquid gushed from the open stab wounds like blood and I stared in disbelief at what I was seeing. I crouched next to the mannequin and rubbed the tip of my finger across one of the punctures in its chest. The porcelain was jagged and red liquid continued to ooze out. I looked at the red circle on the tip of my finger and tasted it. It had a slight coppery taste like blood.

What the fuck was going on here?

The cardboard boxes moved in the corner of the room. At first, I dismissed it as rats or mice and then my phone started making noises of static merged with whispering voices. A claw burst out of one of the cardboard boxes, sending small pieces of packaging foam flying across the room. Then the top of Rosita Ramirez's head poked out of the box with dirty matted hair obscuring her face. Another arm burst out, tight blue skin stretched over her unnaturally gangly arms and she hissed before her head started vibrating side to side, making me feel instantly dizzy and sick.

I fled the room and closed the door behind me. The static on my phone stopped and there was no noise coming from the small room where Rebecca's mannequin was.

"This place is fucking creepy..." I exclaimed, gasping breathlessly. My heart was beating so hard that I thought that it was going to burst through my rib cage.

Then I saw a figure standing motionless at the end of the corridor, where I thought that I had seen someone moving before. I pointed my phone at it and felt uncomfortable at the sight of another mannequin and the large shadow which the light from my phone cast on the back wall.

Several doors lined the corridor. They were labelled as the canteen, toilets, and storage. A sign on the wall said that the factory floor was around the corner at the end of the corridor where the mannequin had been placed. That was where I would head next.

I kept a close eye on the mannequin as I moved closer to it, half-expecting it to jump out at me or something. The sudden noise of a door slamming behind me made me jump and I spun around to see three mannequins standing behind me in the corridor! One had its porcelain hand resting on the brass doorknob of the door which I had come through. The other two mannequins were standing side by side with their arms outstretched towards me.

I moved closer to them, feeling a mixture of bewilderment and abject fear! Nobody could have placed them there that quickly and then disappear the moment I turned around. I reached a hand towards one and froze as my fingers were inches away from one of the mannequin's featureless faces. My phone began to buzz again with static and I retracted my hand, deciding the wiser course of action was to continue my investigation and ignore any paranormal activity. If Rebecca Valentine was right and these were indeed energetic parasites, then I wasn't going to feed them.

I turned around and gasped aloud when there were ten

mannequins crowded in the corner, barring my path. The one which had been standing alone had moved down the corridor so that it was now directly behind me.

I acted without thinking, completely ignoring the cacophony of voices whispering through my phone. I raised my leg and kicked the mannequin in the chest, effortlessly sending it flying down the corridor. Then a mannequin fell on me from behind, its arms positioned under my arms.

I gave an involuntary high-pitched wail of panic as I frantically scrambled to get the mannequin's fingers unhooked from my shirt. As I wrestled with the inanimate object I spun around and now there were at least thirty or so crowding the full length of the corridor behind me. The staffroom door and toilet doors were open, and I could see that these rooms were full of mannequins.

I threw the mannequin to the floor and stamped on its head so that it shattered like an egg with a crack that echoed down the corridor. I turned around and yelled "Fuck!" at the top of my lungs when the outstretched hand of another mannequin poked me in the eye. When I staggered backwards, I stumbled into more mannequins, but I couldn't move them. I spun around again and now there were hundreds of mannequins all crammed into the corridor so that I couldn't even push them over. I spun around again and screamed when the outstretched hand of another mannequin holding a kitchen knife grazed my side, cutting through my shirt and leaving a red gash across the side of my stomach.

More mannequins appeared all around me every time I turned my back until they pressed against me and squeezed the air out of my lungs. I tried to draw my Beretta from its holster, but I couldn't move my arms. I desperately gasped for air until my head felt like it was going to explode! I lost consciousness.

I regained consciousness in the hallway some time later. I awoke with a sudden gasp for air and everything seemed back to normal. The mannequins had disappeared and so had the tear in my shirt, along with the blood. I got back to my feet and decided to continue with my investigation.

I turned the corner and pushed a double door open, which lead to the main factory floor. I shone my torch around and observed my surroundings. Several dust-covered workstations littered the factory floor, clearly unused for a long time. Mannequins were standing along the wall and just the sight of them made my skin crawl. I saw their featureless faces and stiff limbs. They creeped me out.

My phone began making more static noises and I knew that the spirits of the dead were close.

I continued on, shining my torch on a door with some graffiti which looked as though it had been hastily scribbled in red paint. *"This way!"* was all that it read, and I instinctively knew that this was a message that the killer had left for me.

I nervously reached forward, freezing when I heard the faint sound of buzzing and classical music behind the door. I grabbed the brass door handle and pulled the door open.

Inside I was greeted by a plastic curtain which had been attached to the ceiling with either nails or clips. A few battery-powered lamps were on the other side and through the transparency of the plastic, in this light, I could make out several blurred forms hanging from the ceiling.

My heart started racing when I noticed several red droplets on the inside of the plastic and I immediately knew that I had found Crystal Hayes.

I pushed the plastic curtain aside and inside was Crystal Hayes as I had suspected. Metal loops had been screwed into the ceiling with metal chains looped through with large meat hooks attached to the bottom of them. She had been dismembered and each of her limbs were now hanging from one of the four hooks. Her torso lay on a table in the middle of the crudely made operating theater. Her eyes had been gouged out and mannequin arms and legs had been attached to her torso.

Across the room was a painting on the wall. It had been painted using Crystal's blood and it depicted her dismembered body lying in a pile with a wide-eyed psychotic grin plastered across the face of her severed head. Underneath, the title "Beauty fades" had been hastily scribbled in blood.

I felt sick! I raised a hand to my mouth as my eyes stung with tears of bitterness and defeat. I had failed yet another woman! I slumped into a crouching position with my hands tugging at my hair in frustration.

"I will avenge you!" I promised, wiping away a tear that rolled down my cheek with the sleeve of my shirt. "I'm so very sorry!"

I took a deep breath and planned my next move. First, I wanted to investigate the scene of the murder for myself, and second, I would find a way out of here and contact Matthew Perry.

I got to my feet and began to survey the scene. A small metal table stood next to where Crystal's torso was. Several instruments had been carefully organized into a neat line across the tray. These were instruments undoubtedly used by a surgeon. The tools were covered in dried blood and blood spatter was everywhere. The lacerations had been skilfully made, leaving a smooth line where the flesh was cut. Puddles of blood were all over the floor and I had to take great care not to disturb them.

I studied the room and thought about it carefully. It would appear as though the killer had been interrupted or had to rush. The abandoned tools and the painting on the wall suggested that much. Usually the killer had taken his time with his victims, flaying their skin to use as his canvass and using some of their hair in his brushes. Annabelle Green was an exception.

I looked at the tools. It was very interesting to me that the killer had chosen to leave them behind. They looked shiny and brand new. The fact that they had been organized so carefully contradicted the theory that he had been rushing. It suggested to me that all of this was deliberate, like the killer was trying to make me believe that he was interrupted. It didn't make sense. Then why would he post this address to me if his work wasn't finished?

The tools also made a statement in my opinion. It was like the killer was saying to me: "Yeah, I'm a surgeon! What the hell are you going to do about it?!" This raised some interesting questions. How the fuck did the killer know that I suspected that he was a surgeon? The only people I shared that information with was the police! My heart started to race, and I felt lightheaded.

What the fuck is going on?!

I couldn't handle anymore. I left the factory through an old fire escape. The fresh air was such a relief after being stuck in that stale factory. I immediately called Perry and waited for the LAPD to join me on scene.

*

Twenty minutes later and Matthew Perry arrived with Olivia, Barry, and the Grim Reaper.

"Better let forensics investigate the scene first," insisted Larry King. He pulled on a pair of latex gloves. His face was expressionless as always, but even so I detected a sense of excitement within him. 'Don't worry, Jack!" he said with a slight grin, exposing slightly crooked and yellowing teeth. "I'll be able to give you the time of death once I've opened her up."

Grim strode past me, pulling one of his gloves down his wrist and releasing it with a *slap*. I watched him disappear into the factory with a team of forensic scientists where Grim would oversee the collection of important information... or personally see to its disposal.

CHAPTER 12

Country Club

I met with Nicolas Brown and Rebecca Valentine Saturday afternoon at the Blue Bell. I had introduced Rebecca to Nicolas a week before, a couple of days after the discovery of Crystal Hayes. The two were already acquainted. Nicolas impatiently reminded me that he was the one who sent me to meet Rebecca in the first place.

The two of them were now seated in a booth across the table from me. Rebecca was wide-eyed, like a child. She was wearing a green cardigan with a blue pattern sewn into it and black jeans with a pair of brown boots.

Nicolas was wearing his green parker coat and a pair of faded blue jeans. He was frowning and he looked lost in thought. They both waited for me to share what I had discovered in my investigations.

"Here's what I know," I began, regarding my two allies with a solemn glare. "Crystal Hayes was killed the very night that Chad Sullivan and Larry Gyllenhaal were released from police custody, which means there's still a possibility that one or both of them headed over to that abandoned factory to finish the job."

"How the fuck did you manage to let this happen, Jack?" exclaimed Nicolas, reprimanding me with in a sudden outburst of anger. "You had the fucking police watching the entire building!"

"I fucking know!" I snapped back through gritted teeth. His attitude had shocked me. The rise of anger was instantaneous.

"Well it's not fucking good enough, Jack! I warned you that we shouldn't trust the police! I'm telling you I've suspected for a while that the killer has an ally in the police or is a high-ranking member of the police. It wouldn't have been difficult for the killer's ally to have slipped away with her in a police vehicle. I think that girl's death rests heavily on your fucking shoulders, Jack Cucchiano!"

"Stop fucking breathing!" I barked at him like a feral animal.

His eyes narrowed. "You were in there," he screamed with an accusing tone. "Why don't you tell us exactly what happened in there the night she disappeared!"

Rebecca waved her arms to catch our attention. "Guys, please! I can shed some light on what happened!"

We both regarded her sceptically, but we remained silent.

"I went to the art gallery last night. I did some snooping around and I found a hatch with a ladder leading to an old tunnel which was used for maintenance or something. I'm guessing that the tunnel connects to the sewers, which would mean the killer had access to any part of the city from underground."

Rebecca took out her phone and showed Nicolas and myself a video which she had recorded on her cellphone. She had entered the room where the bar had been the night of the fashion gala. Then she swiftly threw open a door with a sign that read 'staff only' and entered a corridor which I immediately recognized. She had slipped through the same door which I did. Rebecca walked through another door and found the maintenance hatch under a rug in one of the storage rooms. When she pulled the rug aside, she discovered the hatch and struggled to open it. She eventually got it open with a grunt and pointed the camera down the hole hidden beneath. A red ladder descended into darkness which the light from Rebecca's phone couldn't penetrate.

"I didn't dare go down there," she said closing her phone. "I was caught shortly after this video. I was escorted from the gallery, banned for life and fined five hundred dollars." Rebecca huffed and rolled her eyes at the memory.

"Don't worry," replied Nicolas, gently placing his hand on hers. "You were there five minutes and you still worked out more than the esteemed detective." I felt a surge of jealousy rush through me.

"Seriously, Nicolas, you can go suck a fucking chainsaw!" I yelled, slamming my fist on the table. "Fuck this! I'm out of here!" I shoved myself up to my feet and was about to storm out of the Blue Bell when Nicolas grabbed my arm.

"Please," he quietly murmured. "I'm sorry. If anyone can catch this guy, it's you, Jack."

I stared at him with a grimace on my face for a moment before I sat down. I wondered whether Nicolas Brown was speaking truthfully. Part of me agreed that I would be the only one to stop this killer once and for all. Then I wondered whether Nicolas Brown was a good ally or whether he was just using me to catch the killer in order to claim his reward from Annabelle Green's family. Ultimately, it didn't even matter.

"I'm sorry," he went on to say. "I'm just stressed that we don't seem to be..." he stopped abruptly. His face staring towards the bar.

"What's wrong?" I snapped impatiently.

"Don't look now," warned Nicolas. "There are two guys in suits who keep looking over at you, Jack..."

Rebecca and I subtly glanced towards the bar where two men in suits were sitting and nursing a beer each that looked untouched. It was hard to say whether or not they were looking at us, but one thing that did catch my attention was Dean Costello. He was standing a few tables away with an enigmatic grin on his face.

"I'm not sure whether they are looking over at us," said Rebecca with a modicum of fear in her voice. She turned back around and cast me an uncertain look, like a child seeking comfort from their parent.

Nicolas was stoic as usual, though their presence seemed to bother him more than me or Rebecca. "I have a plan," he whispered conspiratorially. Rebecca and I leaned in close to see what plan Nicolas had conjured. "Jack, I want you to fake exhaustion. If they are watching you like I suspected, then they will end up yawning as well. Or at least one of them will."

"This is fucking stupid," I complained, yet at the same time I leaned back in my chair and faked the biggest open-mouthed yawn I could. I narrowed my eyes and glanced at the two men who were sitting at the bar. I reasoned that Nicolas had just caught them checking out Rebecca Valentine, but just as I was about to laugh off Nicolas' paranoia, one of the oversized brutes raised a hand to his mouth in a vain attempt to stifle a yawn.

That confirmed it! It was me they were watching, as Nicolas said.

"You were right!" I declared. My heart began racing. The two guys were huge, like two gorillas on steroids. I yawned again and this set them both off yawning again.

"What should we do?" I asked glancing at my allies in search of answers.

"You need to get out of here!" replied Nicolas. "They know we're on to them!"

Everything happened so fast. The two men were already walking towards our table with their eyes fixed on me and their fists clenched tight. Nicolas was on his feet and he charged towards the two goons with a howl that sounded like he believed that he was a medieval warrior charging into battle.

One goon back handed him, and he flew into a table, smashing glasses and evoking screams of panic from the patrons who were seated there. Nicolas went to get back to his feet and Dean Costello grabbed his collar and rammed his fist into his face.

"That's for being a prick!" he yelled before a stool was smashed over his back. He collapsed in agony.

The whole bar descended into chaos. Fists, glasses, and insults were hauled across the Blue Bell as the patrons, band and Nicolas all broke into conflict. I bolted straight for the door, taking advantage of the brawl and using it as an opportunity to escape from the two gorillas in suits who had obviously arrived for me. I ran down the road as fast as my legs would allow. The sound of shoes clicking on the pavement behind me spurred me forwards.

I glanced over my shoulder to see the two men were gaining on me.

"Mr Cucchiano! Stop!" yelled one of the goons furiously.

I almost knocked an old woman over as I desperately dived by her and sprinted down an alleyway. I felt a heavy hand fall on my shoulder and I abruptly stopped and ducked underneath it. The goon continued running and struggled to slow himself down.

"Mitch, he's heading back towards you!"

The other goon was panting breathlessly, and I easily evaded him, heading back towards the Blue Bell. A van pulled in front of the alleyway, barring my path. Rocco was behind the wheel. I turned to face the two assailants rushing towards me and I raised my fists in anticipation of a fight.

"We can avoid anyone getting hurt!" shouted Rocco from the van. "You're outnumbered, Jack! Just get in the van and it will save all of us time!"

"Yeah right!" I spat. "You guys are here to kill me!"

"We're here to take you to Mr Sullivan," replied Rocco calmly, correcting me. "We'd rather you didn't resist. The logical way to look at it is like this, Jack. You are coming with us regardless. Save yourself the bumps and bruises and just get in the fucking van! Mr Sullivan only wants to talk! As soon as you're finished, we can all go home!"

I lowered my fists and willingly got in the van. Rocco's face was a painting of relief. I was nervous, but ultimately Rocco was right. If I'd fought the outcome would've been the same, the only difference being a few broken ribs and a black eye. Going willingly was the only way.

The two goons from the bar got in the back of the van with me, sitting either side of me. None of us spoke a word for the entirety of the trip. What could Walter Sullivan possibly want from me?

The van travelled to Beverly Hills. Beautiful villas and stately homes provided a stark contrast with the slums of Downtown LA. This was where the super rich lived. People like Walter Sullivan.

We arrived at a country club and the van parked in an almost empty parking lot. A few cars were parked here and there, but it was the black Rolls Royce that stood out to me. Clearly the property of Walter Sullivan, the film producer and director with his dirty fucking fingers stuck in a piece of everyone's pie.

We left the van and made our way to the gates which would lead us to the green where Walter Sullivan inexorably waited for us.

Walter Sullivan had his back to us as we approached. He swung his golf club and the ball was sent flying through the air; its trajectory obscured by the harsh brightness of the sun.

Walter turned to face us as Rocco announced our arrival. He was wearing a beige turtleneck sweater and green and red checkered trousers. He had short grey hair covered by a red cap. His eyes were narrow and piercing. He sized me up with disdain while at the same time trying to portray himself as a hospitable host with a large welcoming smile on his face.

"As I live and breathe! Detective Jack Cucchiano!" he declared as though we had been good friends for years. He clasped my hand tightly and gave me a hearty handshake. "It's an absolute pleasure to meet you, dear boy!" He snapped his fingers impatiently. "Don't just stand there catching flies! Someone get this man a drink!" He then turned to me. "What's your poison, Jack?"

"Whiskey on the rocks," I replied with a slight uneasy grin.

"You look nervous, old boy!" said Walter with vague amusement. He placed an arm around my shoulder and walked towards his caddy. "There's nothing more stress-relieving than walloping golf balls around this beautiful green, especially with interesting company! I rarely ever have anybody interesting to talk to, which is a tiresome shame as I'm relentlessly bored out of my infernal mind!"

Rocco opened a large cooler, which contained different bottles of alcohol. He grabbed the whiskey and poured it into a glass filled with ice. He was sweating. His bald head glistened with beads of sweat in the red glow of the twilight sun.

"You sure know how to relax," I complimented Walter as I took the chilled whiskey from Rocco.

Walter nodded and swung his club. It was either my imagination or Walter put more power than he needed in that swing. He grunted as he swung, and the ball went flying with a loud *smack*. Thoughts that Walter was imagining he was knocking my teeth out with that club pervaded my mind.

I took a club and placed a ball down in front of me. I swung at the ball and laughed with embarrassment when my club sailed over the ball, missing it entirely.

"Swing from the shoulders," advised Walter with a chuckle.

I swung again and the ball skipped a few yards diagonally away from us.

"Never played golf before?" asked Walter, patting my shoulder with mock sympathy. "Let an old man show you how it's done!" He took a swing and the ball sailed towards the green. "You don't have children do you, detective?" he asked in a more solemn tone.

At last! I thought to myself with an involuntary grin. We were getting down to business. I drank my whiskey and gestured for Rocco to take my glass. "There's enough shit in life to deal with without the need to add parcels full of it too."

Walter didn't find my joke funny. "Then you could never understand the love a parent has for their child," he exclaimed with a twitch of his salt and pepper colored moustache. "A parent's love for their child is an unspeakable bond, which can never be broken! I don't like my son, I find him insufferable most of the time, so your dislike for him is mutually shared! However, he is still my son and I love him more than anything in this world!"

"You have my condolences," I remarked dryly. I then continued: "Can we just skip the song and dance, Mr Sullivan? I know you brought me here for a reason, so quit beating about the bush."

"I was getting there! But very well then!" His eyes narrowed and his tone became more forceful. "I want you to cease your investigation into my son! He's an idiot and he's made some terrible mistakes, but as I say, he's my son and I love him! Can't put a price on love, detective." He reached into his pocket and produced a check book and a fountain pen. He quickly scribbled into one of the pages and ripped it out, offering it to me with an outstretched hand.

I took the check and laughed aloud when I looked at it. "It's empty!" I observed with some confusion. Walter Sullivan's signature was the only thing he had written.

Walter chuckled again. "Of course it is, dear boy! I want you to use your imagination! Write any figure of your liking and I shall pay it! Please don't be modest, I am a very wealthy man!"

I shrugged my shoulders and reached for the pen still in Walter's hand. He handed it to me with a triumphant smile.

"I knew you'd listen to reason in the end!" he cooed with a satisfied smile. "Investigation weighed up against a nice early retirement is a no brainer! Wouldn't you say so, old chap?"

"Absolutely!" I agreed as I scribbled my price along the dotted line. "Here you are." I handed the check back to him and watched in absolute delight as the smile disappeared from his face and his cheeks flushed red with fury.

"What the fuck is this?!" he demanded angrily. He screwed the check up and threw it in my face. I had written one word: "JUSTICE".

"Those girls your son murdered! I will seek retribution for their deaths! No amount of fucking money is more rewarding than that! I'll never cease my investigation and this little offer you made me only reaffirms my suspicions that your son is responsible for what has happened!"

Walter's eye twitched and he gritted his teeth so hard that I thought that they would shatter like glass. Then he regained his composure and held out a hand to signal his goons, who had started advancing on me, to stop in their tracks.

"Do what you must!" I told him defiantly. "I'd rather die with dignity than sell out for fucking money!"

"A very disappointing decision, Jack..." Walter shook his head with a heavy sigh. "But you're free to leave now."

I was stunned. I looked around uncertainly at the statuesque faces of Walter's goons. "Is that it?" I asked in disbelief.

"That's it," replied Walter. "Did you think we'd murder you, Jack?" He chuckled and wiped a tear from his eye. "I'm a businessman, not a gangster. You're free to leave, but I suggest you do it immediately before I change my mind."

I wasted no time. I left the golf course as quickly as I could with my heart thudding in my chest like a jackhammer. I glanced behind me as I walked away to see Walter watching me with his goons forming a semi-circle around him.

It was starting to get dark now and I was stranded in Beverly Hills with very little money and a dead phone battery. I jumped on a bus and leaned my head against the window. The day's events were troubling me deeply. Walter had just tried to buy me to protect his son! Did this mean that his son was definitively guilty? Or was Walter simply being cautious? In any case I had to be careful. There was no telling who else Walter had got to with his seemingly infinite wealth.

I contemplated my next move and drifted into an uneasy and dreamless sleep!

"Hey! Wake the hell up buddy!"

My eyes struggled to open and I looked the bus driver up and down groggily. "Where the fuck am I?" I asked looking out of the window. It was dark outside. Trees lined both sides of the road. The light from the bus made it very difficult to see them in the darkness outside.

"End of the line, buddy!"

"Where are we?" I asked again, utterly perplexed that a bus would terminate in the middle of nowhere!

The bus driver lost his patience. "Get the fuck off of the bus!"

I huffed and cast him a venomous look before I clambered from the bus and into the cold darkness. The front of the bus displayed "Out of Service" and tore away as soon as the doors hissed closed behind me.

The road stretched for miles in both directions. I scratched my head and tried to figure out where I was. I concluded that the bus must have come from the direction of the city and so that's the way I would walk. A sudden uneasiness come over me and I could hear rustling in the trees at either side of the road. I tried to peer into the foliage to see what was making the noise and as my eyes adjusted to the darkness. I could make out the silhouettes of people standing and watching me from the darkness. At first, I was convinced that Walter's goons had highjacked the bus and brought me out here to kill me, but the silhouettes belonged to women...

I heard someone call my name and I spun around to see Mary O'Reilly standing at the side of the road with a jagged red line across her throat where she had been decapitated. She shimmered and disappeared right before my eyes.

Headlights appeared heading towards me and I frantically waved the car to a halt. The driver looked startled, but he stopped.

"Thank fuck!" I gasped as I dived in the passenger seat. "Are you heading to the city?"

The man, a young man with a slight accent which I couldn't place regarded me with shock. "Yes, of course! Is someone chasing you? You look flustered!"

"I don't know!" I answered as I clipped my seatbelt fastened. He pulled away and I told him where he could drop me off and he nodded eagerly. When I told him about how I ended up on a deserted road in the middle of the woods he looked astounded.

"No buses come through here, this is a drive I do almost every night," he said. I started to have a mild panic attack. My breathing became erratic and hard to control. "Here!" he said, handing me a bottle of water. "This should help calm you down."

I guzzled the water in a few gulps and the friendly Samaritan smiled.

"Must've been thirsty," he remarked, stating an obvious fact.

I grunted with disinterest. Then I sighed impatiently. How far away was the fucking city?! "How long until we reach the city?" I inquired with a yawn.

"Oh, I'm not taking you to the city," he jovially replied with a large smile. He pressed the accelerator and his red Octavia shot forward. The trees started to become a blur on either side of the road and my head began to feel strange.

"I don't feel so good..." I complained as I clutched my stomach.

"Don't worry," said the man. "That's just the sedative starting to kick in. You did drink the whole thing in onnnnne gooooooooo." His voice slowed down and his head seemed to spin around when he turned to face me with a twisted grin on his face.

"Whaaaat arrre the chanceSSssS!" he laughed maniacally. I tried to grab him, but my arms felt too heavy and he easily batted them away like a cat swatting a mouse. "Piiiiiiiiiiickinnnnng upppp thhe maaaaan trrrying to caaaatch meeeeeeee!"

My eyes rolled back as I heard his voice drone in slow motion, and he told me that he was the Artist Killer...

CHAPTER 13

Play Date

I woke up in my apartment drenched in sweat. I frantically looked around and then gave a massive sigh of relief! The woods. The man in the red Octavia. It was all just a fucking hallucination! The encounter with Walter Sullivan had been real though, unfortunately. I couldn't help but worry about what his next move would be. I recounted my steps from the night before and I could remember taking the bus straight home after the encounter at the Country Club.

I checked my phone and raised my eyebrows at the name which stared back at me. "One new message from Olivia Lockhart". It was a pleasant surprise. I had not spoken to Olivia properly for a long time and truth be told I had really started to miss her company.

I clicked the notification with one eye closed. I was still half-asleep and straining to see with the blue light of my phone in the darkness of my bedroom. The message read:

"Jack, this is Olivia. We really need to talk it's urgent!"

I was curious so I called her, and we agreed to meet at a local coffee shop which we both knew and liked. It was a place we used to go to together often. The Toast Office was its name. I arrived fifteen minutes early and I was surprised to see that Olivia was already there.

A broad smile spread across her lips when she saw me, and she eagerly waved me over. "It's so good to see you, Jack!" she said, lightly embracing me and planting a soft kiss on my cheek.

"Shall I order us some food?" I asked with a smile. I didn't have much money, but Olivia was an old colleague and a trusted friend.

Olivia accepted my offer and ordered some poached eggs on toast with tomatoes and mushrooms. She meekly thanked me, but she barely touched any of her food. I ordered myself a full fry up, shovelling it down eagerly as though it would be my last meal.

"I remember when we used to come here all the time," said Olivia with wistful melancholy. "Life sort of just dragged us apart from one another."

I paused, eating for a second and reached across the table, placing my hand on hers. "We've had some disagreements," I replied softly, giving her hand a reassuring squeeze. "But we will *always* be friends, Olivia."

She smiled at that and thanked me for my kindness. "I'm afraid I didn't just invite you here for breakfast."

My curiosity piqued. "Oh?"

"After the interrogation following the disappearance of Crystal Hayes, I followed the guy with the horn-rimmed glasses by car and he went to a warehouse at the docks. Think maybe he owns it or something."

I nodded in agreement and stroked my stubble in deep contemplation. "The strand of rope that Grim found on Emma Fontaine's body!" I declared with a sudden realization. "Of course! The fucking docks!" I hastily dabbed up the rest of my beans with my slice of toast and frantically fumbled in my pockets for some cash to pay for the bill.

"Let me help pay for the bill!" offered Olivia as she pulled out her purse and handed me ten dollars.

I waved it away and insisted that I would pay. As far as I was concerned there was no time to lose. Once the bill was paid, I took Olivia by the hand and rushed her outside to her SUV.

"You drive!" I insisted, diving into the passenger seat. "We're going to investigate that warehouse right now!"

Olivia hesitated for a second, then nodded her head determinedly and scrambled into the driver's seat.

She was in plain clothes, a white button-up shirt with blue jeans and white sneakers. She put her foot down and the heavens opened up on route. The rain bounced from her car like bullets and we both laughed at how close we'd been to getting caught in it.

I must have dosed off during the drive to the seafront because Olivia woke me up upon arrival.

"We're here," she said, gently shaking me awake.

I looked around. We were parked between two rows of old warehouses where thick coils of rope lay scattered around and wooden crates were stacked precariously all around with an abandoned forklift nearby.

The rain still poured torrentially, and the rumble of thunder could be heard in the distance, reminding me of my stomach most evenings.

Olivia unclipped her seatbelt and retrieved her gun from the glove box. "Can never be too careful," she said, tucking it into her jeans.

"Lucky you don't have a pair of nuts, Olivia," I told her with a chuckle. "Could end up blowing them off."

She laughed as we got out of the car into the rain, but she said nothing.

"I don't have my gun with me," I told her, looking around nervously. I stepped into a puddle and cursed when my converse was flooded with water.

"Don't worry about it," she reassured me, instinctively reaching towards the handle of her handgun protruding from her pants. "This is the warehouse." She would then add once we had turned a corner and seen the warehouse she had spoken of: "This is where horn-rimmed glasses came after he was released."

I gave her a hearty pat on the back. "Look at us!" I said dreamily. "Working together, just like the good old days!"

Olivia said nothing but offered a wan smile. Tendrils of her wet hair fell across her face and I tenderly brushed them aside. She pulled her head away and insisted that we focus on the investigation. She had misunderstood my intention. I had simply wanted to show some affection towards a valued friend. She must have thought that I had other ideas...

I dismissed it and followed her into an open door situated at the side of the dilapidated building. Olivia drew her firearm and ushered me to take the lead. I silently nodded and lead the way. I walked through a labyrinth of metal containers until I came into a large open loading area.

"Why on Earth would Larry Gyllenhaal come–?" I abruptly stopped when I heard a click behind me. It was a sound which I knew well. The sound of the hammer of a gun being pulled back. Olivia's gun.

"Don't move, Jack!" she yelled. Her voice was stern and cold, like she was talking to a complete stranger as opposed to someone who was supposed to be a close friend and a colleague.

"Olivia…" I began but could find no words for her. I was hurt and confused. Why the fuck would my best friend lure me here and get the drop on me?

Above us was the manager's office with a metal catwalk which lead around the warehouse. It was there where my eyes were inexplicably drawn when the sound of slow applause filled the cavernous room.

"Bravo!" said a familiar voice with smug satisfaction. "I dare say that you have certainly earned your paycheck, miss Lockhart!" Walter Sullivan was standing there with a malicious grin on his face. He was wearing a navy-blue suit and a black tie. Surrounding him were his goons, including Rocco, clad in black suits and sporting sunglasses. "An absolutely wonderful display of skill on your part!" He continued. "I must admit, I was convinced you'd crumble at the last minute or fail to convince our good friend detective Cucchiano to attend our little play date."

Bitter tears stung my eyes and my soul burned with an ambivalent mixture of intense hatred and the numbness which Olivia's betrayal had brought about. "Why?!" I demanded from her, without turning my head. I couldn't even look at her.

"He offered me too much money, Jack. My mother is sick and the money he gave me will help pay for the treatment she needs…" I could hear the pain in her voice. I could tell from the way her voice trembled that she was upset about what she had done. But it was too late! I would consider her a friend no longer! She was just another enemy now!

I didn't respond to her. Instead, I wrinkled my nose in disgust and spat at the floor.

"It is touching..." said a new voice with mock empathy. The voice was another familiar voice with a southern drawl which I recognized as the voice of disgraced sheriff Hershel Murray. "Remember me, you son of a bitch?!" he asked, stepping into my field of view beside Walter Sullivan.

"You were given a very fair opportunity to cease your investigation into my son, Mr Cucchiano!" interjected Walter impatiently. "You foolishly chose to pursue this fruitless endeavor out of what?! Out of pride? To regain some sort of meaning or purpose?" He shook his head and feigned a sigh and then he looked at me contemptuously and nodded to Olivia. "You're free to go, miss Lockhart. We'll take it from here."

Olivia cleared her throat. "And what's going to happen to Jack?" she asked timidly. "You promised you wouldn't hurt him!"

"That is no longer your concern," replied Walter with a dismissive wave of his hand, as though he were swatting at an annoying fly. "You shall receive your check tomorrow, once Mr Cucchiano has been dealt with. Now go!"

"NO!" screamed Olivia back at him. She moved to my side and adjusted her aim so she was aiming at Walter Sullivan. Her legs were spread to steady herself and she held her gun aiming up at the catwalk, holding it with both hands. "You're a fucking liar! You promised you wouldn't hurt Jack!"

Walter seemed unperturbed by the fact that Olivia was aiming her weapon at him. He gave her a bemused glance and massaged his temples. "I'm a man of my word," he said with a sigh. Then a wolfish grin spread across his face "That's why I brought someone else to take care of Mr Cucchiano!"

Olivia gritted her teeth, her arms trembled slightly and then I watched as Olivia's finger tightened on the trigger. Everything happened in a heartbeat. There was a deafening bang and a blinding flash of light and my face was sprayed with blood.

Hershel spun his colt python around his index finger before

slamming it in its holster with smoke still emanating from the barrel.

I turned my head in disbelief and there was Olivia slumped against a container with a huge hole in her stomach. Blood oozed from the wound and drenched her white shirt claret. Her eyes darted around the room wildly as she struggled for breath.

"NOOOOOO!" I found myself screaming in anguish. I dived by her side and tried to apply pressure to the wound as much as I could. "Hold on! Oh fucking God!" She tried to speak but started to convulse as her body went into shock. "It's okay!" I hushed as I stroked her cheek with my blood covered hand, leaving a red mark. "I forgive you! You were tricked! I forgive you!" And with that she gave a final sigh and she was gone.

"What the hell was that?!" demanded Walter furiously. "We need to get out of here in case someone heard that!"

Hershel shrugged his shoulders impassively. "Fuck her! She was going to shoot you, Walt. I had to put her down."

I held Olivia's head against mine and kissed her forehead. Then I gently rested her head back against the container and closed her eyes for her, so she looked more peaceful. I shot a venomous glance at the men standing above me. "You're all going to fucking die today!" I screamed with spittle flying from my mouth like I was a dog with rabies.

Walter shook his head regretfully. "That's not going to happen, Jack," he replied. "I'm truly sorry for what just happened to that girl. If it's any consolation though, old boy, you're about to be reunited!"

Hershel drew his colt python again and aimed it right at me. "Let's just shoot him and be done with it!" he exclaimed in a complaining tone. He looked astonished when Walter placed his hand on top of the revolver and gently pushed it down.

"No," said Walter with a psychotic twinkle in his eye. He turned his focus back to me and explained: "Money is truly a remarkable thing, Mr Cucchiano. When you are successful enough, you can achieve anything." He paced back and forth in front of his allies as he spoke. All eyes were on him. "Think of cutting-edge medical technology!"

Rocco grabbed something out of his pocket and pressed a button so that a huge shutter in front of me slowly began to open. His mouth was a thin line and it was difficult to tell what he was thinking because of his sunglasses.

"Money could've brought your friend's mother back from the brink of death! Money can pay for top surgeons to perform anonymous operations to make sure that broken bones can be replaced with metal rods and plates," continued Walter. "I know you must be confused, but it was money that inexorably brought you into my clutches, Mr Cucchiano. It was through money that I was able to arrange this little play date for you. Courtesy of our mutual friend sheriff Hershel Murray, who was reinstated as county sheriff because of money."

There was a sudden noise that caught my attention and set my heart off racing. It sounded like a motorbike revving at first, but then it turned into a steady rumble. Anger subsided and gave way to fear as I watched a huge figure shamble awkwardly through the darkness of the adjacent room.

"It was money that I paid surgeons to fix this man's leg so he could provide us with some entertainment this fine day! It was money that I paid Hershel Murray to bring him here," said Walter with a grin revealing all his teeth. "Thanks to your friend's outburst and Hershel's desire to be a gunslinger we won't be able to stick around and watch this reunion. Die well, Jack Cucchiano! Your investigation ends here!"

Walter snapped his fingers and then his men escorted him across the catwalk towards a fire escape at the side of the building where I assumed their motors had been hidden. Hershel lingered momentarily and tipped his hat with a smile when I made eye contact with him. Then he followed Walter through the fire escape, disappearing into the rain.

Heavy footsteps lumbered towards me and the Butcher stepped into the light with a chainsaw held in one hand and a blood-covered severed head in the other. He paused and tossed the head at me and it hit the floor with a wet slapping sound before it rolled to a stop at my feet. The dead eyes of Mike Vance stared up at me sightlessly, a look of horror permanently frozen on his face that provided some insight into his last horrible moments alive.

The Butcher was slower than before. One of his legs was stiff and he couldn't bend it properly. He held up his chainsaw and calmly walked towards me.

I rushed over to Olivia's body, she was still holding her handgun and I thought maybe I could blow the Butcher's kneecap out. I skidded to a stop beside her body, frantically trying to pull the gun from her vice like grip.

"Come on! Don't do this to me!" I pleaded desperately.

The Butcher could see what I was trying to do, and he quickened his pace, brandishing his chainsaw above his head like a battle-axe.

I abandoned the gun and fled between the metal containers in search of the side door which Olivia had led me through. I slammed into it, knocking the wind out of myself. The door only opened enough so that I could see the rain bouncing from the floor outside. Thick chains held the door shut.

My enemies had sealed me inside!

I frantically looked around. Heavy footsteps grew nearer, and panic began to set in. Was this really how I was going to die? I could climb onto one of the containers! I reasoned that the Butcher wouldn't be able to follow me on account of his bad leg.

I scrambled up the front of one of the containers, climbing on the locks and then onto the top of the padlock before I hoisted myself on top and rolled onto my back. I waited until I could hear the Butcher looking for me below and I leaped from my hiding place like a trapdoor spider and wrapped my arms around the Butcher's muscular throat. He effortlessly grabbed my shirt and pulled me away, tossing me to the floor like I was some kind of toy. I rolled to the side as the Butcher brought his chainsaw down to the ground, sending sparks flying into the air.

I got to my feet and ran between two containers, hoping that I had not just trapped myself down a dead end. Behind me the Butcher grunted in pain as he forced himself to pick up pace and catch up to me.

I tripped and hit my head against the floor. My world became blurry and the sound of the Butcher's footsteps and his chainsaw sounded distant. I got to my feet and stumbled backwards into a wall, moving out of the way at the last moment so that the Butcher drove his chainsaw into a water mains pipe instead of into my gut. Water sprayed everywhere, leaving a huge puddle on the ground near where we were fighting.

The water sprayed the Butcher in the face, temporarily knocking him off balance and giving me ample time to escape.

I fled and found myself back to the open space where a forklift was on charge with a transformer and a thick cable running to the electricity mains. My eyes darted back to Olivia's body and I frantically searched her pockets for something sharp.

When the Butcher followed me into the open space he paused when he saw me on my knees beside the forklift. He chuckled to himself and revved his chainsaw while his heavy footsteps thundered towards me at a leisurely pace. His blue dungarees had turned black and his rigger boots left wet footprints in his wake. His hair had grown longer and was soaked.

When he was close enough, I produced a small flick knife and sawed the cable connected to the transformer. The Butcher hesitated for a second, not sure whether to lunge at me before I fashioned my weapon or turn and flee with his bad leg.

Sparks flew from the end of the cable, where severed wires were exposed. I held firmly onto the cable lower down, where the live wires were covered by an outer rubber casing to prevent electric shocks. I smiled menacingly and lunged forward, holding the cable out in front of me as though it were a venomous snake. The Butcher lunged to meet my challenge, driving his chainsaw forward. I evaded it and shoved the exposed wires into his chest, letting go immediately and diving to the side. There was a large jolt and the Butcher shook on the spot and dropped his chainsaw. He fell to his knees as a large puddle of urine grew around him and he collapsed.

This time I wasn't going to chance him coming back. I picked up his chainsaw and rammed it into his throat, ignoring the fountain of blood that sprayed into my face. He made a nauseating gargling sound and then the Butcher was dead.

I wiped my face on my sleeve and grimaced at the sight of my shirt. It was completely drenched with blood, both Olivia's and the Butcher's, but I wasn't finished yet. I was determined to seek retribution for my friend's murder. Walter Sullivan and Hershel Murray both had to die.

I ran back to Olivia's corpse and had to use my teeth to pry her stiff fingers open so that I could take her handgun. I also took the keys to her SUV and the Butcher's chainsaw.

I used the chainsaw to cut the chain around the handle of the door through which I had entered through. The door opened just enough for me to fit the blade of the chainsaw through and apply pressure to the chain. Sparks flew into my face, stinging my cheek as I turned my head away to protect my eyes. It didn't take long for the chain to snap and it slithered through the handle to the ground and I was able to escape from the warehouse.

I sprinted to Olivia's SUV, starting the engine as Hershel's Land Rover flew by shortly followed by Walter's black Rolls Royce. Walter looked at me with disbelief through his rear passenger window as he rolled it up and his horrified face vanished behind the tinted glass.

I sped after them and they started speeding up too, well aware that I was on their tail. Walters tires sprayed water back onto the windscreen of Olivia's SUV, limiting my visibility. Then Rocco put his foot down and separated the distance between them and myself, recklessly overtaking Hershel in his Land Rover.

At the end of the road lined with warehouses came a T junction where Walter and his goons took a sharp left towards the city of LA. Their tires screeched loudly. Hershel took a right and headed towards the interstate. Presumably he was attempting to head back to Texas.

I paused at the junction, wrestling inwardly over who I was going to chase down. I slammed my foot down and the rear tires of the SUV spun and I jolted out into the junction, receiving verbal abuse from motorists who I had almost crashed into as I tore around the corner to the right in pursuit of sheriff Hershel Murray. He was the one who pulled the trigger and killed Olivia. He was the one who I wanted to kill. Walter could wait.

I chased Hershel through the city. Rain continued to lash against my windshield. It obscured my view and made driving very difficult. Hershel erratically weaved in and out of traffic with total disregard for the safety of others. The corrupt sheriff was a menace, a feral dog that needed putting down.

He headed down route five towards San Diego and the road was pretty clear for late afternoon, which enabled me to gain ground on him. He quickly took for the exit, changing his route and deciding instead to take Las Pulgas Canyon Road in his desperate attempt to get back to Texas and shake me.

I caught up to him on Las Pulgas Canyon Road and I drove alongside his Land Rover on the wrong side of the road, driving with one hand and trying to maintain aim with Olivia's handgun. We made eye contact briefly before another car's headlights appeared in the distance shining through the gloom of the terrible weather. I had no choice but to brake and fall back behind Hershel. I cursed my bad luck and instead decided to ram him off the road.

I pressed my foot down to the floor and the SUV shot forward into the back of Hershel's Land Rover, temporarily giving him a short boost. I did it again and Hershel lost control of his vehicle, swerving across the wrong side of the road in front of another oncoming car which he narrowly avoided crashing into. He crashed into the side of a hill where dead shrubs protruded through the earth like tangled mats of hair.

I did a quick handbrake turn and drove back down the opposite side of the road back towards Hershel. I pulled off the road and slowed down until I could see his abandoned vehicle with the driver door hanging open and smoke rising from under the hood.

I slowed to a cautious crawl, edging closer and keeping a look out for the sheriff when suddenly he stepped out from behind a dead tree brandishing a double barrel shotgun.

"Suck my nuts!" he shouted opening fire.

There was a metallic *ping* and I hit the accelerator with the intention of crushing the bastard against the tree which he was now standing in front of. He opened fire again and this time the front windshield exploded into thousands of shards of glass with a deafening *crash*.

I instinctively ducked and the next thing I knew was that the SUV had crashed into the tree. I scrambled out of the passenger door as Hershel stepped into the driver side aiming his shotgun through the doorway.

"Mayhap let me put ya down now, boy!" he called after me. I watched underneath the SUV and could see his cowboy boots as he walked towards the rear of the SUV. Gravel and twigs crunched and snapped underneath his feet. "Walter Sullivan will probably silence the two of us anyway! Should have chased him while he was vulnerable!" he called out to me. "He'll have his place on lockdown now! Him and his son will be locked away tighter than an abstinent girl's pussy hole!" He paused and waited for me to respond, but I didn't say a word. I was waiting! I silently willed him to take a few more steps towards me.

"Come on!" he urged me with a trace of mockery in his voice. "Let me reunite you with your whore of a friend!" He laughed aloud, his beer belly jingling up and down. "I know you're hiding around there! You think I'm dumb enough to walk towards the back of the SUV so you can jump out on me? Fuck you!"

He knew where I was hiding. Olivia's handgun had fallen onto the passenger side floor of the SUV and to try and retrieve it would mean that Hershel could stick his shotgun through the driver side window and blow my brains out.

"Hershel! I surrender! I'm coming out! Don't shoot!" I called out despondently. I was utterly defeated... Or so he thought.

I stepped out from behind the SUV with my hands behind my head. Hershel looked me up and down as though I were the most disgusting thing that he'd ever clapped eyes on. His look turned into a triumphant smile when he raised his shotgun and prepared to fire.

What he didn't know was that in my hand was a fist full of gravel and dirt which I had scooped up while I was crouched behind the SUV and I quickly tossed it into his eyes. He screamed and blindly opened fire, missing me barely and taking all the paintwork off the side of Olivia's vehicle. I grabbed the end of his shotgun and lifted it into the air. We wrestled with it for a while, pulling it back and forth until I drove my shin into his thigh, causing his leg to give way and he collapsed onto one knee.

I gained the upper hand and twisted the shotgun out of his grip, driving the butt of the gun into the bridge of his nose. It exploded and sent him rolling down the hill towards the road.

I flicked the barrel open and cursed when I could see that there weren't even any shells loaded into it. I discarded it and dived down the hill after Hershel, punching him in the face and causing him to drop his colt python which skidded in the dirt. He grabbed the nape of my neck and drove his knee into my stomach. The wind was knocked out of me and I collapsed to the floor gasping for air.

Hershel made a dash for his colt python and I grabbed his boot, tripping him over. From there we crawled over each other in a desperate bid to reach the gun first. Hershel grabbed it and I grabbed his hair and sank my teeth into his throat. He screamed and shook me loose, tossing me to the ground.

He got to his feet and raised his colt python breathing heavily through a blood-encrusted broken nose and I drove my foot into his stomach. He bent low, gasping for air, and I scrambled to my feet and gave him an uppercut in the chin, which knocked him onto his back. Then I stamped on his wrist and his fingers uncurled from around the grip of the revolver and I kicked it away. Then I sharply kicked him in the face, and he fell back into the dirt with his eyes closed. He was still conscious, but barely.

I picked up the colt python and stood over him with the barrel pointed directly between his eyes.

He opened his eyes and forced out a laugh. "You're too fucking honest!" he told me with a mouth full of blood. "You don't have the fucking gu–". He was abruptly cut off when my finger squeezed the trigger and the top left section of his head completely disappeared in the blink of an eye. His left eye and half of his head had been reduced to a mushy pink mess which had spread up the hill.

CHAPTER 14

Probable Cause

My vision became blurry with tears. My wrath had been satiated with sweet revenge. All that was left now was sorrow and a deep emptiness within. It would have been so easy to turn that gun on myself and just die with Olivia.

I stared at Hershel's corpse for what seemed like a very long time until his colt python dropped out of my limp hand and hit the floor with a thud.

I heard footsteps behind me, but I knew that they weren't real. Olivia stood by my side and looked down at the corpse of the sheriff with a sad expression on her face.

"I know this isn't how we're supposed to do things," I sobbed, wiping my eyes with my blood-soaked sleeve. "I knew if I let him get back to Texas, I'd never see him again! I couldn't just let him get away after what he did to you." I reached out to touch her and my hand passed right through her. I fell to my knees and sobbed like a child.

Once I had wept, I sprang into action and dragged Hershel's corpse behind a small dune to prevent anybody from happening to spot his body as they drove by. I didn't want this bastard to have a proper funeral. I wanted his body to become carrion for crows and food for wild coyotes or some other beasts. I didn't give a fuck what happened to him as long as it wasn't a decent burial. He didn't deserve that!

Afterwards I climbed back into Olivia's SUV and drove back to the city of LA. I don't even remember half of the drive. I looked around at the houses of LA and wondered how the fuck I'd managed to even get there when I sort of phased out for the best part of the drive.

Once I entered the city, I became paranoid that I would be pulled over by the police. I was still sodden with blood, which had begun to dry and turn my shirt into a dark brown color. My shirt also felt like cardboard the more it dried. Explaining this to a police officer would be very fucking difficult.

I strategized in my head. I decided that declaring my presence at the warehouse bloodbath would be a grave error that would prove to be my undoing. I also decided that the police could no longer be trusted. If Walter could turn Olivia against me then there was no telling who else would be overcome with his promises of wealth.

I parked the SUV a few blocks from my apartment building down a back alleyway situated behind a row of shops. It was getting dark now and most of the shops had drawn their shutters, meaning that it would be unlikely that I would be disturbed.

I waited there until the early hours of the morning and then took to the backstreets and alleyways as much as possible to avoid bumping into someone, like a police officer, who would surely want to know why there was a man running around just after midnight soaked in blood.

I got back to my apartment amazingly without being seen. I got undressed, threw my clothes in the sink and jumped straight in the bath. I washed all of the blood out of my hair and from my skin, scrubbing furiously because it seemed as though all of the blood had dyed my skin a red tinge.

Once I was washed, I changed into a black sweater and some black jeans. I tossed my blood-soaked clothes and converse into a bag and swiftly headed back out to the streets, making my way to the alleyway where the SUV was parked behind the shops.

I drove the SUV to the forests near LA and set it ablaze with my blood-soaked clothes inside. I stood and watched the flames engulf the vehicle and its contents, completely mesmerized by the flames and the way they seemed to dance around. It was beautiful, but the smell of burning paintwork turned my stomach and sent up thick plumes of black smoke, which was bound to attract unwanted attention.

After that I called the police anonymously from a phone booth, claiming in a panicked voice that I'd heard gunshots from the warehouse at the docks. Gunshots and screaming. I gave the address to the lady on the phone, but once prompted to give my name I hung up and left as quickly as possible.

*

Olivia Lockhart's funeral was held a week later after an inquest into her death was made. Matthew Perry swore in the name of God in front of the whole LAPD that he would find the man who shot his trusted friend and colleague and bring down the heavy boot of the law upon his throat.

It was frustrating for me, knowing who was responsible for her death, but not being able to say anything. I kept to myself at the funeral, thinking back to all the good times I'd had with Olivia. She was like a younger sister to me and now I was putting her in the ground.

Matthew Perry made a touching speech at her funeral. His voice trembled as he spoke, and his eyes welled with tears like rivers threatening to burst their banks. I was silent during the whole funeral. I helped to carry the coffin and lower Olivia into the ground and the priest said a prayer for her while we all stood respectfully silent.

"Something just doesn't add up!" said Perry with a scowl once he had lit up a cigarette in the car park after the service.

"No," uttered Grim in agreement.

"What do you mean?" I ventured, trying to seem confused. I really didn't want these guys to know that I had been there.

"Well..." sighed Grim as he inhaled cigarette smoke deeply and looked at me with his beady eyes. "Olivia's time of death and the anonymous phone call we had were hours apart. And the phone booth used to make the call was on the other side of town."

"You must have seen her before she died, Jack!" retorted Perry with a raised eyebrow. "We checked her phone and the last person she contacted was you, saying that she had to speak urgently with you. Care to share what the two of you talked about, Jack?"

My heart started racing and I could feel my cheeks burning as they flushed red. I raised my hand to my mouth to take a drag of my cigarette and realized my hand was shaking. I tried to sound as natural as possible with my response, but I cursed myself inwardly for neglecting the fundamental fact that I was the last person who Olivia was known to have contact with.

"She wanted to talk about the case," I told them, my gaze shifting between Grim and Perry. "She had been investigating Chad and Walter Sullivan. She told me that Walter had offered her money to cease her investigation. If we look into her financial records we should be able to determine whether a large payment was made into her bank account, and if so, whether that money was paid into her account by Walter Sullivan. If the answer is yes, then I'd say it's a safe assumption to make that Walter had Olivia killed."

Perry's expression became more relaxed. He had some of his cigarette and tossed the butt on the floor, scraping his shoe over it.

"I say it's time!" I declared, taking a step towards them. "Let us gather a group of like-minded individuals and do a raid on the Sullivan mansion! We can plant cocaine to justify our presence there!"

Perry shook his head vigorously. As I'd expected, he was too much of a stickler for the rules to even consider such a prospect. If we raided the Sullivan mansion, I suspected that Walter and his goons would fight back and there would be our justification to shoot all of them, which is what I wanted. Sometimes justice had to be taken into our own hands.

Grim had a look of contemplation on his face. "I like the idea," he added with a shrug. Like Perry and myself, he had known Olivia since she had first started on the force as a beat cop. Even though Grim rarely ever showed any emotion, it was abundantly clear how much respect he had for Olivia.

"This isn't the wild west!" snapped Perry with a belittling snigger. "That's not how justice works! We do this properly by finding evidence and taking them through the courts!" Perry was determined. He gave Grim and me a look of concern before he added: "Don't get any ideas about revenge! Any act of vengeance taken outside of the law will be treated as any other felony," he warned us ominously. "Act within the constraints of the law or find yourself inside of a jail cell! It's that simple!" And with that he got into his car, ignoring my protests as he drove away. He knew as well as I did that no judge would ever convict Walter Sullivan. The man would just bribe his way out of it. If Perry wanted evidence, then I'd fucking find some.

*

I rented an Astra and drove to the Encino neighborhood in the San Fernando Valley region of LA, which was the area where Chad Sullivan lived and where Annabelle Green had lived before she was found dead in the reeds by the lake. I parked across the road from Chad's house, watching for activity within the house.

If my hunch was right, then Chad would have been whisked away by his over-protective father and taken to his mansion in Beverly Hills. The mansion was surrounded by a fence and protected by Rottweiler dogs, so it was exceedingly difficult, if not impossible, to break in or launch an assault without help.

After a couple of hours, I got out of the rental vehicle and stood in front of the property which Walter had purchased for his unruly son to live in. I smoked a full cigarette while I leaned against the Astra, formulating a strategy in my mind. This investigation had become a mental game of chess and it was now my move!

I looked around and after a little while a rusted Chevrolet Malibu pulled to a stop and Nicolas Brown wound his window down, squinting at me in the sunlight. He was still wearing his green Parker coat, even though it was a gloriously sunny day.

"You're late!" I remarked with a scowl. "We need to act fast. You know the deal, right?"

Nicolas nodded with a sour look on his face. "A share of the reward money offered by Annabelle's parents," he recited the terms of our agreement, previously arranged shortly after Olivia's funeral. He spoke the words as though they made his mouth taste like turd. "You drive a hard bargain, Jack! But fair enough! I like the plan. Let's do this!"

We walked around the back through a fancy cast-iron gate surrounded by an archway of rosebushes. Out back was a huge back garden with a large patio area and a barbeque. Next to the patio was a swimming pool with crystal blue water shimmering in the sunlight with a Jacuzzi hot tub installed beside it. Empty beer bottles littered the patio and stood in small clusters around the hot tub.

We walked to the back door and Nicolas reached into his parker coat pocket, producing two thin pieces of metal which he jammed into the lock and juggled about until the door gave a satisfying click and swung open.

"Thanks, Nick," I said, giving him an approving glare and a fond pat on the shoulder. "Help me look for any clues that we can use to convict Chad. Any judge presented with compelling evidence will have no choice but to convict him even if tempted with a bribe."

Nicolas nodded in agreement but said nothing. He was keen to get to work and gather the reward money. He had previously told me that he didn't care for the hustle and bustle of such a busy city. He wanted to get this case over with so that he could retire to a quainter area and to be honest who could fault him?

We entered the house into a large open kitchen with marble work surfaces and mahogany cupboards. There was a large oak dining table with a red cloth draped over it. The kitchen was cluttered with mess. An open archway led into a living room with top-of-the-range leather sofas and a large stuffed bear in one corner, which made Nicolas yelp with alarm, much to my amusement.

"I've always found taxidermy to be the most distasteful form of art, if it can even be considered as art," grumbled Nicolas as he observed the bear and looked around at various other creatures mounted on the walls as trophies.

"Probably from his father's hunting trips," I said, passing a glance over the room. There were wolf heads and the heads of magnificent stags planted upon the wall.

"I'll search upstairs," I told Nicolas. "You search the ground floor."

Nicolas nodded in agreement, turning his attention to a side table which had a letter and a small card sat on top of an open envelope. "What's this?" he murmured with curiosity. "Jack, come look at this!" he added once he'd picked it up with a gloved hand. His eyes grew wider as he read through the letter.

I walked over to him and had a look. The small card was his invitation to the fashion gala and the letter read as follows:

"Chad, now is the time to make our move. Everything has been prepared for the game. You know what you have to do. I promise we will meet soon. Sincerely:

Your tutor."

"This is some pretty concrete evidence," said Nicolas with a satisfied glare in his eyes.

I shook my head in disagreement. "It's too vague," I grumbled with discontent. "It may work well alongside something more concrete! Keep searching, I'll go investigate upstairs."

I made my way into the hallway where a grandfather clock ticked away monotonously. The sound of it already started to drive me crazy within the time it took me to ascend a couple of stairs.

There were no framed pictures in the hallway, which I considered to be odd. It seemed to me that Chad must not have even been here that often.

I searched his bathroom. Nothing was out of the ordinary. His medicine cabinet was full of grooming products and a jar of prescribed methadone. I closed the cupboard and continued into the bedroom.

The bedroom was a mess. Clothes lay scattered around in disorganized piles and the bedsheets looked stained and dirty. A vague smell of sweat hung in the air.

Newspaper clippings covered a cork board. All of them were segments from articles which contained information regarding different serial killers who have operated in the city of LA. Unsurprisingly, most of these clippings were articles about the Artist Killer, the latest psychopath to terrorize the streets of LA.

I took a photo of the cork board and then moved over to a chest of drawers. The first drawer contained mundane items, which were of no interest. The second drawer contained a leather-bound scrapbook tied by string. I unwrapped the string and opened the cover to find notes to do with his case. There were letters from his attorney Moe the Jew and various threatening letters and a letter from Annabelle Green's parents. On the end was a small envelope which I took and opened.

"That settles it..." I grumbled as I squeezed the essential piece of evidence in my hand. "Chad Sullivan is the Artist Killer!"

In my hand was an unstamped train ticket from Chad's local train station to an air force base near New York. Chad never took the trip, which meant that my deductions were correct, and Walter had bribed a few people to make false alibi statements that Chad had attended training the day Annabelle was killed.

If that weren't enough, there were several Polaroid photographs of Annabelle Green playing in her garden or skipping in the streets. Most of the shots looked as though Chad had been hidden behind shrubs so as not to be seen. The bastard stalked her out!

I took the scrapbook and headed back downstairs to Nicolas. I showed him my findings and his eyes lit up. We both promptly headed to the back door, where we had entered.

Nicolas left the latch off and closed the door behind us as we left. Then he took out his handgun and smashed the window with the grip before opening the door again with a gloved hand so as not to leave fingerprints.

I called Matthew Perry and executed the final stages of my plan. Everything else would fall into place.

Chad was hiding at his father's mansion when the police took him in front of several different news teams which had arrived once word had spread that several riot vans had appeared outside the Sullivan mansion at early hours of the morning. There was a momentary standoff where Walter outright refused to have his son taken into custody.

"I will not have my son paraded in front of the media like a confounded animal!" he roared from his bedroom balcony, clad only in a purple dressing gown and slippers. "Some false evidence arises, and the police and media become a lynch mob!"

I stood beside Perry with a satisfied smile on my face. He was clad in full riot gear, fearlessly barking orders at Walter Sullivan like a Roman general on the front lines of an impending siege.

I yearned for blood. I was calm on the surface, but underneath raged a violent storm of hatred and a lust for vengeance. I wanted all of them to die for the part which they played in Olivia's death and the cover up of Annabelle's murder.

Much to my disappointment, Chad surrendered himself to the police before Perry could order snipers to execute several of Walter's goons. Walter barked at his son like a ravenous dog as Chad walked down the winding path lined with fancy cut hedge plants.

Chad was violently slammed onto the bumper of a police car with a satisfying thud. He squirmed uncomfortably when the officer pinned his arm behind his back and applied pressure. He made eye contact with me for a second and I revelled in his fury. That tear-filled expression of hatred forced a grin across my face.

Chad was read his Miranda Rights and shoved into the back of a police car. Walter marched down the path towards his cast-iron gates, which had closed electronically behind Chad. He was furious.

"You have my son! Now get the hell away from my property!" demanded Walter. He took a double glance when he happened to spot me standing beside Perry next to a riot van. "Matthew Perry and Jack Cucchiano! I'll have your badges! I'll have you both imprisoned for harassment and the perversion of justice! I run this fucking city!"

His outburst was mainly aimed at me. I'm sure that there was a subtle threat against my life hidden in there, but it didn't matter. I had already won.

"There is one more matter to settle before we leave," exclaimed Perry dryly. "Your Rolls Royce will have to be taken into police custody to be thoroughly examined by a forensic team!"

"So I am to be tarred with the same brush as my son? This is clearly an attempt to frame us and tarnish our family name with these insidious accusations! It is repugnant that the police force would resort to such an unnecessary measure to aid an alcoholic schizophrenic's delusion!"

Perry sighed. "We checked the financial records of those who provided an alibi for your son. They all received a substantial payment from an offshore bank account while Chad was on trial for murder. I can't prove it was you, Walter, but I know you made those payments. I know your Rolls Royce left that partial tire print at the reservoir where Annabelle was found. You're an accessory to murder! And you're coming with us downtown! You can either come willingly or we'll enter your property and drag you out!"

Walter looked shocked but nodded his head reluctantly. When he looked up at me and Perry, he had the grin of great white shark. "I shall surrender willingly. My team shall stand down." He raised his hands and continued to grin.

He knew what I knew! No judge would ever convict him! He

would just bribe, blackmail or threaten his way out of a conviction. He looked at me as he began taking steps towards the gates. His look seemed to say: "*I know what you were trying to do, and you failed! Next is my move, Cucchiano!*"

But he was wrong. I'd already anticipated a peaceful surrender scenario and I'd taken steps to ensure my victory was absolute. My grin spread to match Walter's and his face dropped in confusion.

A subtle whistle was audible as something sailed overhead the crowd of armed officers and Walter staggered backwards with an audible thud. He looked down in shock at the crimson circle that spread wider across his velvet dressing gown. He staggered backwards with his arms outstretched and landed in his pool with a *splash*. Plumes of blood rose to the surface, followed by the corpse of Walter Sullivan bobbing up and down on the surface like the turd that he was!

"Who the fuck fired that shot?!" screamed Perry into his walkie talkie with absolute fury. He cast me a suspicious glare and picked up his microphone to address Walter's goons and they all surrendered their weapons.

Justice had been served to a satisfactory level. Walter died for the part he played in Olivia's death and, with his death, Chad's protection would now completely dissolve. No more bailouts from daddy and no more expensive lawyer.

*

"So here we are again," sighed Barry with a raised eyebrow.

I sat beside Barry in interview room one and Chad was seated opposite us. I knew that Matthew Perry was standing behind the one-sided mirror across the room, watching earnestly.

Chad's demeanor was completely different this time around. After just watching a rogue officer shoot his father dead, Chad's attitude had reduced to nothing more than a bubbling wreck. He sobbed audibly with his shoulders rising and falling.

"Are you crying for your father? Or crying for yourself?" I taunted him. I was leaning back in the chair with my arms folded.

"Let's start with the evidence!" said Barry, eagerly taking the reins and pushing the scrap book which I had found across the table to

Chad. He flicked through the pages and showed him the letters which he had received from an unknown party and photographs of Annabelle Green both alive and dead. Then the paperwork which showed that traces of Annabelle's dried blood were found in the trunk of Walter's Rolls Royce. "The photos of Annabelle?" asked Barry. "What's your explanation for this?"

Chad sobbed and wiped his snotty nose across his red leather jacket sleeve. His crystal blue eyes were brimming with tears. "I killed her," he whimpered, pulling a face like a child who was exaggerating sadness. "I followed her and snatched her when I had a chance."

Barry nodded calmly. His facial expression remained neutral. "And what about traces of DNA evidence discovered by forensic investigators? Annabelle Green's hairs and fibers from her clothes were found in the trunk of your father's Rolls Royce?" inquired Barry. "Was your father complicit with the murder?"

Chad nodded and wiped his eyes with his fingers. "My father helped me to move her. We dumped her at the reservoir after we made the ransom note," he explained. "Daddy was the one who came up with the idea to write the note so nobody would suspect me. Why would a rich kid demand money? Am I right?"

What the fuck was that look he just gave us?! Was he just seeking approval? I clenched my fists but remained calm. I glanced at Barry to see what his reaction was, but Barry remained unreadable.

"We burned her clothes and the ones I wore when I strangled her after we dumped her," continued Chad.

I was astounded. He was just giving up. If he was willing to give himself up, then maybe he would give up his mysterious "tutor" who I suspected was Larry Gyllenhaal. "What about your 'tutor'?" I prompted, eagerly leaning across the table. "You have a chance to reduce your sentence, Chad!" I offered him. "Just tell us who your accomplice is!"

Chad eyeballed me reproachfully. Tears still streamed down his cheeks and his bottom lip quivered like a leaf. He was like a neutered dog in my eyes. He was utterly pathetic without the security which his father had previously provided for him. "I don't know his name. I never met him in person. He kept telling me where to meet him, but never actually showed up. He told me to meet him at the Budapest

Hotel, then again at the fashion Gala. He never actually met me though!"

"You expect me to believe that bullshit, Chad?! Where did you go to college, Chad? You have no surgical experience! Most victims were discovered with incisions only a skilful surgeon could execute," I challenged with a hostile tone.

Barry prompted me to calm down and slid a piece of paper across the table to Chad. "This is a confession paper," he explained, completely disregarding my line of questioning. "Sign it and you may be eligible for early release." Then he added sniggering maliciously: "Whenever that will be!"

Chad looked it over and reached for the pen which Barry had extended to him. His blue eyes flicked from line to line and then suddenly widened with shock. "There must be some mistake!" he exclaimed in disbelief. "I can't sign this! I didn't kill those other girls! I only killed Annabelle! I swear! I just wanted to be famous like the Artist Killer! Please!"

Chad's plea was definitely convincing. So convincing that I actually believed him. He stared at Barry and myself pleadingly with his wide blue eyes. I could find no sympathy within myself for this pathetic creature. Even though I knew what was coming next, I made no move to stop it.

Barry nodded at Perry behind the mirror and I instinctively knew that all recording equipment had been turned off. Barry got to his feet and stretched before tightening his belt. He was a bear of a man in comparison to Chad Sullivan.

Barry was a big guy and his punch had impact. He rammed his fist into Chad's face with a satisfying *crack* that sent Chad flying backwards off his chair so that he hit the floor. "Sign the goddamn confession!" he shouted angrily.

Chad whimpered and I got to my feet and left the interview room. I barged into the observation room where Perry and a few others watched intently through the one-sided mirror.

"Please, give us a few minutes!" I gestured to the door and the other officers looked at Perry uncertainly before he finally nodded and gave his consent. The officers all begrudgingly left. "What the fuck is all this?!" I demanded furiously once I had closed the door behind the other officers. I looked through the mirror to see Barry had Chad pinned in a corner. They each had their hands around the scruff of each other's collars. Barry was planting more punches into Chad's face and stomach while Chad tried fruitlessly to protect himself.

"What is this?" repeated Perry, pressing his hands together. His voice was distant, and he never took his eyes off Chad getting his ass kicked. "This is justice, Jack!"

"Justice?!" I spat in disbelief. "This isn't justice, Perry! This kid is some sad act rich boy who became obsessed with the Artist Killer and tried to become a copycat killer! To make him sign that confession and take responsibility for all those other murders as well isn't justice because then it becomes a closed case and the real Artist Killer will get away with it!"

Perry turned his head sharply towards me and his face twisted with fury. "You have some nerve talking to me of justice, Jack! You don't think I know that you had something to do with Walter's death?" he accused. He paused to look back through the mirror as Barry had Chad on the ground in the corner of the room, his two giant hands thundering down upon Chad as he screamed at him to sign the confession. "Any trust I had in you went straight out of the window with that fucking stunt!"

"I don't know what you're talking about," I replied, trying to look shocked. "I was standing beside you the entire time!"

"Oh, fuck off, Jack! I'm not a fucking idiot! You have access to the armory here and for some reason you chose not to wear full riot gear like the rest of us! So, either you had someone execute Walter, or you set up a rifle to fire on a timer or by remote! I will get to the bottom of this!"

I shook my head and snapped back at him angrily. "How is any of this relevant to what's happening in that interview room?! You can't really preach to me about justice and doing things by the book when you're having your pet gorilla beat a false confession out of him. Chad is a piece of fucking shit and he deserves a good punch, but, Perry, we have to focus on the bigger picture! A serial killer is still out there!"

Perry would hear none of it. Our friendship hung in the balance with the recent events that had transpired. He knew that I had something to do with Walter's death, but he will never know how I did it. He didn't trust me anymore and I didn't trust him either.

*

Chad Sullivan eventually signed the confession reluctantly and he was taken to court and sentenced to serve ten years for each murder committed in the name of the Artist Killer. Chad Sullivan would spend the next sixty to seventy years in a maximum-security prison.

I watched his trial feeling giddy but with a sense of trepidation at the same time! It was a very strange feeling. On the one hand I was happy that the killer of Annabelle Green was going to rot in a cell. And on the other hand, I felt like the LAPD had just done the real Artist Killer a great service by forcing Chad to take responsibility for every single murder. All the Artist Killer had to do now was nothing and he had won.

I couldn't let that happen! After Chad's conviction I stood among a crowd of journalists as captain Matthew Perry was given awards by the mayor (a fat prick named Thomas Danforth) for outstanding bravery and police work. Perry took the microphone on the town hall steps and made a pompous speech about how he was proud to serve his city and how much of an honor it was to put the Artist Killer behind bars.

I growled and walked away, deciding once again to take the investigation into my own hands and continue my hunt for the Artist Killer. Larry Gyllenhaal must have been feeling very comfortable now that Chad had taken the fall for all the murders instead of just the one which he had actually committed.

Don't get too comfortable! I'm coming for you next, Larry Gyllenhaal!

CHAPTER 15

Closing the Net

Nicolas met with me at the Blue Bell Tavern and withheld his end of our bargain. We met in the day when the bar was relatively quiet, save for a couple of die-hard regulars who would be too drunk to notice us. We sat opposite each other in our usual booth and Nicolas subtly used his foot to push a shoulder bag full of my half of the reward money under the table to me.

"I have to say, Jack, you've done a fucking good job!" he said as he extended his hand towards me. I reached across to meet him, and he clasped my hand tightly. "We pulled it off and put the fucker behind bars!"

"'Probable cause' is a police officer's best friend," I replied with a smirk. We clinked our bottles of beer together and drank in celebration.

My plan had worked. Walter was dead and Chad was imprisoned for the rest of his miserable little life. A whole lifetime to reflect on his shitty life choices. I had reported to Perry that I had heard an intruder breaking a window at the rear of Chad's house and I went to investigate, accidentally stumbling upon some evidence that would put Chad away. I don't think that Perry bought it, but at the end of the day it wasn't about what he knew but rather about what he could prove.

"What will you do now?" I asked him before I guzzled down the rest of my beer.

"I'm not sure," he replied with a disinterested shrug. "Now that the Artist Killer is behind bars and the case is over, I guess I'll move somewhere much quieter."

I shook my head. "The case isn't over yet," I corrected him. "Chad killed Annabelle Green, but he didn't kill those other girls! The killer is still out there and I'm going to find him!"

Nicolas cocked his head and gave me a puzzled look. "What do you mean? Do you have any suspects?" he inquired. He looked troubled, as though the revelation had deeply disturbed him.

"Just one for now," I replied. I started to tell him about how I suspected Larry Gyllenhaal but stopped myself before the air escaped my lungs. I decided instead to keep my information to myself. Larry Gyllenhaal was an enemy. I wanted to deal with him personally.

"Best of luck with your hunt," he said as he got to his feet, ready to excuse himself. "You have my cellphone number, Jack. If ever you need any help with your investigation, I'm sure we could come to another agreement."

We shook hands once again and left the Blue Bell together. He went one way and I turned to head back to my apartment with my shoulder bag containing my half of the reward money. When I turned, that was when I saw Matthew Perry parked across the road in an unmarked police car. I pretended not to see him and allowed him to follow me home. I hoped that he wouldn't pull over and demand to know what was in the bag and thankfully he didn't.

*

It took a week of sneaking around, avoiding Perry's watchful eye, before I could properly continue my investigation into Larry Gyllenhaal. I threw Perry off by pretending to go to the Blue Bell and get drunk every night. Eventually he either got bored and gave up or had someone else start tailing me instead.

It was evident to me that a dumb schmuck like Chad Sullivan wasn't responsible for the murders of those girls and Reece Pemberton. The killer had to be somebody with advanced surgical knowledge. Based on that knowledge I thought that it would be prudent to start by investigating different colleges and universities within LA to search for Larry Gyllenhaal. If he had ever been a professor or a student, then the relevant university will surely have this information on record.

There was a possibility that Larry Gyllenhaal had taught or studied medical surgery elsewhere, but I was hoping that wouldn't be the case.

Another week into my investigation and my labor bore fruit. Larry Gyllenhaal had taught medical surgery at the University of California, Los Angeles. I took a page from Walter Sullivan's book and bribed the receptionist to give me all information relevant to Larry Gyllenhaal, including his address, which he'd refused to share during his interview.

I should have known that a university would contain books and books contain names, names with addresses. I now knew where the fucker lived. I thanked the receptionist and promptly left to stake out Gyllenhaal's house.

I parked across the road in another rental car and I watched the windows intently. Gyllenhaal had done well for himself. He had a nice house in a more 'refined' area of Compton. His garden was big with a flower bed containing different herbs and spices which Gyllenhaal had planted. A sprinkler sprayed water across the grass to keep it vibrant and green. A metal trailer with a sailboat firmly strapped to it sat on his drive and I'd bet my life that there was a coil of thick hemp rope on there, the kind which had been used to strangle his victims.

A light was on in the kitchen and I watched as discretely as possible as Larry Gyllenhaal walked into what I assumed was the dining room with a large tray of food. He was wearing a beige sweater and his horn-rimmed glasses reflected the light.

Then my jaw dropped when a woman with a blue tank top and blonde hair tied in a bun entered the room and kissed him on the cheek. A young boy and a teenage girl with gothic attire and too much makeup entered the room and seated themselves around the table.

"He has a fucking family..." I muttered in disbelief. Did this diminish his chance of being the Artist Killer? Or was his family life merely a cover up for his dark secrets?

I got out of the rental Mercedes and cautiously approached the house, diverting from the front door to vault upon the trailer with a grunt and investigate the boat which was strapped to it. As I had predicted, a coil of hemp rope sat on the deck. The end was frayed, indicating a length of rope of an unknown size had been removed from the coil. I narrowed my eyes and climbed back down, making my way across the lawn to the path.

I pressed the doorbell and waited patiently until a blurred figure appeared through the frosted glass in the mahogany door.

The woman answered the door and I politely asked if I could speak with Larry Gyllenhaal. He came to the door with a puzzled look on his face. He didn't look pleased to see me.

"Detective..." he uttered under his breath. He gained his composure and cleared his throat. "What do you want?"

I forced myself to smile and almost replied through gritted teeth. My hatred for this man was absolute because something in my gut told me that this was the guy! "I came to apologize," I said, trying my hardest to sound sincere. "Chad Sullivan was the Artist Killer all along. He signed a confession and took responsibility for the murders. I thought I owed you an apology for the inconvenience I caused you."

Larry raised his eyebrow suspiciously. Perhaps he suspected my insincerity, or perhaps he was feeling uncomfortable that I had invaded his private space as I suspected that he had invaded mine when the killer broke into my home. "How did you find my address?" he sternly asked. He was standing as rigid as a board. "Why are you really here?"

"I genuinely came to apologize. I have no other reason to be here now that the killer has been captured," I smiled at him warmly. "May I come in?"

Just then I heard a familiar voice excitedly call my name and my heart sank. This was the worst possible scenario that I could have ever imagined. I heard Rebecca Valentine whistle at me and call me again. I turned to face her, absolutely terrified that someone close to me would be revealed to the Artist Killer.

When I turned back to look at Larry, he had a broad grin on his face. The light from the porch reflected from his glasses, giving him a menacing look. "What a wonderful specimen..." he whispered to himself so only I could hear him. My anxiety worsened and I feared for Rebecca's safety. "Well isn't this a splendid coincidence!"

Rebecca clicked her way up the path in a pair of black stilettos and a black coat which came to her thighs. Her hair had been dyed auburn red and fell down to her back. Her eye makeup accentuated the beauty of her eyes. "I was in the neighborhood," she panted with a smile. She lived in Compton herself, so it wasn't too much of a stretch to bump into her I supposed. "Aren't you going to introduce me to your friend?" she asked playfully, thumping my arm and cocking her head when I said nothing.

"You really must come in!" piped up Gyllenhaal. His tone had completely changed, and I could tell that he was revelling in my discomfort. "We're having turkey with all the trimmings!" he jovially exclaimed.

"This can wait until another time, Gyllenhaal," I retorted dismissively. I took Rebecca by the arm and began to walk away. She resisted and tried to subtly warn me of my rudeness.

"Nonsense!" snapped Larry. "I really must insist! There's plenty for the both of you."

"Jack..." prompted Rebecca.

I sighed and relented. I would have to figure out some way to warn her later. We entered the house into a white tiled hallway with extravagant clay pottery on display. Larry Gyllenhaal boasted of his artistic talents to Rebecca, taking credit for any artistic piece that we spotted in his house. To me the house looked very clinical with a modern chrome decor, which seemed to be the theme of every room.

"I see my house as a canvas through which I can express my artistic talent," bragged Gyllenhaal. He gestured for us to be seated across from his two children in the dining room, another chrome room filled with sculptures and paintings. "This is my wife, Rose." He gestured to the tired-looking woman in the blue tank top. She nodded curtly upon introduction. "This is my son, Billy. He's six. And my daughter, Paris, a moody teenager who never has much to say." Paris rolled her eyes at his remark. "This is detective Cucchiano of the LAPD and his lady friend. Cucchiano and myself are well acquainted." Larry seated himself at the head of the table and gestured to his wife. "Wine!" was all he said, and Rose dutifully headed into the kitchen. She appeared a few moments later with an expensive bottle of red wine and a handful of crystal wine glasses.

THE DARK SIDE OF BEAUTY

Rose poured a glass for each of us, excluding the kids, and proceeded to serve dinner. We had roast turkey glazed with red wine with stuffing and potatoes. A separate tray held vegetables such as carrots, parsnips and sprouts.

"Eat! Drink! Be merry!" said Larry pressing his fingertips together.

We ate and made small talk at the table until Rebecca inevitably asked how Larry and myself knew each other. There was an awkward silence until Rose asked if we would like dessert.

"I don't care what you say about me, Jack!" remarked Larry in a snide manner as soon as Rebecca had left to help Rose wash the plates and trays. "I won't have you saying I wasn't an auspicious host!" He smiled at me and took a sip of his wine. I took note of his kids casting each other a glance. Was there something to that?

"Seems you two are getting on just fine!" called out Larry to Rose and Rebecca after he heard them talking away to one another in the kitchen. "Rebecca, you should come visit us more often!" he said as he grinned at me again.

What was his angle? Was Rebecca in any danger? I grabbed a napkin and stuffed it in my pocket when Larry started making remarks about Paris not eating enough food. "I'm just heading to the restroom," I said, excusing myself. I got to my feet and Larry told me that the toilet was through the door at the top of the stairs. Once in the bathroom I took a pen out of my jacket and scrawled a note on it to Rebecca.

"Beware this man. I suspect him of being the true Artist Killer," was all I wrote. Then I headed back downstairs and seated myself next to Rebecca for pudding. I nudged her and passed her the note under the table and watched as the color drained from her face and she went as rigid as a board.

"What's the matter?" inquired Larry with feigned concern. "Passing notes? Isn't that a little rude?" His face dropped and he flared his nostrils. "Rose, take the kids and go to your rooms!"

Rose looked confused. "But we haven't even started our pudding yet..." she responded quietly.

"Fuck off to your rooms, cunt!" snapped Larry angrily. "Don't make me fucking ask twice! I wasn't asking the first time!"

Rebecca and I watched in shock as his family pushed their chairs back in unison and silently left the room to head upstairs. Larry straightened his collar and his smile returned.

"You must forgive me," he said with a false chuckle. "Disobedience is the cornerstone of stupidity. And I despise the stupid." He got to his feet and walked to Rebecca's side. He towered over her, taking deep breaths until he held out his hand beside her. "I'm going to count to three..." he growled in a shaky voice. "When I reach three, I expect any notes you've been passing between you to be placed in my hand!"

Rebecca looked at me. Worry in her eyes. Her hand was shaking, and she reached across to hand my note to Gyllenhaal, my pleas of protest falling on deaf ears.

"There's a good girl," he said with a condescending pat of her head. "So, you still think I'm a killer?" asked Larry laughing after reading my note. "I should've known that my hospitality would be wasted on such a fool. What did you hope to accomplish by coming here?" He smiled at us like a wolf grinning at cornered prey. "Rebecca, look at me!" he cooed from across the room. "LOOK AT ME!" He slammed his hand on the table and she flinched fearfully, turning her head to face him with tearful eyes. "That's better! I'd love to capture your beauty on canvas." He laughed aloud at the worried exchange between Rebecca and me. Then his face became serious and he narrowed his eyes hatefully. "Now get the fuck out of my house!"

We silently got to our feet and left his house without saying a word to each other or Larry. Larry followed us out and lingered on the doorstep until me and Rebecca were in the rental car.

"What the hell, Jack?!" asked Rebecca, melodramatically as she watched Gyllenhaal disappear into his house. She took deep breaths and fanned her face with her hands. "That's the bastard who killed Mary O'Reilly?"

I nodded my head grimly. "That's what I suspect. I've been investigating him for a while now. He was at the gallery the night Crystal Hayes disappeared too! So was Chad. I reckon Chad must have nabbed her and thrown her down that maintenance ladder," I speculated with a shudder. "They must have returned for her once they were released from police custody."

Rebecca shuddered and goose bumps appeared all over her bare arms. Then her face twisted with anger and she furiously beat at my chest. "Why the fuck did you let me go in there?!" she demanded as her eyes began to brim with tears once again.

"Don't worry, if you like I can stay with you for a while," I offered as I delicately placed one hand on her slender shoulder and cupped her chin with the other.

"I'm angry with you, Jack!" she snivelled. "You staying over is a nice idea, but it would complicate my work arrangements..."

I recoiled my hands and shifted in my seat uncomfortably. I cleared my throat as my cheeks burned with embarrassment. "It's fine," I replied composing myself and smiling. "At least I didn't endanger your life in vain," I said this last sentence with a chuckle, nervously trying to make a joke out of the dark situation. I reached into my pocket and retrieved a set of house keys which I had swiped from a wooden plaque lined with hooks for keys as I had excused myself to go to the bathroom. "I'm going to head back there later tonight when Gyllenhaal and his family are asleep," I told her.

"Please be careful..." cautioned Rebecca as she planted a soft kiss on my cheek. "Let me know what you find out." Then my heart sank as she started to get out of the car. "I can walk from here, Jack. I doubt Gyllenhaal will bother coming to look for me."

I earnestly offered to keep her company for the night instead of investigating Gyllenhaal and couldn't hide my disappointment or hurt when she told me that it would cost me three hundred dollars. I drove back to my apartment frustrated and angry. I tried to push thoughts of Rebecca from my mind and focus on my investigation. Tonight, I would break into Gyllenhaal's house and search for clues.

I drove back at two in the morning, taking a detour by Rebecca's house to see her lights were still on, and parked a few houses away from Gyllenhaal's. I walked up to the ship and took photographs of the rope and its frayed edge. Then I walked to the front door and let myself in, closing it quietly behind me. I checked a door under the stairs and shined a torch down into the basement. I descended the wooden staircase and swept my torch across the room to see several canvases covered over with cloth. A quick peek revealed the paintings had no relevance to my investigation. Aside from that all that could be found were paints and other bits and pieces used to make clay pottery and such.

After that I crept upstairs, freezing absolutely still when one step creaked loudly. Dread rushed through my body and I waited to see if I could hear movement from any of the sleeping Gyllenhaals. Nothing. I crept upstairs and avoided any doors that I could hear snoring behind. One bedroom door was ajar with blue light flashing here and there with the faint sound of gunshots coming from a television set. As I crept by, there was Paris sitting cross-legged on the floor in front of a huge plasma-screen television mounted onto the wall. She wore striped pyjamas and a large pair of skull candy headphones. She couldn't hear me.

At the end of the hallway was a locked door with an ornate metal plaque on it which read 'Study. Keep Out!' I fiddled around in my pocket and produced two small pieces of slender metal, which were my lock picks. I fiddled around in the lock for what seemed like an eternity until it gave a satisfying click and began to open.

The study was decorated traditionally, with wood-panelled walls and a navy-blue carpet. Wooden bookshelves lined the walls. Each shelf was filled to the brim with books of varying sizes. An ornate wooden desk stood against the window with paperwork neatly arranged into piles on top of it. A huge self portrait of Larry Gyllenhaal was positioned over a fireplace with small bright embers still visible on the blackened logs within.

I swept my torch over the books. Gyllenhaal had an extensive library. There were books containing information on art, philosophy, law, and a collection of books kept together with red covers which contained information about surgery. My eyes widened when I saw the name of the author: *Heinrich Wulf*. This was the same alias which the killer used at the Budapest Hotel. I took photographs of the books and continued my investigation.

I headed over to the desk and searched through Larry's paperwork. There was his framed graduate paper in surgery, and I took a photograph of it. I also found a ledger in which Larry Gyllenhaal kept records of his financial affairs. I took photographs of the relevant pages as I hastily flicked through. I was nervous that I was going to be discovered at any moment. I took photographs of a page containing records of receipts for the fashion gala. He had purchased four in total. One for me, one for himself and one for Chad. What about the forth one? His wife? I couldn't recall seeing her at the gala but judging by how Larry treated her at dinner it wouldn't be a stretch to say he'd abandoned her there.

I took a photograph of another page which contained records of his mortgage payments. Larry Gyllenhaal was paying mortgages on his house, another property, an art studio situated in the Downtown region. And the final mortgage was on his sailboat.

This art studio Downtown, could that be where Larry Gyllenhaal conducts his darker form of artistic expression? Could that be where him and Chad committed their murders?

I took another photograph of a page containing records of the booking of room 526, the room adjacent to the room where Emma Fontaine was found dead and the dates matched up too.

I put the ledger back where I found it and left the property as quickly as possible without being detected. I placed the keys back on the hook and headed back to my rental to investigate the address of Gyllenhaal's second property.

*

The studio was tucked away in a dingy area of downtown, situated at the top floor of a block of studios. Some were to let. I took an elevator to the top floor of the block to the studio which Larry Gyllenhaal had purchased. I slid the mesh elevator door open and approached the metal door of the studio.

With my trusty lock picks in hand I got to work on opening the door. It was a sturdy lock and at one point my lock pick almost snapped, but eventually it creaked open.

It was a small studio with a single window on the far wall overlooking rooftops. There was a table in the center of the room and I immediately recognized this as the place where Reece Pemberton was mercilessly shot in the head by the true Artist Killer as I witnessed in the tape which he had left for me when he broke into my apartment.

I walked to a shelf which held jars containing the eyes of the Artist Killer's victims. I took photographs of the jars with shaking hands, anger and uncontrollable remorse building within me.

There were dark red blood stains all over the studio and I took photographs of all of them as evidence. A small drawer contained several blood-covered surgical tools and I took photographs of them. Another drawer contained a hatchet covered in dried blood.

"This is the place!" I muttered in disbelief. A victorious smile began to spread across my face when I was reminded of the death of all those girls. Their dead eyes stared at me reproachfully. "Larry Gyllenhaal, I've fucking got you!"

I walked into a small bedroom which contained several different outfits and wigs. One outfit was a police officer uniform.

"The first police officer on the Budapest scene..." I murmured as my eyes widened. "So that was this fucker all along! He got the security guard out of the office because the security guard thought he was a police officer and he wiped the security footage! You sneaky bastard!" I took pictures of all the costumes and another picture of a small stand containing a box full of different colored contact lenses. It seemed that Larry Gyllenhaal was a master of disguise.

I made my way into the kitchen and froze when I heard the door to the studio open. I pressed myself tightly against the wall next to the doorway and peeked to catch a glimpse of someone in a long blue trench coat and a trilby hat. They were wearing shoes and black trousers and a scarf across their mouth and nose so that only their bright blue eyes were visible.

I took cover as they looked my way and there was a moment of silence that lasted forever. Before I took cover, I caught a glimpse of two metal jerry cans. I heard the Artist Killer grunt as he lifted one of the jerry cans and a splashing noise followed. My nose was assaulted by the overpowering odor of turpentine and petroleum spirits.

I leaned around the corner again to see him dousing the entire studio in flammable liquid! So, Larry knew I was on to him and now he's making a desperate attempt to eradicate the evidence.

I drew my Beretta 9mm and stepped out from my hiding place with my gun held high. "Don't fucking move!" I ordered as I cocked the hammer, so he knew I was serious.

He raised his hands slowly but didn't turn around.

"Thought you could get rid of the evidence, didn't you?" I sneered with a bitter chuckle. I had the drop on the Artist Killer! Now I had the choice of shooting him in the back or taking him in.

It happened in the flash of a second. He darted for cover as I felt my finger tighten on the trigger. There was a deafening bang and a blinding flash of light and then splinters of wood flew from the wall, leaving a small hole.

I heard a click and saw a metal Zippo lighter skid across the floor, igniting the petroleum spirits that spread across the wooden floor. Flames leaped into the air, licking at my face. I was forced backwards with my arms shielding my face from the intense heat.

The Killer had barred his own escape in his desperation to destroy all the evidence. Flames swept across the room, creating a barrier of intense heat between the two of us and the only way out. The only way out now was through the window overlooking the rooftops.

That was what the killer sprinted for. He ran towards me and rammed himself into me as I tried to fire another shot. I was knocked to my back and my gun went skidding across the floor and was consumed by the flames that hungrily crawled towards us. Everything would be destroyed.

The killer braced himself and leaped through the window with a crash that sent glass flying everywhere. I got to my feet, struggling for breath. The room was full of thick black smoke and it stung my eyes.

I followed the killer, abandoning my firearm and all the evidence to be consumed by the flames. I leaped through the window and skidded down a sloped roof until I landed on a flat roof. The killer was hoping over the gaps and heading down the roofs.

I spurred myself forward and gave chase, willing myself with every fiber of my being to go faster. My lungs burned and my legs ached, but eventually I caught up to him and dived for his legs and took him down to the ground.

He turned and punched me in the chin, sending my world spinning. He got to his feet and drew the same Glock which he had used to execute Reece Pemberton. I rolled across the floor as he fired a shot. Flecks of asphalt stunk my face.

I grabbed a handful of grit and tossed it into his eyes. He blocked it with his arm and instinctively turned his head away. I got to my feet as he took aim and I slapped his hand so that he fired at the floor instead of at me. My intention was to knock the gun out of his hand, but his grip was firm.

He raised the gun and I grabbed it, wrestling with all my strength to pull it from his grip. He rose his knee into my stomach and all the wind was knocked out of me. I let go of the gun and sank to my knees, gasping for air, when the killer struck me across the side of the head with his Glock. My vision went blurry and I collapsed onto the roof and lost consciousness as the blurry silhouette of the killer disappeared across the rooftops and down a fire escape ladder.

*

"Wake up, Jack!" said a gentle voice. I felt delicate hands shaking my shoulders.

My head was pounding, and I struggled to open my eyes. I mumbled something incoherently as I was shook again, more violently this time.

"Jack, it's time to wake up!" Little fingers pried my eyes open and I could see the blurry form of a child smiling at me.

"Annabelle...Green..." I muttered with a raspy voice. I sat up and opened my eyes. I was no longer on the rooftops. Instead I was in a dining hall of some kind. Stone columns stretched seemingly forever into a ceiling that was not there. Instead, they disappeared into darkness. There were no windows and no doors. Just stone walls and columns. The dining table was made of a dark red oak.

"We need to talk, Jack. No games this time." Now that I was more coherent, I could hear the demonic whisper in her voice. As she spoke, she sounded as sweet and innocent as Annabelle would have when she was alive, but everything she said was overlapped with a faint demonic whisper that repeated her words as she said them. "Take a seat!"

I couldn't move. I was routed to the point where I was standing. A chair skidded across the floor from the darkness and knocked me off my feet so that I was sitting in it as it scooted across the floor and came to a screeching halt at the table. There was a creaking sound as wood grew from the arms of the chair and the legs and stretched around my wrists and ankles. The wood merged back to the chair, pinning me to it uncomfortably.

"Please..." I begged her. "I found your killer! Chad Sullivan is going to spend the rest of his life in prison!"

"Do you think that's enough?!" screamed Annabelle angrily. "As long as the real Artist Killer lives then more women will die, and more Chad Sullivans will kill in aspiration! You really need to shut your fucking mouth and listen!"

She outstretched her hand and I screamed in terror as skin began to stretch across my mouth until my screams became garbled muffles of protest. Annabelle outstretched her hands and floated above me. Her head went limp and her eyes glowed red. As she spoke, only the demonic voice came through, but this time much louder and clearer. The sound of her voice seemed to come from every direction rather than from Annabelle's mouth. Her lips didn't move as she spoke.

"We have lost patience with you, Jack Cucchiano," she said. Annabelle paused as a series of screeching noises echoed throughout the room. More chairs skidded towards the table from the thick darkness at the room's outskirts. Seated upon them were Scarlett Jones, Mary O'Reilly, Rosita Ramirez, Emma Fontaine, and Crystal Hayes. They were all rigid, like mannequins, with exaggerated grins on their faces.

"Your investigation still hasn't got any closer to the capture of the killer. So, we are giving you three more days!" warned Annabelle. "After three days, if the Artist Killer is not captured or dead, then I'm afraid we are going to claim your soul, Jack!"

She laughed menacingly at my groans of terror.

"Three days," she reiterated. "After that your body will be found dead under mysterious circumstances."

I watched wide-eyed, but couldn't talk or even scream, as their flesh began to decompose right in front of my eyes. Scarlett's face ripped itself open into the Glasgow smile. Mary's head rolled off. They were all becoming horrific looking. That was when I noticed that their fingers were scalpels and other sharp implements as they all crawled upon the table towards me. Their horrific faces filled my view, contorted with agony and suffering. They each dug their claws into my arms and shredded the flesh to ribbons so that my arms looked like a lattice pastry with jam leaking out of it.

Then Annabelle grew exponentially. She didn't stop until her head was well out of view and a giant hand swept me up and hoisted me into the air towards a giant gaping mouth. She threw me into her mouth and chewed me up. My bones were crushed, and my body was pulverized beyond recognition, but I was still somehow conscious and observing the horror. I was watching my own body get crushed and mangled by Annabelle's giant teeth. Then she spat me out and as the tangled pile of mush that was my body splattered onto the concrete my eyes shot open.

*

I was back on the roof. I tried to open my left eye and it was swollen shut. Blood had congealed across my forehead and down my cheek where the butt of the killer's glock had split my head open. My vision was blurry, and I was afflicted with a crippling headache.

An inferno raged behind me and red and blue lights flashed in the distance. The fire brigade and the LAPD would be here any moment. I decided to make a move, staggering precariously towards the fire escape ladder which the killer had fled down. I felt as though I had been drinking, but the hangover had arrived early!

I cautiously climbed onto the ladder, almost losing my grip as my world suddenly began to spin out of control. That was when I first caught a glimpse of my arms, all shredded and bleeding profusely. What the hell? Had Annabelle's threat been real?!

I got so far down the ladder and let go of the rungs. I tumbled downwards and bounced off of the side of a pair of garbage cans. I hit the concrete with a thud and the air was knocked from me. A searing pain in my chest and a shortness of breath indicated to me that I'd broken a few ribs, possibly even punctured a lung.

I lost consciousness as two uniformed officers discovered me trying to drag myself to the roadside.

*

I regained consciousness in a hospital bed with Perry standing over me. He had a look of concern on his face, which immediately disappeared and became a suspicious glare once he realized I wasn't going to die.

"Perrrry..." I croaked.

"Don't give me that fucking shit, Jack!" snapped Perry

impatiently. "What the hell were you doing near that burned studio?"

The studio!

"Perry," I explained trying to sit up and grunting in agony. "Larry Gyllenhaal! I was... I got evidence! Check my phone!"

Perry scoffed at that. "I can't. Your phone was smashed when you hit the deck."

I couldn't believe it! All that hard work was for naught. My only hope was to be frank with Perry and confess my investigation into Larry Gyllenhaal. Perry handed me a glass of water and I gulped it down greedily, flinching as my head started to throb. I told Perry everything about Larry Gyllenhaal and how I entered his house and found the ledger containing his financial records.

Perry listened intently; his expression unchanging. "Jack..." he softly said. "I can't issue a warrant to search Gyllenhaal's house based on your word! It isn't something I trust much at the moment." He paused and took a deep breath. "Besides... Larry Gyllenhaal's house was also burned down last night." He paused again as though he was letting the gravity of his words sink in. "Three bodies were found charred to a crisp in the wreckage. We've been unable to identify them as of yet."

My heart sank. That was it... All the evidence had gone up in smoke. What shocked me the most was the extreme length Larry Gyllenhaal went through to protect himself. He had burned down his own home with his family still inside to hide his guilt.

"And you've just confessed to being present at both scenes where the arson took place," exclaimed Perry, narrowing his eyes at me.

CHAPTER 16

Suicide

After a day of agonizing chest pains, I was finally able to check myself out of hospital. A doctor prescribed me some strong pain killers and recommended that I take it really easy for three to four weeks until my rib healed.

I didn't have the luxury of time on my side, especially if Annabelle Green's threat was genuine and not some paranoid delusion that I had conjured in my mind. Her ghost, or whatever it was, had always seemed very real to me. Any injury she inflicted upon me always carried over into reality.

For example, Annabelle had appeared at the foot of my bed late last night. Her very presence brought a crisp chill to the room that made me shiver and curl up in my blankets. My flesh was covered in goose bumps and my breath escaped my lips in a foggy plume. Annabelle repeatedly whispered that I had three days. Then I watched helplessly as her silhouette prodded a dainty finger into my knee. Searing pain shot up my leg and I gripped the thin bedsheets between my teeth to stifle the scream. Thankfully her ghost didn't visit for long. As quickly as she appeared, she was gone, but even after reality returned to normal the pain in my knee lingered.

The morning following Annabelle's ominous warning, I awoke to see that my knee was bruised and swollen. The doctor asserted that I must suffer from sleep walking and night terrors. He erroneously reasoned that I had imagined the whole thing and went for a walk in my sleep. According to him I must've slipped and bashed my knee as I was climbing back into bed. He said that it was amazing that a nurse never spotted me with a forced laugh that made me cringe.

I remember stepping out of the hospital doors that morning. It was a beautiful morning. Beams of sunlight cut through the clouds like golden spears. I closed my eyes and took a deep breath as a gentle breeze caressed my face and blew through my hair.

I hobbled to a shop downtown where I left a shady looking gentleman my phone in an attempt to have it repaired and recover some of the evidence that was lost during the fire. All the photographs were hidden away inside that broken lump of plastic. I intended to have them back in my possession.

The shady gentleman informed me that my phone would take a day to have the screen repaired. I begrudgingly accepted his unreasonable time frame and his exorbitant prices. A hundred dollars to repair a damaged phone screen! Fucking ridiculous! What choice did I have? I had to accept. That was a day wasted in hospital and a day wasted waiting for my phone to be repaired of the three days which Annabelle had so mercifully afforded me.

I went home despondent and full of dread. I think that I even started biting my fingernails for the first time ever. I definitely smoked my own bodyweight in cigarettes so that my apartment smelled like an old ashtray. Thankfully, I managed to stay away from the booze, in spite of my stress and worry.

It was later that night that something interesting happened. It must have been around eight in the afternoon. I was resting. The cigarettes which I had smoked had made my chest pains much worse. Each labored breath seemed like it took too much energy. That was when I heard the frantic knocking on the door. It was an urgent rapid knock. I responded by staring at it and waiting for whoever it was to go away. Eventually, when the knocking was paired with a man angrily shouting my name, I relented and pried myself out of my seat.

I looked through my keyhole and there were two people outside my door. One was an angry looking man who looked like he'd been snorting cocaine. His green shirt was too tight for his muscular chest and broad shoulders. He was jittery and kept sniffing and rubbing his nose. He was holding a briefcase in one hand.

The woman who accompanied him was heavily pregnant. Her hands rested on her bulging stomach, which protruded from under her stripped shirt. She looked bedraggled. Her brown hair was a tangled mess and her eyes looked puffy like she'd been crying.

I asked what they wanted through the door and it was the man who responded. "Jack Cucchiano? Please, we need to talk!" His eyes had beamed hopefully, and he rested a caring hand on the woman's shoulder.

I opened the door and the man thrust his hand out and grabbed mine. My swollen eye didn't perturb him whatsoever. He gripped my hand so tightly that I thought he would crush it in his vice-like grip and he shook my hand so vigorously that I thought that he was going to rip my arm off.

"Come in..." I croaked as I cleared my throat. I stepped aside and let them enter, my curiosity taking precedence over my anxiety and paranoia. I wanted to know what they wanted.

They sat together on my leather sofa. The man had placed the briefcase on the floor and took his wife's hands in his own. I can assume that she was his wife because of the expensive-looking wedding ring on her finger.

I sat in my chair opposite them. I had no intention of offering them a drink of any kind. I was in too much pain to play the part of gracious host. "Start by telling me your names," I ordered them. I had a pen in my hand and my notebook on the table. I had been looking over my notes when they arrived.

"I'm Jeremy Irons," replied the man in a confident voice. He puffed his chest as though to say that his own name brought him a great deal of pride. "This is my wife, Lucy."

His wife looked up at me and offered me a smile and a curt nod. From what I could see there were no signs of abuse. In fact, with the way in which they were sitting and touching each other constantly I'd say that this was a deeply affectionate relationship. "We understand you used to be a private detective?" said the woman.

When I looked at her properly, I could see that she had a lot of natural beauty. She had striking eyes. "Indeed," I replied.

"We were hoping you could help us," she continued. "Let me start from the beginning. I was fuelling up my car when I was approached by a man in a suit. He told me that he was late for a meeting and was desperate for a ride," she sighed. "I agreed, he flung his briefcase on my backseat and then excused himself to go to the bathroom before we left. When he was gone, I got a sharp pain in my stomach and I thought I was going into labor. I immediately drove to the nearest hospital."

The man took over. Anger was in his voice and he clenched his fists as he spoke. "It turned out to be a false alarm. She wasn't going into labor and she came home afterwards."

"I didn't even think about the man who wanted a ride until I got home and discovered his briefcase was still on my backseat," added the woman.

Jeremy lifted the briefcase and placed it on the table between us. "We figured if we opened it, we could find some details about the person it belonged to. THIS was what we found." He opened the briefcase and my eyes widened at the contents within. All it contained was a pair of latex gloves, a hatchet, and a length of thick rope.

"Did he give an alias? What did he look like?" I asked eagerly. I was now perched on the edge of my seat. "Did he have blue eyes? Horn-rimmed glasses?"

The girl shook her head. "No glasses. But bright blue eyes. I remember those. We went to the police first, but they totally dismissed us."

I huffed. That was hardly a surprise. The police were still getting inundated with calls about people claiming to know who the killer was. That fact coupled with the fact that they're all incompetent and there we have the expected results.

"May I keep the briefcase?" I inquired. I wanted to study it more closely. They agreed and thanked me for my time. I promised them that I'd do my best to catch the person who did this. And I intended to stick by that promise.

*

The next day my phone had been repaired and I eagerly went to collect it and recover the photographic evidence which I had obtained. Unfortunately, in repairing my screen my phone had been reformatted and all my photographs were gone. A bit disappointing to say the least. FUCK!

I damned myself to hell for not uploading the images to an online storage file. In all the excitement I'd never even considered it, and this was the result. A punishment for my lack of foresight.

I poured a drink. My head rushing with thoughts about how to proceed with the case. Where was Larry Gyllenhaal? And was he the only one? Was that fourth ticket really for his wife? It was possible that Larry removed his glasses in favor of contact lenses so that it would completely change his appearance. I had to find him!

My phone rang.

An unknown number flashed upon the screen. I hesitated at first, but I reluctantly answered it. I didn't say anything and all I could hear was breathing.

"Jack..."

"Who is this?" I recognized the voice. It was a man's voice. The voice of a man who had an air of arrogance about him. This was the voice of Larry Gyllenhaal.

He sighed. "I was a leading surgeon at one of the most prestigious hospitals in LA," he said. His voice carried a complete lack of remorse for his family who had recently been incinerated by an arsonist. An arsonist? Or a desperate man trying to eradicate his guilt? I told him to shut his fucking mouth and he ignored me and continued: "I was to perform life-saving heart surgery on a young girl no older than ten. Instead, I was instructed to operate on mayor Thomas Danforth, someone whose heart condition was due to his insatiable gluttony and his sedentary lifestyle. The child died waiting for an operation which an obese zounderkite stole from her! While she waited, she had painted the most beautiful thing I had ever seen. A magnificent piece created by a truly talented individual! I lost my faith in humanity that day," he paused, likely reflecting back. "What a shame! I considered that her beauty couldn't be captured in a painting. That brilliant creative essence was what set her apart from the mundane. That is why she deserved to live!"

I listened intently, trying to think of ways to keep him talking. If he was emotionally vulnerable right now, I could prey on that and manipulate him somehow. Was that even possible? Did this monster even have emotions?

"Larry, your family..." I ventured. I had to be sure. I had to hear him say the words. I couldn't believe that a man would be capable of killing his own children.

"What of them?"

"They were killed in a fire at your house. Did you have anything to do with that?"

"My hand was forced, detective. You left my study open following your endeavor and my wife just couldn't keep her hornbill-sized beak out of my affairs. She was suspicious that I was having an affair. I guess my absences had begun to arouse suspicion in her. But ultimately you were the one who killed them, detective. Consider myself the gun and you the trigger-happy cowboy who squeezed the trigger."

"But what about your kids?!" I spat in disbelief. My heart began to race with anxiety and anger welling inside me. I was shaking. He had actually fucking done it.

"Oh, those two were not my spawn," he replied as though the subject were a trivial matter. "I was their step-father, not that that title entitled me to the respect I deserved! None of them appreciated the art I made. The two spawn were destined for destitution. They had no future other than sitting in the street begging for handouts for crack and stinking of excrement."

This man sickened me. "Where are you? Hand yourself in!" I prompted him. I spoke as I fought back the urge to be sick.

"Yes. It's about time we spoke face to face. Just the two of us. Everything will be made apparent once we do. Bring your gun if you like! We'll have a little chat and sort out all this unpleasantness!"

What was his angle? Was this a trap? "Where are you?" I thought it best not to mention that my gun was incinerated in the artist studio.

"I'll text you the address to the hotel I'm staying at," he replied. Larry paused again and then continued: "But, please... come as fast as you can, detective."

The phone went dead and I stood there frozen for a moment. I was in complete disbelief. Then the phone buzzed with a text message from the same number. It was a dingy hotel on the other side of the Downtown district.

I didn't call Perry. I wanted to do this on my own without his authoritarian attitude impeding my freedom of choice. I wanted to be the judge of whether this prick lived or died. I would have to be careful though. I was mindful of the gun which the killer had in his possession.

I looked at myself in the mirror. I was standing in a pair of joggers and I had no shirt on. My chest was purple. I'd broken some ribs when I fell, and my eye looked like a telescope. I was in no position to fight anyone. Was it really wise to go there alone?

I had no choice. I had to call Perry. It was the sensible thing to do. I implored him to give me this one chance to prove that I was right, and that Chad wasn't guilty. I would have Perry and his team wait outside Larry's hotel room while I eased him into a false sense of security or have him confess to me so that Perry and the others could hear.

Perry agreed, albeit very hesitantly. What pissed me off was that it took him a full half hour to pick me up! I hobbled down the stairs and got into Perry's police Sedan without saying a word. I gave him the address and he pulled up a few blocks away.

"The building is surrounded," Perry told me bluntly. "Barry and the others are in plain clothes and lingering around the building trying to look inconspicuous. I'll drop you off here and you can walk the rest of the way." He taped a wire to my chest and encouraged me to encourage a confession out of him."

"Have you got the money to pay for my cab fare there?" I remarked sarcastically.

Perry rolled his eyes and slammed his hands on the steering wheel furiously. "I've had enough of your dog shit attitude, Jack!"

He told me to fuck off and I obliged, slamming his car door in defiance, which was probably not the best way to treat my only backup.

I hobbled to the hotel and asked the receptionist which room I could find Larry Gyllenhaal in and she told me that he was in room four.

I went to the room and knocked on the door. As I stood there waiting for Gyllenhaal to answer the door I reflected on my attitude towards Perry. At first, I had thought that his idea to drop me off a few blocks away was out of spite. Then I realized that he was right. If this was a fake location and Larry was watching from afar to see whether I would involve the police, then this should encourage him to give me the correct location.

I knocked again.

Where the fuck is he? What would happen if I kicked down the door? Was it rigged to explode like in the movies?

I sighed. I was thoroughly bored of waiting. I knocked again and still no answer. I decided fuck it! I kicked the door wide open.

I sighed again, more loudly this time. "Perry, you can come in. I think you should see this," I paused and looked at Gyllenhaal with disgust. "And get hold of Grim! We're going to need him here!"

*

Suicide. A gunshot wound straight through the head. The last thing that I was expecting to see. It was a small room with a bed against the window and a small table with a kettle and things to make tea and coffee. There was half a bottle of wine on the table and half a glass.

Larry Gyllenhaal was sprawled half across the bed and half across the floor. The left side of his face was pressed down against the floor with his right eye staring lifelessly at the door. A gun rested near his limp right hand and the exit wound had blown the left side of his head wide open. Blood spatter and chunks of brain clung to the wall. He was wearing a green suit with a purple tie and brown loafers.

"Well that's that," said Perry as he straightened his pants, pulling them up by the belt with a grunt. "I guess if he is the Artist Killer as you suspected, then it's case closed."

"Jesus Christ!" retorted Barry with a wrinkled nose and a distasteful grin on his face.

Something wasn't right. I could sense it. I can't see Larry Gyllenhaal shooting himself in the head like that. Was this a last attempt to cast suspicion on me? Or perhaps to discredit me? I really had no idea.

When Grim arrived, he handed Perry and me some gloves to begin investigating. Afterwards he would take Gyllenhaal down to the morgue for a more thorough examination.

Perry searched Gyllenhaal's blazer pocket, finding a note and a tape recorder. He placed the tape recorder on the table and pressed play.

"*My name is Larry Gyllenhaal. I am the Artist Killer. I conspired with Chad Sullivan to kill all those women. I confess to all the crimes and take full responsibility for what I've done. I set my own home ablaze and killed my family and eradicated all traces of my guilt. May my essence be forever captured in my creative works.*" Then there was a gunshot and a thud.

Perry pressed pause on the machine and gave me a questioning look. I was suspicious, and I think that my facial expression made that quite clear.

"The note," said Perry, handing me the small piece of paper. "It's garbage."

He handed it to me, and I looked it over with a raised eyebrow. Perry was right. It was garbage. It had nothing but an inconsequential list of alchemical ingredients from the periodic table. Despite sensing that it was useless I folded it up and put it in my pocket. The note read as follows:

"**Nickel:** *A metal found in most meteorites. Silvery white takes a polish. Used in alloys and for coins.*

Cobalt: *A brittle, hard metal, resembling iron and nickel. Used to harden alloys. Brilliant blue color pigment.*

Lanthanum: *A very reactive, soft, rare-earth metal. Used for high intensity lighting.*

Sulphur: *A pale yellow, odorless, brittle solid, which is insoluble in water. Strong odor as Sulphur oxides.*

Bromine: *The only liquid non-metallic element. A heavy, mobile, reddish-brown liquid with a disagreeable odor.*

Oxygen: *An abundant gas which makes up 21% of the Earth's atmosphere. Extremely reactive and necessary for life.*

Tungsten: *A steel-grey to tin-white metal. Filaments used for lights and electronics.*

Nitrogen: *A gas that makes up 78% of Earth's air. Odorless and colorless, but important to life as a fertilizer.*"

"What do you make of it?" asked Perry. I could tell by his tone that he dismissed the whole situation.

"I think the whole thing stinks!" I replied sharply. I wasn't just bitter because I'd been denied retribution against this man. It was the unsettling feeling that I had that this was a murder scene, rather than merely a suicide. Looks like that fourth ticket wasn't for his wife after all.

"Oh fuck off, man!" snapped Barry with a sneer. "He fucking blew his own brains out, case closed. Let's get coffee and donuts and let Grim and the forensic team do their jobs."

Perry ignored Barry and turned to me. "Go on then? What do think?"

I thought back to my confrontation with Gyllenhaal at the fashion gala. He was holding a glass of wine back then. He loved wine. So why didn't he finish the glass on the table before he offed himself? That was my starting point.

"Firstly, I doubt Larry Gyllenhaal would have left half a glass of wine on the table. People who intend on committing suicide generally don't leave things like this unfinished," I said.

"Maybe it was spontaneous," chipped in Barry with a shrug of his shoulders.

"No... there's more. The gun!" I pointed at the gun lying beside Larry Gyllenhaal's hand. "Larry shot himself with his right hand, as you can tell with the gun and the exit wound at the left side of his head."

"What's your point?" asked Perry impatiently.

"When I spoke to Larry at the fashion gala, he was holding a glass of wine in his left hand. He shifted it to his right hand to shake my hand. Larry Gyllenhaal was left-handed, so it makes no sense that he would shoot himself in the head using his right hand."

"Maybe he was ambidextrous," retorted Barry. This time his interruption made my blood boil. Was he purposefully trying to discredit me?

"Come on!" I beseeched them with my eyes looking into theirs pleadingly. "Would Larry Gyllenhaal have really gone to the trouble of blowing his own brains out and then *rewinding* the tape recorder back to the beginning?"

Barry and Perry cast each other an unreadable glance before they scratched their heads and thought about my words.

"Larry Gyllenhaal was murdered!" I exclaimed in an explicit manner, just in case my point hadn't sunk in yet. "In his financial ledger he kept a record of everything he purchased. He had purchased four tickets for the fashion gala! That's one for me, one for himself, one for Chad Sullivan and one for an unknown party." I narrowed my eyes. "This unknown party is the true Artist Killer! Or at the very least an accomplice who killed Larry to protect himself."

"This old spiel again..." snickered Barry, giving Perry a sideway glance to see whether he approved of his mockery.

"Do you have any suspects?" asked Perry, completely ignoring Barry's ridicule.

That was the tough part. I didn't have a clue. The only thing which I was certain of was that Larry Gyllenhaal was murdered and it had been made to look like a suicide. I was on to Larry and the Artist Killer wanted to silence him.

"The tape probably rewound itself, he was probably ambidextrous, and he did this to fuck with you, Jack! Case closed, man!" Barry's attitude had now taken on a more understanding approach, bordering sympathy.

It wasn't case closed! But it would be for me if I didn't find the true killer by midnight tonight! Midnight would mean the end of my three-day allotted time period. I had to think! I had to think hard and fast!

The coroner, Grim, came for Gyllenhaal's body and later I went back home in great pain.

It was later in my apartment that a sudden realization hit me. Suddenly, I thought back on a few things certain individuals had said and done leading up to this point. It hit me like a freight train. So hard that I spilled my drink all over the carpet and collapsed, struggling to stand!

I knew who it was! I fucking knew who it was! That clever son of a bitch!

I heard whispering. It was midnight. Annabelle and the others were coming. I braced myself and tried to scramble to my feet as the walls around me began to bend and twist unnaturally. Paintings appeared on my walls, all showing the sneering face of Larry Gyllenhaal.

"We're going to get you!" This was what each painting was saying to me. My front door swung open and there was Annabelle, floating inches from my floor towards me. The wall behind me became like liquid and formed into several hands which gripped me and pulled me inexorably towards them.

"Please!" I pleaded with them. "Give me one more day! Just one more day! I know who he is now!"

The hands released me from their grip and Annabelle dissipated while whispering, "Last chance!"

I opened my eyes. A new surge of enthusiasm swept through my body and I got to work arranging what would be the final confrontation between the Artist Killer and myself. I would gather all my closest and most trusted allies and in their presence I would expose the killer and end the case once and for all!

CHAPTER 17

Confrontation

The meeting place was a small, secluded cabin not far from Shaver Lake. From the cabin's porch you could see the sunlight glimmering on the surface of the water as though it had been littered with golden coins. Trees and greenery could be seen as far as the horizon. A gentle breeze carrying the faint aroma of pine caressed my face.

I had brought with me the following: my case notes, a compilation of all my research since the case began and the diary of Mary O'Reilly. I also brought the cassette player which I had bought along with the tape which I was sent of the killer executing Reece Pemberton, who had recently been found in a canal. He was decomposed to the point where no forensic evidence was obtainable.

Nicolas arrived first. He stepped out of his car and smiled at me as he walked up the gravel path to the cabin. Stones crunched underneath his black shoes. He hopped up the steps and offered me a firm handshake.

I started coughing again. I'd been chain smoking on the porch, waiting for the others to arrive. That last cough was pretty violent. So violent that I lurched forward and honked like a goose. Nicolas slammed his hand against my back in an attempt to sooth me. I looked at the remainder of my cigarette and scraped it under my shoe.

Perry and Grim arrived one hour later. Both of them were in police uniform. Perry looked pissed off, which was normal for him. To be honest, I was surprised that he had shown up. Grim's face was emotionless, as always. He offered me a polite nod and a handshake. Perry did not.

"We're still waiting on a few others," I told the three of them. None of them knew why I had brought them here, but they all knew that it was important.

We entered the cabin and I had set everything up ready to use in my little demonstration. The video was ready to play at the click of a button and the files were compiled on a table beside a little surprise which I had arranged. That surprise was an open briefcase with the piece of rope, hatchet, and rubber gloves. It was just on display there, for all to see.

I carefully studied each man's reaction as they walked in, attempting to gage any signs of shock or recognition. The real Artist Killer would immediately recognize this briefcase.

Grim passed it first, not even looking at it. His eyes lacked any emotion of any discernible kind. But could that have been to cover how he truly felt about it?

Perry asked what the fuck I was doing with that. He marched past it angrily and joined Grim by the sofas near the small television set hooked up to the cheap VCR.

Nicolas looked over it with vague interest before silently joining the others.

I walked over to an old jukebox and put on some music. It was a classical piece, which I really enjoyed. Moonlight Sonata by Beethoven. I found that the soothing melodies of classical music helped me to concentrate.

"What the fuck is this?" snapped Perry, his patience already as thin as a thread.

I smiled at him mischievously. "I have a flare for the dramatic," I told him with a chuckle. "Besides, we're still waiting on a few others, one of whom I need here."

One of those who I had invited was Rebecca Valentine. I still had deeply rooted affection for her. I wanted her to witness my greatest moment as a police homicide detective. After I exposed the killer, I had images in my mind of her wrapping her slender arms around my neck and pushing her soft lips against mine. That wouldn't happen though, not unless she turned up.

I had been in contact with her frequently since Gyllenhaal's dinner, relaxing considerably since his alleged suicide. She had refused every offer I made to keep her company, insisting that she would be safe.

I stared wistfully out of the cabin window overlooking the gravel path and willed her to appear at the end of the winding road obscured by trees.

"Jack, can we just get this shit over with? I'm about to leave!" Perry was serious. He looked at Grim and nodded his head towards the door.

"Just wait," I urged them. "In a moment, somebody is going to walk through that door. When they do, I can begin with the exposure of the Artist Killer!" I turned to Nicolas and Perry. "You two brought your guns, didn't you?"

Perry nodded, his hand instinctively reaching for his firearm. He stroked the grip for luck, as he always did when he was nervous.

Nicolas opened his green parker to show his gun resting in a brown leather holster. "Mostly for display..." he muttered at Perry when he caught the man giving him a reprimanding glare. Nicolas coughed uncomfortably and drew his parker closed, obscuring the gun from view.

The cabin door began to creek open. I rallied Grim, Perry and Nicolas by my side and we all watched as a beam of sunlight suddenly stretched across the floor of the cabin, the shadow of a man in its center. The man was a shadowy silhouette standing in the doorway. No features could be discerned as the sun forced us to shield our eyes as the man entered.

He stepped into the cabin and slammed the door behind him. Once our eyes adjusted, we could all see who the man was.

"You!" barked Nicolas sharply across the room. "So, this is the fucking chump who murdered those girls!"

Dean Costello stood with his back to the wall, arms folded with a grin on his face. He was wearing his signature white suit with a fancy bow tie. He ignored the others and only acknowledged me, giving me a nod and saying: "So, here we are..."

He was here! It was time to begin! My eyes narrowed and I started to speak in a clinical tone. "You stand accused of the murders of Scarlett Jones, Mary O'Reilly, Rosita Ramirez, Emma Fontaine, and Crystal Hayes. You're also responsible for the shootings of Reece Pemberton and the murder of your ally, Larry Gyllenhaal. How do you plead?..." I left a pause as a grin forced its way across my lips. We all stood in a row, eyeballing Costello as I listed the various victims of the Artist Killer. There were others, of course, those whose deaths were caused indirectly such as Annabelle Green and even Olivia Lockhart who ultimately died because of the Artist Killer. My sworn enemy! The man who I had hunted for several years! The man who ruined my career and reduced me to an alcoholic shell of a man. Now I would have retribution!

"How do you plead?" I asked again, shifting my gaze from Dean Costello to Nicolas Brown. All heads turned to follow my gaze.

Nicolas looked as though he had been slapped across the face. The shock in his face was evident as the color drained from his face. He stammered and struggled to express himself. Grim and Perry also turned to face Nicolas, both of them clearly surprised by the turn of events.

Dean Costello kept smiling. He had been made aware of my plan from the beginning. Without him this little exposé wouldn't have been made possible. This was his cabin after all. He used his hand to gesture for Nicolas to speak. "This should be good!" he exclaimed.

Nicolas sighed and took off his parker coat. He ran a hand through his shaggy mousey hair and took a seat. He was wearing a white shirt and faded jeans. "May I have a cigarette, Jack?" he asked with a smirk. The sheer brass balls on this cunt astounded me.

"Fuck off!" I shouted indignantly.

He looked up at me sharply with a look of hatred in his eyes. He was slightly trembling. I noted this with some satisfaction. Though whether it was through anger or fear I could not be sure.

"Let's start with Larry Gyllenhaal, shall we?" I asked rhetorically, receiving unnecessary nods from Perry and Costello. Grim was still stoic, his expression unchanging.

"Larry Gyllenhaal was definitely a close ally of the killer," I began, pacing back and forth in front of my gathered allies. They all watched me intently, as did the Artist Killer. "In the end, Gyllenhaal implored me to meet with him at the hotel where his body was found, suggesting to me that he knew Nicolas would see him as a loose end. I mean, I sincerely doubt it was the Artist Killer's plan for Gyllenhaal to expose himself to me at the fashion gala. Nicolas knew I would stop at nothing to continue my pursuit of Gyllenhaal and that's why he had to die!"

"Bullshit!" snapped Nicolas, pushing himself to his feet in defiance. His eyes searched the room, pleading with the others not to believe me. "Can you really believe the word of a delusional psychopath?! What evidence is any of this even based on?!"

Perry looked at the floor with uncertainty. His look made me feel uneasy. Had I lost Perry already? I smiled mischievously. I had a little something that could sway Perry and any other doubters present as to the accuracy of my claims.

From my pocket I withdrew the small piece of paper which had been found in Gyllenhaal's pocket when he died. The list of alchemical ingredients. I felt a surge of excitement rush through me. Would this be all that was necessary to convince them? Or would it require more evidence? I was willing to go as far as it would take.

"This piece of paper was on Gyllenhaal's person the day he was found," I explained, walking around the room and making sure that everyone could have a good look at it. "It seems inconsequential, just some random note about chemistry. However, this piece of paper is a vital piece of evidence!" I turned to face Nicolas Brown and pointed an accusing finger at him. "Larry Gyllenhaal knew you would remove any notes or messages left for me. So, he cleverly incorporated one into a seemingly unrelated note about chemistry."

I read the note aloud for the whole group to hear: "Nickel: A metal found in most meteorites. Silvery white takes a polish. Used in alloys and for coins.

Cobalt: A brittle, hard metal, resembling iron and nickel. Used to harden alloys. Brilliant blue color pigment.

Lanthanum: A very reactive, soft, rare-earth metal. Used for high intensity lighting.

Sulphur: A pale yellow, odorless, brittle solid, which is insoluble in water. Strong odor as Sulphur oxides.

Bromine: The only liquid non-metallic element. A heavy, mobile, reddish-brown liquid with a disagreeable odor.

Oxygen: An abundant gas which makes up 21% of the Earth's atmosphere. Extremely reactive and necessary for life.

Tungsten: A steel-grey to tin-white metal. Filaments used for lights and electronics.

Nitrogen: A gas that makes up 78% of Earth's air. Odorless and colorless, but important to life as a fertilizer."

Perry rolled his eyes impatiently. "Jack, that note is garbage! There's nothing in there that we can use."

I shook my head in disagreement. "All this," I gestured to all the information about the different elements from the periodic table. "All this is garbage, as you say. A mere smokescreen to hide the code that was intended for me to find. See if we take all the elements and transfer them into how they appear on the periodic table then the message from Gyllenhaal is very different!" I got a pen and grabbed some paper, writing out the list of elements included in Gyllenhaal's notes. Beside each element I wrote its symbol from the periodic table. When I was finished, I held the paper up for all to see and read it aloud once again. This was how my new list was presented:

"Nickel: Ni.

Cobalt: Co.

Lanthanum: La.

Sulphur: S.

Bromine: Br.

Oxygen: O.

Tungsten: W.

Nitrogen: N."

Everyone's eyes seemed to widen together. Perry shot a narrow-eyed glare towards Nicolas Brown and his hand instinctively went for his gun.

Slow clapping filled the void of silence that followed my revelation. "Bravo, Jack!" declared Nicolas with a wolfish grin that completely surprised me. "You certainly have everyone here fooled!"

He shook his head and rested it in his hands. "You're all fools!" barked Nicolas aggressively at the other three men present in the room. "The Pied Piper has played his tune and you've all danced along to the music without even considering the fallacy behind Jack's accusations!"

"And what fallacy is that?!" I snarled through gritted teeth.

Nicolas chuckled. "The fallacy that you would trust the word of a confirmed suspect!" Now Nicolas prowled back and forth in front of the bystanders, like a wild animal asserting dominance. He didn't take his predatory eyes off me for a second. "The fact that you're so eager to push for me to take the blame for Gyllenhaal's murder only reaffirms what I've suspected for some time already!" He pointed a finger at me. His eyes were bulging as though they were going to pop out. The man looked deranged, but even so the bystanders clung to his every word. "I am actually a hired investigator!" he retorted, hectically removing a handful of his tacky business cards and tossing them onto the ground. "I was hired by the families of the victims to bring the Artist Killer to justice! Jack Cucchiano has been my suspect for some time!"

"Evidence?" asked Perry plainly. It was uncertain what he made of Nicolas Brown's claim, but I knew for definite that he didn't trust me...

Nicolas smiled. "Oh, I've got evidence! Evidence that can prove Jack is a killer! And I'm not talking about false evidence, like the testimony of a confirmed suspect!" Nicolas paused and chuckled ominously. "It is clear that Jack Cucchiano and Larry Gyllenhaal were secretly in cahoots with one another." He walked over to his parker, which was draped over a wooden chair. He retrieved a brown envelope, containing several photographs. He flicked through them and found the particular one which he wanted. "Here we are..." he said, smirking at me.

I cocked my head inquisitively. What was this guy's angle? And why was he so confident? What was his A-game?

Nicolas presented the photograph to Perry and Grim. He never showed it to Dean Costello, who he must have known was my closest ally at this point. "Here we can see Jack and his lady friend leaving Larry Gyllenhaal's house!" he stated with an accusing glare.

Nicolas pointed at Gyllenhaal. "Just look how complacent he is! This is not the actions of enemies! I'd say these two were clearly allies!"

Uncertainty washed over the faces of the spectators. And for good reason! The poor lighting concealed Rebecca's expression of concern and I was staring blankly. The bastard had been following me and building some kind of counterattack portfolio!

This was my theory: He had staked out the Budapest Hotel after he had murdered Emma Fontaine. After that he waited for me to arrive and followed myself and Olivia to Reece Pemberton's house. That was how he found him. It must have been when Olivia dropped me off home later that day that he discovered where I lived.

I felt sick! I felt like I'd been violated! Goosebumps crept down my arms and the hairs on the nape of my neck stood on end! That was how he found me at the Blue Bell! How he knew that I was at Club 88 the night Chad and his goons attacked me!

I ground my teeth together furiously. Then I composed myself and challenged his claim. "I was there investigating! I went there under the guise of being apologetic on account of the 'Artist Killer' being arrested. I don't think that he bought it, but he enjoyed playing games with me, for he couldn't resist."

The more this went on the more I considered the possibility that Larry Gyllenhaal had in fact not set his own house alight. I considered that maybe he had only said those things to me on the phone so that I would hurry up and get to him. It was my theory that Nicolas Brown had torched Gyllenhaal's house with the impression that Larry Gyllenhaal was still inside it. Maybe I was just kidding myself because I didn't want to believe Larry Gyllenhaal was capable of such malice. Surely if he was capable of killing his own family, he couldn't have cared about them, and if he hadn't cared about them then wouldn't it have made more sense for him to just leave? He clearly had the financial means... Right now, I couldn't worry too much about that! This was the final battle and I had to succeed!

"He sold you out in his code, Nicolas!" I continued. "I'm guessing he wrote a fake note which you would've mistaken as his actual message to me!"

Nicolas gave a dismissive snicker in response to me. "Come on, Jack! You could've written that stupid code yourself once you'd already murdered Gyllenhaal! Are these people expected to believe that Larry Gyllenhaal had written it based solely on your word? Let's face it, that's not exactly trustworthy, is it?"

"Let Jack continue!" droned Grim. "Do you have anything else, Jack?"

"Yes, Jack! Please do tell us what other evidence you're going to astound us with!" remarked Nicolas, putting his hand on his chin and staring at me intensely.

I ignored his mockery and began with Rosita Ramirez's case. "Her lock was picked! As was mine when the killer broke into my house! It was evident by the scratches under the door." I produced three of my own photographs. One was of Rosita Ramirez's lock, another was of the door lock to my flat and a third one was of the door at Chad's house. I had secretly gone back there and took pictures of Chad's lock after Gyllenhaal's death. Nicolas had picked it when we broke in to look for evidence that could convict Chad.

"These three photographs are of scratches around locks. One is Rosita's lock and another is of my own, both of which the killer picked. Look at this distinct scratch pattern." I indicated the similarities in the photographs. "It shows the killer has a particular method when it comes to picking locks." I then showed them the third photograph of Chad's lock. "This is of Chad's lock. Nicolas and myself went there looking for clues. I lied about hearing a break in, as if that isn't obvious by now. At least we convicted Annabelle's murderer. At the time I had truly believed Nicolas was a private detective."

"That's not true!" came Nicolas' stern defence. "He's lying! I was never there!"

Perry was clearly sceptical. He shook his head doubtfully. "It's clear these photographs are taken where you say. But unfortunately, yet again we have nothing but your word to tie Nicolas to any of this! It's your word against his! I don't trust either of you!"

"It's clear one of them must be the Artist Killer," added Grim calmly. His attitude reminded me of a tranquil ocean resting under a thunderous storm. The rest of us were the storm.

"It's Nicolas!" I practically screamed. The scream was so shrill that my voice was hoarse afterwards and my chest was pounding in pain. "He's the one Larry Gyllenhaal bought the fourth ticket for! He took

Crystal Hayes down a maintenance shaft and dismembered her in that abandoned factory!" My eyes frantically darted from person to person, searching for acknowledgment. "I stake my reputation on my supposition that that partial footprint in the Budapest Hotel would match a print of Nicolas' shoes!" I thought of mentioning the fact that Nicolas was at the Hotel disguised as the first officer on the scene named Kenneth, another alias and a disguise, which he had cleverly used to trick the security guard into leaving the security office so that he could wipe the footage.

Nicolas shook his head "Stake what reputation? You're nothing but a loser, Cucchiano. I didn't kill those girls and you fucking know it! You're the only killer here and I intend to prove it!"

Dean Costello was the next to speak. He lashed out in anger at Nicolas Brown, telling him to shut his lying murderous mouth. "You fucking killed Scarlett! You and that deranged fella Gyllenhaal!"

Nicolas looked down upon him as though he were observing an insect. He took a few paces towards Dean with his arms outstretched. "Oh, and we all know who you are, don't we?"

"That's not true," interjected Perry, turning to face Costello. "Who the fuck are you supposed to be?"

"A killer for hire!" piped up Nicolas before Costello had a chance to say a single word. Nicolas turned to face Perry. "Jack gave Costello his riot gear and a gun from the police armory! That alone should be a felon!" He turned towards me with a condescending smile as he slowly retrieved a photograph of Costello and myself in an alleyway close to the LA police department.

I felt my heart sink into the pit of my stomach. It was true! I had told Costello my plan, knowing that he'd been in the army previously and had killed before. I knew that he wouldn't have any objections to killing someone who had played a part in Scarlett's death. It was easy to convince him. I offered him a monetary incentive to begin with, informing him of my agreement with Nicolas to share the reward money offered by Annabelle's parents once her killer was captured. Costello had listened to my plan thoroughly without saying a word. The entire time his hand was on his chin in contemplation. We had never been friends. To begin with, following the murder of Scarlett Jones, I had even suspected him of being responsible and pushed for his prosecution.

"I like the plan," he finally said with a conspiratorial grin. "If Walter has to die in order for us to convict Scarlett's killer, then I'll do it. So long as you guarantee me the reward money and that nobody will discover my role in this if things go south."

"I fucking knew it!" screamed Perry at me. His face turned red with absolute fury and he drew his firearm and aimed at me apprehensively, his arms shaking. "You're a fucking murderer, Jack!"

I raised my hands in the air. Perry turned his gun on Costello and gestured for him to move next to me. Costello looked at me in disbelief. I was sure that my evidence would be enough to convince them.

"If you suspected Jack, then why did you initially accuse this guy in the white suit?" asked Grim in a clinical tone.

Nicolas replied faster than I could snap my fingers, explaining that he also suspected Costello and was waiting for the right moment to expose me. The bastard had an answer to everything! This silver-tongued monster was swaying the influence of the crowd. Or at the very least he was convincing the one person who had a gun. I wasn't finished yet, though. I still had more cards up my sleeve.

"Costello, show them what's inside your pocket!"

Costello slowly reached into his pocket and retrieved something too small for the others to see. He threw them on the floor at Nicolas' feet and muttered: "You dropped these when I punched you!"

Nicolas looked down at his feet where two brown contact lenses were staring back up at him.

"The diary!" I urged Grim, frantically pointing to the diary of Mary O'Reilly on the table. "Brown isn't his natural eye color!"

Grim stiffly strode to the table and picked up the diary by the corner with his index finger and thumb. He walked over to Perry and handed it to him. Perry lowered his gun and started reading, mumbling so that he was barely audible.

"Nicolas Brown is Bright Eyes! Ralph Lawrence!" I panted. Perspiration was thick on my brow and dark circles had appeared under my armpits.

Perry looked at Grim and gestured for him to go check. Grim walked towards Nicolas and held out his hand until Nicolas took out his contact lenses to reveal bright blue eyes.

"Yes, I wear contact lenses," shrugged Nicolas, trying to downplay what that indicated. "The two of them set this up together! They obviously knew I wore contact lenses when Costello punched me!" He protested, rubbing his chin as though the mention of the punch brought back the sting. "Jack probably wrote that diary himself, or had Costello write it! Again, this is not tangible evidence!"

"You're a fucking piece of work!" snarled Costello.

"Keep your dog on a leash, Cucchiano!" shouted Perry. He tossed the diary aside and frantically waved his gun at Costello and myself. We raised our hands again in panic.

"I've had enough!" shouted Nicolas. He withdrew a photograph and handed it to Perry. "This should prove, irrefutably, that Jack Cucchiano is a killer!"

I couldn't see the photograph, but Perry stared at it for a long time. Tears formed in his eyes and at that moment I knew that I'd been utterly defeated. Perry cocked the hammer on his pistol and spoke to us in sheer anger as tears rolled down his cheeks. "I'm taking you both in!"

"As you can see in the photograph, Jack murdered a police sheriff. I don't know who he was, but I'm assuming that he must have been working with someone in the LAPD." He paused and I caught the slight glimpse of a smirk on his face. "A woman? What was her name, Jack?"

"Olivia!" answered Perry on my behalf through gritted teeth. "So, you fucking killed her! I can see her SUV in the fucking photograph, Jack! You're already covered in blood! I'm taking you in!"

I shook my head. "You'll have to shoot me!" I'd rather die than spend the rest of my life in prison for the crimes of the Artist Killer. No! I'd much rather die! Not that it mattered anyway. Even if I went willingly, Annabelle and the others would come for me.

Nicolas drew his own weapon and moved to Perry's side. "I know I said this was just for display, but it's actually loaded!" he explained, aiming it at Costello and then at me. A surge of dread rushed through my body as Perry stepped forward towards Costello and me, but Nicolas lingered back.

"Perry! His gun! Check his gun for prints!" I pleaded.

Nicolas scoffed. "Of course you will find my prints on my own gun!"

"Perry! Check for MY prints! I was wrestling with the killer the night I got this!" I pointed at my swollen eye. I looked at Nicolas and smiled. "I let you have your fun," I told him. "Like I said earlier, I have a flare for the dramatic! I wanted to present all the evidence to Perry before I revealed my 'Opus Magnum' if you will." I gestured to the video cassette player. "Please Perry, may I? If you still don't believe me after this then I'll come willingly!"

"You'll come willingly anyway, Jack! You're a murderer!" Perry's gun followed me as I moved across the room. "And you!" he said, turning his gun on Nicolas. "Put your gun on the table and move next to white suit!"

Nicolas graciously obliged without saying a word.

I played the tape of the Artist Killer shooting Reece Pemberton. I paused the video as the killer outstretched his hand and was about to pull the trigger. "If my prints on the gun aren't enough to convince you, then look at this! The Killer's gun is a Glock, the same as Nicolas Brown's! I know that isn't evidence on its own, but if you look really carefully you can faintly see the model and serial number on the side. It should match up with the model and serial number on Nicolas' glock!"

Grim squinted his eyes and leaned inches from the television screen. "It's true!" he replied. "If you really concentrate you can just make them out." I handed him a pen and he quickly jotted them down. Then he purposefully strode across to the table where Nicolas Brown's gun was. "It's a match!" confirmed Grim.

Perry turned to Nicolas, thrusting his gun in his direction. "So, you are a fucking killer! Let's see you talk your way out of this one!"

"Perry," I asked gently. "What about Walter?" He looked at me wide-eyed and with his hands shaking. Thick stress lines stretched across his brow. He was silent and so I tried to appeal to him through his love and respect for Olivia. "Walter bribed Olivia so that she would lead me into a trap at that warehouse. Olivia's mum is really sick and Walter used that to manipulate her actions. Olivia felt as though she had no choice. In the end, when she realized that Walter had intended to have me killed, she tried to defend me and was shot dead by that sheriff in the photograph. I was covered in blood in the photograph Nicolas showed you because I had cradled her in her final moments. I took her SUV and killed the bastard! He killed my best friend, Perry! He killed our Olivia! He shot her with a colt python revolver!"

"That checks out," added Grim with a nod in my direction. "During her autopsy I found a bullet that was fired from a gun of that caliber and .305 shell casings were found at the scene."

"I think Jack stole my gun!" protested Nicolas as Perry held out both arms aimed at him. "That's how he got his finger prints on my gun! He's fucking guilty!"

"I'll deal with Jack later! First, we need to deal with you!" replied Perry, giving me a quick sideways glance. "How were you intending to deal with him?" He asked.

"I was going to fucking lynch him with his own rope," I replied flatly, indicating to the briefcase on the table.

Perry holstered his gun and shook his head. "I can't allow that!"

"Take him in then, if you want." I shrugged.

"Fine…" mumbled Nicolas, barely audible. "I am the Artist Killer and I would like to surrender." He held his hands up and began to snicker. "Tell me, Jack, how's Rebecca Valentine?"

My heart sank. She had still not arrived, despite my invite. My anxiety began to escalate into fear and dread. "What have you done with her, you sick fuck?!" I launched myself forward and punched him in the jaw, pulling my chest and collapsing in the process.

"She's safe…" replied Nicolas, wiping the blood from his lip. Then he smirked malevolently. "At least for now!" he jeered, giving a wide-eyed, extravagant wave of his hands. "She's out here! She's among nature! And if you don't hurry up and find her, she'll be returning to the Earth soon!" Nicolas began to laugh maniacally. He ignored our orders to shut his mouth. "I don't know how much oxygen she'll have left by now. But if you let me take a car you have my word that

I shall send her location to your phone. I just want to get out of here. I won't talk in prison, and I certainly won't talk if I'm dead. This is your only chance to save her! Let me go now, or Rebecca dies a horrible, slow and painful death in the dark and the cold."

Perry looked at Grim and suggested that they get some donuts. "Good luck, Jack and Costello! I want you both out of LA within a week. If I see either of you again, I will have you arrested. I'll have every officer under my charge to search under every leaf in this forest!"

Perry and Grim both left without even looking at any of us, let alone saying another word. And as they disappeared so too did any chance that Nicolas Brown had of living.

I called Nicolas' bluff and grabbed his Glock from the table. I used it to blow out his kneecap to make him an easier target for Costello, who grabbed the cut length of rope and wrapped it around Nicolas' neck, cutting out his screams of agony. Costello dragged Nicolas across the floor, grunting like a wild bull. He kept saying that he was going to kill Nicolas for what he had done to Scarlett Jones. Nicolas uselessly kicked at the floor, his working leg leaving scuff marks on the wood from his shoe. His tongue protruded as he choked hopelessly for air and his eyes bulged until they went red and rolled back into his head. And even after Nicolas Brown was long dead, Dean Costello kept strangling him. And I kept watching.

We used the hatchet to dismember him, putting his body parts into bags and dumping them into the lake at nightfall. We vigorously cleaned the cabin and then went our separate ways. I was the greatest homicide detective in LA. And I had just made my finest accomplishment. I just hoped that in doing so I hadn't inadvertently caused the death of Rebecca Valentine. That was something that would haunt me for the rest of my days, and so even though I had victory, it would be nevertheless bittersweet...

CHAPTER 18

Epilogue

Perry had warned us to leave town as soon as we'd finished with Nicolas Brown. His strong sense of justice couldn't allow for him to coexist in the same city as Costello and myself. Costello left immediately, completely disappearing without a trace. I had managed to convince Perry to let me stay for one more week so that I could see whether or not Rebecca Valentine was found. Perry reluctantly agreed.

There was a sharp knock at the door, a rhythmic knock which I recognized. I opened the door and fondly greeted Grim with a smile, a handshake and a warm pat on the back.

I invited him in and made coffee for the two of us. Then I asked the inevitable question, the question which I wasn't sure I wanted answering. Was Rebecca alive?

"We searched the forest all week, Jack," replied Grim with a regretful shake of his head. "Perry is still searching for her now! He's been at it all night!" He cleared his throat and continued: "I took the liberty of having Michael O'Reilly's DNA cross referenced against that of Mary O'Reilly, whose DNA we have on file. Well, there was no match. Mary O'Reilly couldn't have been Mary O'Reilly. She's back to being Lady Mystery."

I was lost for words. Grim stared at me for a few more awkward moments before uncomfortably excusing himself and heading towards the door. I quickly got to my feet, grunting in pain because of my chest. I caught up to Grim and stopped him, grabbing the sleeve of his white shirt. "What does that mean?" I asked desperately. "What does that have to do with Rebecca Valentine?"

Grim shrugged his shoulders. "I'm sure you said the two of them were friends." He then blinked expressionlessly and offered me another handshake. "Good luck, Jack!" said Grim, smiling at me for the first time in several years. "You did really good! Any plans for the future?"

"Sky's the limit!" I replied jovially, although in truth I had no idea where I would go or what I would do now. I felt without purpose. I perceived a certain emptiness in my soul. We wished each other luck again and then parted ways for the final time.

Back to the silence and solitude of my apartment... I sat myself down in my sofa and pondered over this interesting new development. Mary O'Reilly was not Mary O'Reilly! What did that even fucking mean?! Was Rebecca Valentine still alive out there? Or had I indirectly caused her death when I mercilessly had Nicolas Brown killed? I had solved the case and yet there were more questions than answers!

I tugged at my hair in frustration. Where the fuck is she?! *Who* the fuck is she?! I got to my feet and paced back and forth through my flat.

Think! Think! Think!

I thought about every likely outcome and considered the possible scenarios based on what I knew so far. "Nicolas Brown was the one who said he questioned a friend of Mary O'Reilly... Rebecca Valentine put me on the track to hunting down Mary's detestable father. The diary..." I said aloud.

I paced back and forth some more. This was my concluding theory: Rebecca Valentine was either a victim or a culprit. I think that it could have been possible that she knew Nicolas Brown was the Artist Killer and possibly blackmailed him into helping her expose Mary's father. Except it wasn't Mary's father! There was no match with the DNA! That told me that Rebecca Valentine was actually Mary O'Reilly! That's the only logical explanation!

Rebecca Valentine, or Mary O'Reilly rather, had used the Artist Killer to send me to her, so she in turn could use me to expose her father's pedophile ring. I made quite a few arrests that day! So, who was Rebecca Valentine? Was Lady Mystery the real Rebecca Valentine? This was all so very confusing!

That was my theory as to her identity, her true identity. I developed two theories on what had actually happened to her. The first theory is that she was kidnapped by Nicolas Brown, possibly in an attempt to silence her. Nicolas must've buried her alive somewhere with barely enough oxygen to survive. I cringed at the thought of Rebecca, or Mary, being trapped and doomed to die because of me.

If that were the case, was the woman who I loved a necessary sacrifice to put an end to the Artist Killer?

My second theory was much more idyllic. She simply got away. After Larry Gyllenhaal had been whacked, she must have scarpered somewhere, leaving all her personal belongings behind and making a break for a new beginning. Perhaps she had wanted to escape the clutches of the psychotic Nicolas Brown. Perhaps she wanted to escape the clutches of the psychotic Jack Cucchiano... Perhaps she felt that I would have had her arrested for conspiracy or something. I didn't care. I just hoped that she was safe.

Should I dedicate the rest of my life to finding her? I quickly decided against it. It wouldn't be worth it. If she had wanted me to go with her, she would have asked me.

The more I thought about it, the more I realized that I didn't actually care whether or not she was an ally of the killer. I loved her and that was just the simple truth of the matter. I couldn't spend my life looking for her even if I wanted. If Perry saw me in LA again, he'd not be so lenient with me. I had to leave.

I could hear rumbling. An implacable sound that completely dragged me out of my deep thoughts. That was when I noticed the door that shouldn't have been there. A door to a room that didn't exist in my apartment. I knew that it didn't exist!

Whispering filled the air and I slowly got to my feet, slowly walking towards the mysterious door which swung open by itself as I continued to walk. I made no resistance. Whatever would come next was an inevitability.

I glanced behind me and I could see the faces of all those who had died pushing their noses against the glass, eagerly waiting for what fate would befall me. Their dead eyes studied me intently and they left hundreds of handprints on my window. The ghosts of the others. They had come for me regardless of the outcome! I should've known they wouldn't have been reasonable!

The door swung open more violently and inside the small room which I had never entered before I could see easels with half-finished portraits of Mary O'Reilly. Not Lady Mystery Mary, but Rebecca Valentine Mary. Whichever was which. Who the fuck even knows anymore?

I kept walking, inexorably drawn to this mysterious room as the window shook in its frame as the disgruntled spirits of the dead relentlessly banged against it.

Annabelle Green appeared inside the room. She looked normal with a warm smile on her face. "Come on, Jack!" she urged me excitedly. She reached out and took my hand, drawing me into the easel room.

"It's time now, Jack!" whispered Annabelle softly. She looked to the center of the room and my gaze followed hers. Our eyes rested on the rope that hung from a wooden beam that made up part of the ceiling. "It's time to come home!"

I agreed dreamily, staring straight ahead as I stepped onto the wooden chair below the noose. I grabbed the rope and draped it over my head.

"My dearest Mary O'Reilly, or Rebecca Valentine, whatever your name is! If you're on the other side, then I'll meet you there! I'll find you!"

And with that I stepped from the stool with a contented smile on my face. My neck didn't break right away. My face was twisted sharply upwards as the rope slid closed around my neck and felt like a boa constrictor.

I knew what people would say when they heard. "He did it out of guilt!" "Jack was actually the Artist Killer!" "He couldn't satisfy Mary!" "Jack had a little dick!" I really didn't care what the others thought! I knew the truth.

THE END

Printed in Great Britain
by Amazon